Praise for *Talk to the Paw*

"Filled with romance and adorable kitty antics, *Talk to the Paw* is a light and cozy read that is awesome to curl up with, particularly alongside your own mischievous cat!" —*Modern Cat*

"This adorable romance featuring a spunky, matchmaking kitty will steal readers' hearts. Metz's descriptive writing expresses clearly the point of view seen through the eyes of MacGyver, the adorable tabby cat. MacGyver is a pet full of personality and his voice shines through loud and clear in the story, thanks to Metz's buoyant writing. Both Jamie and David are endearing in their honesty and vulnerability. Lively, amusing secondary characters will have readers laughing along with one adorable feline who will simultaneously have readers' hearts melting. A fun-filled, sweet, heartwarming read." —*RT Book Reviews*, **4 Stars**

"Fans of cozy romances will root for these realistic and appealing characters." —*Publishers Weekly*

"The surpassingly cute story of a matchmaking cat determined to pair off his human with a neighbor through the power of stinky laundry." —*Kirkus Reviews*

"Witty . . . inspired by reports of real-life klepto kitties, this cute book is sure to put a smile on your face." —*Catster*

"There's no time to pussyfoot around! . . . the cat's meow."
—*Closer*

"If the adorable cover doesn't have you picking up this book to read, then the witty, charming story that plays out inside should have you begging for more. . . . If you want fun, cute and memorable, this is the book."

"Mac is the cats pajamas." —*Dea*

Also by Melinda Metz

Talk to the Paw

The Secret Life of Mac

Published by Kensington Publishing Corporation

MAC ON A HOT TIN ROOF

MELINDA METZ

KENSINGTON BOOKS
www.kensingtonbooks.com

KENSINGTON BOOKS are published by

Kensington Publishing Corp.
119 West 40th Street
New York, NY 10018

All Kensington titles, imprints, and distributed lines are available at special quantity discounts for bulk purchases for sales promotion, premiums, fund-raising, educational, or institutional use.

Special book excerpts or customized printings can also be created to fit specific needs. For details, write or phone the office of the Kensington Sales Manager: Kensington Publishing Corp., 119 West 40th Street, New York, NY 10018. Attn. Sales Department. Phone: 1-800-221-2647.

Kensington and the K logo Reg. U.S. Pat. & TM Off.

ISBN-13: 978-1-4967-1902-7 (ebook)
ISBN-10: 1-4967-1902-6 (ebook)
Kensington Electronic Edition: December 2019

ISBN-13: 978-1-4967-1900-3
ISBN-10: 1-4967-1900-X
First Kensington Trade Paperback Printing: December 2019

10 9 8 7 6 5 4 3 2 1

Printed in the United States of America

For the fabulous Laura J. Burns, my oft-time co-author and longtime friend. When a family emergency caused me to stumble while working on *Mac on a Hot Tin Roof*, Laura came to my rescue. (She has a little MacGyver in her!) She saved the day with long conversations about cats and kittens, why people fall in love, and other crucial plot points. I must now turn to E. B. White and Wilbur to express my gratitude. Just substitute "Laura" for "Charlotte":

"It is not often that someone comes along who is a true friend and a good writer. Charlotte was both."

CHAPTER 1

MacGyver stared at his person's face. He could always tell when Jamie was faking sleep, and she wasn't faking. He used to think she didn't appreciate the necessity of frequent naps, but now she napped even more than he did. And that would be fine with him—if she didn't nap when it was his breakfast time!

He leaned closer, so close his whiskers brushed against Jamie's cheeks, then he opened his mouth as wide as he could and yowled. He reserved his yowls for true emergencies, and *this* was a true emergency. His stomach was empty!

Jamie made a grumpy sound, and her eyelids twitched, but she didn't wake up. Mac gave her a tap on the nose with one paw, claws in. She brushed it away, but she still didn't wake. He considered his options. He knew he *could* wake her up. A little scratch would do it. But Jamie was his person, and he wasn't going to do that to her. Unless she started making this kind of disrespect a habit.

He leapt off the bed. There were lots of humans around who owed him a meal. Make that a meal a day for life! When he saw a human struggling to manage the basics of life, Mac stepped in.

He felt it was his duty as a higher being. Now it was payback time.

Mac decided to pay a visit to Gib. When he'd first met Gib, he'd known the man was lonely. One whiff had told him that. It didn't take long for Mac to figure out the person who should become Gib's packmate. Now they were sharing a house. Yes, Gib had a debt to repay. Gib also always had sardines.

Diogee galumped into the room and started whining as he stared at Jamie, who was still sleeping. Mac could take a detour and knock over the treat jar so the dog could eat. And maybe he would, but later. Cats before dogs. He was getting his own belly filled before he took pity on the bonehead. He trotted to the bathroom, jumped up to the window ledge, and flicked the round window open. From there it was a smaller jump to the closest branch of the cedar, his personal staircase. He scampered down, then loped toward Gib's, the slight breeze ruffling his fur and the dewy grass tickling his toes. He could almost feel those oily little fishies going down his throat.

Mac heard . . . something. He slowed down, one ear flicking back. The sound came again. A mew, so weak it was almost inaudible, but definitely a mew. He stopped. There was a kitten in trouble. And no one but Mac was going to take care of the situation. Sigh. The sardinesies would have to wait.

He took a few moments to calculate the direction the mews had come from, then broke into a run. As he got closer, he realized the mews weren't all coming from the same kit. There could be two or even three.

O, holy Bast! Mac was hardly ever wrong, but this time he was. When he found the kittens under some scrubby bushes by the place where he could usually score a few bites of chicken, there were four babies, all tan-and-gold tabbies like Mac. Two of them began to mew louder when they saw him. One didn't mew at all. It didn't even open its eyes. The fourth stepped forward and arched its little back, its tail as bushy as a tiny tail could be. The kitten opened its mouth and hissed. Hissed at Mac, who had to outweigh her by eight pounds.

Ignoring the challenge the kitten was trying to give him, Mac breathed in deeply, using his tongue to flick air into his mouth, gathering information. The littlest kitten was alive, but extremely weak. The others were healthy, but they hadn't eaten recently. The mother cat had been gone for several days. If she'd been able to come back, she would have.

The kittens wouldn't survive on their own, even the sassy one hissing at Mac. Their tummies had to be a lot emptier than Mac's. And no one was going to be around to teach them the basics— hunting, stealth, or making the big eyes humans couldn't resist. He was going to have to take care of them. There was no choice.

First, he needed to get the babies into a safer place. He could smell other cats, cats who might be insecure enough to find a bunch of kits a threat to their territory. There were dogs, too. Diogee would probably drown the little ones with slobbery licks, but Diogee was a wimp. He'd seen Diogee run away from a Chihuahua. A *Chihuahua.* The bonehead could have swallowed it whole, except he was a wimp.

A car drove by, reminding Mac of another threat. He had to move fast. He picked Sassy up by the scruff of the neck, ignoring her puny growl. Where to take them? Moving as fast as he dared, he started toward home. He didn't want to take the kittens there, though. Jamie wasn't even capable of feeding him and the bonehead right now. Or cleaning his litter box. David had to do it. Mac really had to figure out what was wrong with her. She'd been smelling strange for months. Not sick. But not like herself. He'd deal with that later.

Right now, he needed a safe place, somewhere with no animals or humans. Not all humans were like Jamie and David and Mac's friends. They had to be observed and thoroughly smelled before they could be trusted.

Sassy wriggled, trying to free herself. Mac ignored her, brain whirring as he moved through his neighborhood. Where, where, where? He caught a whiff of rotting cloth, cardboard boxes, wood, and mouse droppings. The kittens weren't much bigger than mice, but once the squeakers smelled Mac in the area, they'd get themselves gone.

He veered toward the small building that was the source of the smells. It was about the size of the room where Jamie and David slept, but the roof was much higher. Mac had come across it on one of his nighttime jaunts. He took the wiggly kitten through the narrow tunnel he'd discovered when he'd first investigated the place. He deposited her on an old piece of carpet, then he returned to the others. None of the others wriggled as much as Sassy had. The last one hadn't moved at all. But he was still alive. They all were. And Mac was there to make sure they stayed that way.

That meant food, and home was the easiest place to get enough. He knew where the pouches of tuna were. That would do to start. He wasn't supposed to take food from the cupboards. Jamie would call him a bad cat—if she woke up long enough to notice—but that never bothered him.

Most of the time being a bad cat was fun. Right now, it was necessary, although it wouldn't be for long. He'd teach the littles what they needed to know, then he'd match each of them up with a human. He knew lots of people, and he was excellent at matching. Those kittens were lucky it was MacGyver who'd heard their mews for help.

Serena slid the key into the lock, then paused. She was about to enter the place she would be living for the next year. She'd never stepped inside. She'd never even been to California. Not that Atlanta was a small town. But this was *Hollywood*. The Hollywood sign was right over there to prove it.

She turned her head and took a long look. "Breathe it in," she whispered. It was this thing she'd done since she was about twelve, something her mother had taught her. Every day she tried to find at least one amazing thing. Then she'd say—or just think—"breathe it in." It locked whatever she'd experienced in her mind, upped her appreciation of it. It had turned out to be really useful as an actress. Now she did it anytime she wanted to store the feelings and sensations of a moment, good or bad.

"Breathe it in," she whispered again as she turned the key in the lock. She smiled as she swung open the door. A circular staircase dominated the large, round room, a dining room/kitchen combo. It spiraled up, up, up. Four floors up. "Breathe it—" she began, then stopped. There was too much to see and experience. She couldn't break it into moments. She'd just have to let the experience envelop her and hope she remembered everything, everything, everything.

Instead of exploring the first floor, then moving on, she followed the impulse to run to the stairs. The second floor was smaller—just the way you'd expect it to be living in a lighthouse. She was going to live in a lighthouse! Well, not a working lighthouse, but a house designed to look like a lighthouse, complete with red-and-white candy-cane stripes outside and a widow's walk around the cupola. All the houses in Storybook Court were unique. She hadn't gotten a chance to look at all of them, but that was at the top of her list. Her favorites so far were the one that looked like it belonged in the Shire, round, with round windows and a round door, and a thatched roof, and the one that looked like a witch's cottage with a peaked roof and windows, and a door knocker shaped like a spider with a center of faceted ruby glass.

Serena took in a funky pot-bellied stove and cozy overstuffed chairs and sofas before she continued up the stairs. On the third floor she found the bedroom. She abandoned the staircase to test the bed—just the right amount of bounce—and run her fingers over the patchwork quilt that covered it, enjoying the feel of the different textures of the fabrics. Then she was up again, taking a quick peek at the bathroom and its claw-foot tub. "Breathe it in," she told herself, because she had to.

As she returned to the staircase, she heard a low *ohhhhh-waaaaah*. Fog horn. No, doorbell that sounded like a fog horn, she realized as the sound came again. She hurried back down the stairs and opened the door. A fifty-ish woman with short black hair shot through with gray, bangs almost touching her eyebrows, stood there, a friendly smile on her elfin face.

"Ruby Shaffer?" Serena asked.

"But of course," Ruby answered. "Here to welcome you and see if you have any questions on the requirements of the award."

Serena stepped back to let her in. "I'm sure I will have, but I've gotta admit, my brain is pretty much at capacity right now. Many, many new things."

"Understandable," Ruby answered. "I don't want to strain your brain. You know the basics—you get to live here rent free for a year. All you have to do is show that you're pursuing creative goals. Acting in your case. Just keep track of auditions, classes, and whatnot, and we'll go over everything once a month. Then I'll send a report to the Mulcahys, who created the Lighthouse Foundation. There's not too much else to know, and I'm only a few blocks away if you need me. Also, I have a phone, and you have the number."

"I do." Serena had spoken to Ruby several times since she'd received the notification that she was that year's recipient of the Lighthouse Award. "Can I get you . . . a glass of tap water?" she asked. "Wait. I'm not sure I have a glass. Can I offer you the chance to stick your head under the tap and slurp up some water?"

Ruby laughed. "You have glasses. You have cups and saucers, too. Plates, sheets, towels, everything you need. The Mulcahys even had me stock the kitchen so you wouldn't have to worry about going out for groceries. I should have told you that. Sorry."

Serena nodded, then nodded again. "No, you did. I remember now. I'm just having a little trouble taking it all in. Did I say that already? It's too much goodness."

"Hey, that's Hollywood—a very small percentage of the time, for a very small percentage of people," Ruby answered. "And I'll take some mint tea, which is in a pitcher in your fridge."

"And my fridge is right over there." Serena headed to the beach-blue retro fridge positioned between two sections of curved countertop. A big wooden table that had been painted a soft green in the same palette as the fridge dominated the room. Comfy-looking flowered chairs circled it. "I love the way the place is decorated, what I've seen so far anyway. I just got here a few minutes ago."

"I thought you were getting here around noon."

"Delays." Serena surveyed the well-stocked fridge, then pulled out a Pyrex pitcher with a pattern of pink diamonds circling around and around. It fit perfectly with the table and fridge. Ruby grabbed a few glasses and pulled a Ziploc of fresh cookies out of her enormous bag and dumped them on to a plate. When they got settled at the table, Serena let out a "whew."

"I feel you," Ruby said. "I had a thirteen-hour meeting yesterday with the production team of a movie I'm doing set dressing for. Thirteen. Hours. Actually more, because I dreamed I was still in it last night, and it felt so real that it has to count."

"Absolutely," Serena agreed. "Dreams can really take it out of you sometimes. I've had a few where I've had a fight with someone and when I wake up, I'm still mad at them. I have to sort of talk myself down and remind myself that the person didn't actually do any of the horrible things in real life." She took a bite of one of the cookies, and a delightful mix of lime, coconut, and pineapple got her taste buds tingling. "So, you must know, since I am an actor, that I want to know all the details of the movie, especially if there's a part for me. Did I wait an appropriate amount of time before I asked that? I did respond to the dream part of what you said first."

"You're fine. The movie's, well, it's kind of hard to describe. Try to picture a Wes Anderson-ish take on the Old Dark House tropes—secret passages, a killer at large, witty banter," Ruby said. "All the principals have been cast, but I'll keep an ear out."

"That sounds amazing. And I'm not just sucking up." She laughed. "Which I guess means I am partially sucking up. But also wanting to get to know you, and wanting to know more about movie making. I mostly did theater in Atlanta, and even that was years ago. I've been mostly teaching acting for the last almost four years, not acting myself." She shook her head. "Four years. It feels like twenty, except for when it feels like about a month."

"The contradictory nature of time," Ruby commented. She used her finger to draw an infinity sign in the condensation on the side of her glass.

Serena liked her. She was one of those people. All you had to do was talk to them for a few minutes and you already felt a bond. "What made you decide to go back to acting?" Ruby asked.

"It's not exactly like I decided to step away from it," Serena explained. "I picked up a job teaching to pay for some little extras—like rent."

Ruby snorted. "Been there."

"It turned out I really liked it, and I got good evaluations," Serena continued, "and I got asked to take on more classes, and then—*poof*—four years later."

"So, you just came across the Lighthouse Award info somewhere and decided you wanted to get back to acting again?" Ruby added to the artwork on the side of her glass.

"No. I did a thorough search of all the grants I might qualify for and applied to them all," Serena answered. "One day after class, I overheard two of my students talking. About me." Ruby raised her eyebrows. "About how even though they liked my class, maybe they should study with a working actor. They went on about how I had to be almost thirty, and I obviously wasn't going to make it as an actor or I would have already. And maybe they shouldn't take classes from someone who obviously didn't have what it takes."

"Ouch." Ruby ran her palm down the side of her glass, wiping it clean.

"Yeah. Especially because they were right. Without even realizing it, I'd given up on my dream of being an actor. I'd kept on accepting more teaching work, and it ended up being full time, and I stopped auditioning, and . . ."

"*Poof.* Four years later," Ruby said, echoing what Serena had said earlier.

"Exactly. So, I decided to do what I advised my students to do. Get out there. Don't give up. Every audition is like buying a lottery ticket, and you can't win unless you buy a ticket."

"And here you are. You beat out a lot of applicants, I'm sure you realize that."

"I'm still in a state of shock. A year rent free and a stipend for expenses? Who ever gets that? Nobody. Except here I am." Serena took a few seconds for a silent "Breathe it in." "And all I have to do is do exactly what I want to do—work at becoming a full-time actor."

"Not becoming a star?" Ruby asked.

"Well, sure, that would be great. But we both know that's very rare, and there's a lot of luck involved. If I can make a living doing what I love, that's a beautiful thing. I don't need to be famous."

Ruby nodded. "Good to hear. There've been years where I

had to do a lot of handing out tissues to weeping women who were devastated when they didn't become an overnight sensation."

"Why are only women eligible for the award? Not that I'm complaining."

"The Mulcahys had a daughter who wanted to be a director. She died in a car accident shortly after she came out here to take her shot," Ruby answered. "Her parents set up the award in her honor, and it was their call. Maybe they wanted to balance the scales a little. You know the stats on male directors versus female."

"And the salary inequity in pretty much every field." Serena chose a second cookie, a chocolate one. The last one had been delicious, but it hadn't been chocolate, and, really, nothing could be as good as chocolate. "Hey, we got totally off the subject of you. I said I wanted to get to know you better, and then I just talked and talked and talked some more."

Ruby glanced at the yellow kitchen clock, complete with thermometer and timer. "There's a community meeting over in the courtyard in a few. Want to come with me? We can talk more on the way."

Serena stood up. "Absolutely. After all, for this whole year, I'm a part of the community." She actually lived here now! In Hollywood. In Storybook Court, which had to be the most adorable neighborhood in the city. And she was getting paid to go after her dreams. She couldn't stop a grin from spreading across her face, a grin so wide it made her cheeks ache. How did she get to be so damn lucky?

"How did I get so damn unlucky?" Erik muttered. He slashed an annoyed glance at his partner.

"Why are you looking at me like that?" Kait asked. "All I said was that at least you already know Storybook Court, and a bunch of the people, so our job will be easier." The city had decided to try having beat cops again, at least on a small scale, something they'd given up about eight years ago. The Court was part of Erik and Kait's territory. They were going to hold a community meeting to introduce themselves and give some basic safety tips.

"I don't give a crap about that. We could go into any neighborhood and make it work."

"You're absolutely right," Kait said quickly. "I was just trying to show that there was a bright side."

"I don't give a crap about the bright side."

Kait sighed. "Stanford did a study on how improving kids' attitudes toward a subject actually made their brains—"

"I don't—" Erik interrupted.

"Give a crabcake about the studies," Kait finished for him.

"Crabcake was not the word I had in mind."

She ignored him. "I'm not spending every day absorbing your negativity. I need my brain working at top capacity for the detective's exam. And so, by the way, do you."

Erik only grunted in reply as he squeezed the patrol car into the one empty space on Gower Avenue. As he got out, he saw a rat's bright black eyes staring down at him from the palm tree. He almost pointed it out to Kait, who hated any animal that didn't have hair on its tail, but refrained. It's not like it was her fault they'd been assigned here. "Let's get this over with."

"That's the spirit." Kait slapped him on the shoulder. At least she hadn't brought up Tulip. At least she hadn't tried to point out it had been three years, and according to some study—Kait could cite a study for every situation—he should be over Tulip by now.

Anyway, he *was* over her. He just didn't feel like thinking about her, and being here was going to make it hard not to think about her.

"We've got a decent size crowd going," Kait commented as they entered the courtyard. If she kept trying to show him the bright side, he was going change his mind and show her the rat.

He paused and scanned the group gathered around the fountain and saw some familiar faces. Al and Marie. David and a very pregnant Jamie. Those two had gotten together around the time he and Tulip—Erik didn't let himself finish the thought. There was Ruby standing next to a woman he didn't know. The woman's hair was a pale red, and it was tousled like she'd just walked off the beach. Her pale green dress had thin straps that showed off her shoulders, but was loose and flow-y, going almost down to her feet. She'd knotted it on one side, a little below the knee, so he got a glimpse of leg, a glimpse that left him wanting to see more. If only the dress were a little thinner. . . .

"Don't even," Kait warned.

"Don't even what?"

"Don't even look at the women who live in the Court as possibilities for one of your three-date specials," Kait said. She made air quotes around the word "date." "Stick to counterpart.com. Don't defecate where you masticate."

Erik let out a bark of laughter. "You are such a priss. And I was just looking at who's here, not searching for a spot to . . . defecate."

"I'm a cop. I am good at reading people, and I'm especially good at reading you. You were sizing up the one with the red hair," Kait shot back. "Now, let's do this." She walked over to the fountain and jumped up on the wide lip. Erik joined her. He didn't let his gaze drift back to the redhead, although he wouldn't have minded a longer look.

"Welcome, folks!" Kait called out. "I'm Officer Tyson. Kait. And this is my partner, Officer Ross."

"Erik. Good to see some familiar faces." He waved to the group, and noticed Marie giving him an approving nod. He made a mental note to stop by for an iced tea and a chat. Marie knew almost everything that went on at the Court, and what she didn't know, she could easily find out. He hoped when he was in his eighties, he'd be as sharp as she was.

"We've done some reorganizing down at the station, and we're going to try getting more beat cops out in the neighborhoods around here. Erik and I—we're yours."

"That means you'll be seeing a lot of us," Erik jumped in. "We want to get to know all of you, and we want to hear any concerns that you're having about safety in your neighborhood. Anytime we're around, feel free to come up and talk to us."

"We'll give you our cards, too, so you can call or email," Kait added. "Anybody have any questions?"

"What's the point?" a man asked. He looked familiar, but Erik didn't remember his name. "There's no crime in Storybook Court. Not if you don't count when MacGyver was stealing everyone's underpants."

"Is this MacGyver someone we need to keep an eye on?" Kait asked softly.

"MacGyver's a cat. I'll explain later," Erik answered under his breath, then raised his voice. "Even though Storybook Court can feel like its own little town, it's part of a big city, and there's crime in every big city. We don't want to scare you. We just want you to keep an eye out for each other, and to tell us if there's anything in the neighborhood that's bothering you."

"It bothers me that Ed Yoder weeds while wearing a bathing suit!" someone yelled, and everyone laughed.

"Sorry. We aren't the fashion police," Erik answered, getting some laughs himself.

Kait got them back on track. "Today, we want to give you a couple tips about staying safe."

"Say I'm a door-to-door salesman, and I knock at your door." Erik raised his fist and made a knocking motion in the air.

"This could easily happen," Kait told the group. "Thirty percent of companies who sell security systems report that ninety percent of their new business comes from door-to-door salesmen."

"You open the door." Erik gave a friendly smile. "Hi, I'm Erik and I'm with Safe and Sound Security. I—" He stopped in mid-spiel, the way he always did. "Hey, this would go better if I were talking to an actual person. Can I get a volunteer?" And dead silence. Using a volunteer was a good way to up the crowd engagement, but when no one stepped up, it got kind of uncomfortable. Where was Hud Martin? If he were around, the former TV star would have taken the opportunity before Erik had the word "volunteer" completely out of his mouth.

"Nobody?" Erik asked.

"Serena will do it!" Ruby called, nudging the redhead forward.

The woman laughed. "Sure, Serena will do it!"

"Great! Come on up here." Erik waved her forward.

"Don't even," Kait mumbled. Erik heard her, but pretended he hadn't. He reached out his hand to help the woman—Serena—up on the edge of the fountain beside him, and was surprised to feel an almost electric jolt of attraction when his fingers touched hers. It's not like he never got that buzzy feeling, just not usually so fast, with such casual contact.

"So, this salesman shows up at your door," Kait said, like she thought he'd forgotten what he was supposed to be doing. Which he hadn't. He'd just been distracted for a split second.

"Right. Okay. Just do what you'd do if I showed up at your door," Erik told Serena.

She nodded. "Got it."

He did his air knock again.

"Um, your hand is going too far forward," Serena told him. "From where you're standing, the door would be here." She swept her arm down. "Try to picture it. Then try again."

Was she busting his chops or actually trying to be helpful?

Didn't matter. He had to go with it. "O-kay." He repeated the knock.

"Better."

"Hello, I'm Erik Ross. I was over on Magic Beans Street handling an issue with a false alarm. My company is going to be in the neighborhood over the next few weeks, replacing older alarms, the ones that are giving people trouble."

Serena crossed her arms, and shot him a challenging look. "Why are you telling me this?"

She was really getting into it. And she had the attention of the crowd. "Well, here's the thing. I'm looking for a few home-owners to help me promote my company. All you'd have to do is put this sign with our logo and phone number in your yard."

"Not interested. Do you know how much time I've put into my yard? I'm not ruining it by sticking a sign in the middle." Her voice was unfriendly, but her eyes were sparkling.

"I was admiring your roses as I came up the walk," he answered, playing along. "Here's the thing. In exchange for placing our sign in your yard, my company will install a Safe and Sound security system in your home."

Serena raised her eyebrows. "For free?"

"Absolutely free. In exchange for putting a sign, a small sign, in front of your home."

She nibbled on her lower lip. He couldn't help noticing it was a little fuller than her top lip, which was . . . shapely. Just perfectly . . . shaped. The bow, he guessed it would be called, clearly delineated.

And, yeah, he was staring. Had she said something while he was trying to find the right way to describe her mouth?

"Hmm. I don't know. It sounds too good to be true."

"It sure does," Marie said loudly, getting some applause from her neighbors.

Good. He hadn't screwed up. He was still on track. "We

both get something out of it. Safe and Sound gets advertising, you get the security system. In order to get you set up, I need to know how many doors you have."

"Two," Serena said.

"The backdoor is where most break-ins occur," Erik told her. "Because they're more secluded. Could I take a look? I need to get the specifications for my team."

"I . . . guess so."

She'd made him work for it, but she'd given him what he needed. Erik turned away from her and looked out at the group. "And now I'm in. I'm going to get a good look at the house. And then—" He turned back to Serena. "What time will you be home tomorrow?"

Serena handed him the perfect answer. "I won't be home until late."

"And now I know the best time to break in."

"We're not saying all door-to-door salesmen are thieves," Kait said. "What we're saying is that you need to be aware of what information you're giving to a stranger."

Serena hopped off the edge of the fountain. "Let's all give our volunteer a hand!" Erik called out, and everyone clapped.

"Something else to be aware of is—"

Erik had to force himself to pay attention to what Kait was saying. He wanted to move quickly once she wrapped this up.

"I'm just going to go over and tell the woman who helped me out with the door-to-door salesman thing thanks," Erik told his partner as soon as she finished.

"Don't pretend like you don't remember her name. This is me you're talking to." Kait gave an exasperated sigh.

"I'll be back in a few." Erik jumped down from the fountain and headed for Serena. She and Ruby were already heading down the street. "Hi," he said when he caught up to them. "Just wanted to thank you for volunteering."

"You should be thanking Ruby for volunteering me," Serena answered.

"Thanks, Ruby! Good to see you." Although it wasn't. He liked Ruby, but most memories he had of her involved Tulip.

"You too. I'm glad you got assigned here. I've missed you," Ruby answered, then stopped walking. "This is my street. We need to get together, Serena. How 'bout if I take you out to breakfast day after tomorrow?"

"I'd love that." Serena waved as Ruby started across the street.

"New to the Court?" Erik asked as they continued.

"New to the Court, new to the city, new to the state," Serena answered.

Woman new to the city. She'd want to see all the hot spots. He was more a quiet pub, or beer on the porch guy, but . . . "Been to the Frolic Room yet?"

"I don't think you know me well enough to ask that!" Serena pretended to be scandalized. At least he was pretty sure she was pretending.

"It started out as a speakeasy run by a guy named Freddy Frolic," Erik explained. "It's the ultimate dive bar. A Charles Bukowski hangout, of course. Everyone who lives in Hollywood has to go there at least once."

"What happens to me if I don't?" Serena asked. "Will you have to arrest me?" She kept a straight face, but he thought a smile was tugging at the corner of her lips.

"Not the trendy dive bar type. Okay. Let me think." He studied her for a moment, reviewing the spots he'd met up with counterpart.com women. The only time he went anywhere that might be considered cool was with one of them. "I'm thinking the Edison."

"The power generation museum? I've heard so much about

it! And I'm a huge fan of electricity!" Her eyes glowed with excitement.

"I'm having trouble telling whether you're messing with me right now." She was keeping him on his toes, just the way she had in their little role-playing thing.

"It's a gift. And I was definitely messing with you." She laughed. "Unless there actually is a power generation museum around here. Like I said, I'm new. What's the Edison?"

"Bar. People say it created cocktail culture. The bartenders are called alcohol surgeons," Erik answered. "It's also on the list of most beautiful bars in LA." He immediately felt like a jerkoff. Had he actually said "list of most beautiful bars in LA"? He'd gotten that from one of the women he'd taken there. Sam? Thalia? He should be able to remember these things, but the dates, and if he was honest, the women, started to run together.

"I'm not so much of a bar person," Serena said. "Although Atlanta definitely has a bar scene. I got taken to a place with a 'beverage director' once. Is that above or below an 'alcohol surgeon?'"

"I have no idea," Erik admitted. "I'm actually not so much of a bar person, either. But when dating, they are pretty much obligatory."

"What do you do when not dating?" she asked. "No obligatories."

He considered lying a little, to make himself sound at least somewhat interesting, but decided to go with the truth. "I hang out at home. Read. Watch TV, pretty much just sports. Cook. Work in the garden. I even have some 'spectacular roses,'" he said, doing a call back to what she said when she was playing the suspicious homeowner. "But that doesn't mean I never want to go out," he added.

"That's me too. My friends would complain about how they had to pry me out of the house. It's not that I don't want to go out sometimes, like you said. But I need my home time. Although cooking? No. Unless you count my expert microwaving skills."

"Sorry. I can't," he answered. "Just to make sure you don't starve, would you want to come over for dinner some night?"

"Well . . . I don't know." She did that thing where she gnawed on her lower lip. "I just went to a talk on safety. It doesn't seem wise."

They turned a corner and the lighthouse came into view. Erik's stomach tightened. "Well, there will be a cop present the whole time," he answered.

"In that case—yes."

Her answer swept away the tension looking at the lighthouse had started up. "Great. Next Friday?"

"Next Friday," she agreed. "This is me." Serena stopped at the walkway that led up to the red-and-white-striped building.

"This?" The tension was back. Now his chest was tight, too. "This?" he repeated. He took an involuntary step backward, away from her. "You know what? I just remembered I have something on Friday." Lie. "A date." Another lie. "So, we'll do it some other time." Big, big lie.

Her brown eyes widened, but all she said was, "Okay." He hurried off, giving her a wave without turning around.

CHAPTER 2

Mac gave Bittles one last lick, then took a sniff. Good. The smallest kitten now smelled like Mac. Anyone who got close would know immediately that this kitten—and his sisters and brothers—were under Mac's protection. Well, not humans. Humans' noses barely functioned. Sometimes they couldn't tell food was rotten before they put it in their mouths.

Bittles gave a yawn and snuggled closer to his sister Lox. Mac called her that because the delicious fishy was one of his favorite things. David liked to eat it—and had gotten Jamie to eat it, too. Which meant Mac got double treats. Bittles was what Jamie had called Mac when he was a kitten not much bigger than these, which is how this Bittles got his name.

Mac surveyed his charges. After getting fed and bathed, they all looked ready to fall asleep, even Zoomies, the one who was always running, zig-zagging, going under and over furniture. Mac liked to do that sometimes, especially at night, and David always blah-blahed that Mac had the zoomies when he did. It seemed like a good name for the fastest kitten.

Finally, Mac could take a break and get fed himself! He

squeezed through the tunnel and out into the sunshine. The dew had dried, and the grass was warm under his feet.

But there was an unpleasant tang in the air, the odor of a human who wasn't doing well. He took another whiff. There was no scent of illness. Just another human who didn't know how to make itself happy. Mac was about to let the human find its own way out of whatever was bothering it. He had four kittens to look after. But one last sniff told him he knew the human. It was the one called Erik. Mac almost hadn't recognized his scent. The odor of his unhappiness, unhappiness mixed with anger, was too strong.

It had been a while since Erik had been in Mac's neighborhood, but Mac remembered that Erik knew the exact spot Mac liked to be scratched—under his chin, a little to the left. He also used to eat sitting by the fountain with the human called Tulip, and he always shared. Not her, though. Mac could almost taste the bites of the tuna, the ham, the turkey.

Erik was one of the good humans. Mac was going to have to help him. It's not like anyone else was stepping up to do it. Maybe he needed a kitten. Possibly Sassy. She might be able to handle human problems when she got a little older.

But Mac wasn't going to let one of his babies go to anyone who smelled the way Erik did right now. None of them were ready to handle that yet. Once Mac had fixed Erik, he might be a person who was worthy of one of MacGyver's kittens.

"I can't believe she lives in the lighthouse."

"So you've said three times since we got in the car," Kait answered. "And watch your speed."

"It's not like I'm going to get a ticket," Erik shot back.

"I don't care about a ticket. I care about dying," Kait answered. "As I've told you before, speeding is a factor in thirty-one percent of—"

Erik completed the statistic with her. " 'Fatal crashes.' But what you've never been able to tell me is what percentage of that percentage is exceeding the posted speed limit by five miles per hour or less. Because right now, I'm at about four over."

The familiarity, and absolute Kait-ness of the oft-repeated conversation began to suck all the bad stuff, all the anger, and old hurt, out of him. At least temporarily. He slowed down to 40 mph. "Sorry," he said. "I know speeding stresses you." He flexed his fingers on the wheel. "Going to Storybook got to me more than I thought."

"You weren't expecting to be attracted to a woman who lives in the same place Tulip used to," Kait answered.

"Yeah. Well, at least you won't have to keep reminding me not to get involved with Serena. There's no possible way I'm getting within ten feet of another Lighthouse Award recipient."

"I don't think you have enough data to make a correlation between one Lighthouse Awa—"

"Can we just not talk about it?" Erik cut in, the bad junk already bubbling back up again.

Kait gave a shrug in response, and began streaming "I Know You Know." Her jazz obsession had started with *La La Land*. Lately, she'd been exploring women in jazz, both in the 1930s and contemporary performers like Esperanza Spalding. That was her MO. She found something that she liked and she went deep with it. When she was in her Shakespeare phase, she read every play, watched every movie adaptation, and caught as many plays as she could get herself to. Eventually, something else caught her attention, and she moved on. With the exception of psychological studies and comics. He didn't think she'd ever get enough of either of those.

"Home again, home again," Kait murmured as Erik pulled into a parking spot in the precinct lot. He gave a grunt in response. "Use your words," Kait joked, her tone softening as she added, "Storybook is only part of our beat."

"I'll get used to being there. It's no big deal." And it wasn't.

Tulip had left him more than three years ago. He was over her. Being back in her old neighborhood, standing in front of her old house, where he'd spent so much time, it had just gotten to him. But only because it was the first time he'd been there since he was with Tulip. He'd be fine now that he'd gotten that behind him.

"She broke your heart, Erik. There's no reason to pretend she didn't." Kait waited until he looked over at her, then added, "Not with me."

This was absolutely not a conversation he was having. He grunted, then got out of the car and started into the building. He heard her sigh as she followed him.

He'd fallen hard for Tulip. That much was true. She was so vivacious, so *alive*. It's almost like he'd become another person when he was with her, sucked into this magical world she seemed to create.

But that didn't mean she'd broken his heart. Yeah, she'd hurt him, but that was because she was his first. Not his first girlfriend, but his first love. He'd thought he'd been in love a few times before he met her—sex could do that to you, especially when it was all new—but when he and Tulip had gotten together, he'd realized he'd been wrong. What he'd felt before hadn't even come close.

It was normal that losing that had knocked him off balance for a while, probably because when she left LA—and refused to let him come with her—it had been clear she didn't feel anything close to what he did. That love he'd felt, it was pretty much one-sided, or she'd never have been able to walk away from him.

"You just walked past the door!" Kait called to him.

And yeah, he'd gotten so far up his own butt that he had. Why had he let himself start thinking about True Love and all that Tulip bullshit? It was in the past. Seeing the lighthouse didn't change that. It was just a building.

He turned around, and followed Kait into the glorified supply closet where the two of them, and the other cops who'd been assigned beats, were headquartered. Only a few neighborhoods were getting beat cops who'd mostly patrol on foot in the same neighborhoods every shift. It was something their field officer had wanted to try. It's not like it was new. But using beat cops had fallen out of favor the last few years, and the FO wanted to show it was worth going back to. He'd gotten approval to give it a shot on a small scale.

Since it was a trial run, there was a lot more documentation that had to be done, more stats to gather. So, instead of doing most of their paperwork in the car the way they were used to, he, Kait, and the rest of the new beat cops now had a few beat-up metal tables and a few beat-up computers assigned for their use, along with a Mr. Coffee from the late 80s. Jandro Flores was pouring himself a cup when Erik and Kait came in, and Erik paused to give him their obligatory horizontal-high-five-fist-bump-heart-thump greeting. They'd been doing it since they became friends at the Police Academy. Jandro had spent a few years in the Marines, and he'd gotten Erik through the first couple days at the academy, when Erik didn't even know what getting into formation meant. Not something that had been covered in his AS from Los Angeles City College.

"How'd it go out there?" Jandro asked.

Jandro knew Erik wasn't exactly thrilled to be going back to Storybook Court. And he knew why. He'd spent way too many nights sitting around while Erik cried in his beer over Tulip. 'Cause he was that kind of friend. The kind who'd listen to you say the same damn thing thousands of times until it was out of your system. Things like: "I wasn't enough to keep her here." "Why wouldn't she let me go with her?" "Why did she turn out to be psycho?" "How did I get to be so pathetic?"

Before he could answer Jandro's question, Sean Hankey

spoke up. "It was awesome. Found this place called Carousel. Best lamb shawarma ever."

"He ate so much I keep expecting him to baa," Sean's partner, Tom, added. "His idea of walking a beat is eating his way up and down the streets."

"Hey, I was making contact with local businesses. You can't stop by a restaurant and not at least have a mezze. That's disrespectful," Sean said.

"Mezze?" Kait asked.

"Appetizer," Sean told her.

"He's a polyglot, as long—" Tom began.

"Ooooh. SAT word," Sean exclaimed.

Tom ignored him and continued. "He's a polyglot. As long as the words involve food." Sean gave a loud belch in response. In response to that, Tom grimaced. "I can still smell the lamb."

"And when you fart, I can smell the kale and beets." Sean belched again and patted his flat stomach with satisfaction.

"A vegan and a carnivore walk into a bar," Jandro's partner, Angie, muttered, without looking up from her phone.

"So how was it?" Jandro asked Erik again.

Erik shrugged. "It was what it was." He was going for indifferent, but Jandro knew him too well to buy it.

"You going out with, whatshername—Brittany—again?" he asked. Jandro had thought the best way to get over Tulip was to get with someone else. Even though it had been years since they broke up, Jandro kept pushing, probably thinking if Erik kept at it, he'd meet someone as great as Jandro's wife.

"Bettina." Kait pulled a bottle of water out of her messenger bag. "And that was two women ago."

It was actually three. He hadn't mentioned Amy to her. He hadn't wanted to hear her disapproving huff. Kait talked a lot, but she could communicate as much with her air output as she could with a sentence.

"So, who's up to bat right now?" Sean asked. "I want details. I want dimensions. Is her shoe size bigger than her dress size? That was always one of my must-haves."

Kait gave a disapproving sniff. She could also communicate a lot with air input.

Sean looked at her. "What's the problem?"

"You're married," Angie answered for Kait, while continuing to scroll through her phone.

"Damn right, I'm married," Sean shot back. "That's why I need details from Erik. It's not like he'll give me any." He jerked his thumb toward his partner.

"A horndog and a gentleman walk into a bar," Angie mumbled.

Kait snapped her fingers at Erik. "Paperwork."

He grabbed a cup of coffee for himself and sat down next to her. As she began to type, he pulled out his phone and checked his counterpart.com account. He'd gotten a heart from a cute woman named Amber in Los Feliz.

"Yeah. Definitely yeah." Jandro had stepped up behind Erik and was looking at the pic on his phone. Erik sent a heart back. Not because he still needed help getting over Tulip. He got over her a long time ago. Seeing the lighthouse had brought up some bad memories, that's all. Some momentary bad memories. Just momentary. Pretty much already forgotten.

At least until he had to go back to Storybook Court.

"I think I'm going to have the flight of wee waffles," Serena told Ruby when they met up for breakfast on Thursday. "Partly because flight of wee waffles is very fun to say." She repeated it again, just for the fun. "Flight of the wee waffles. It sounds like an adorable animated short. Also, one of the wee chive waffles involves smoked salmon and dill cream cheese, and that sounds amazing."

"I'm going for the gluten-free vegan waffle," Ruby said.

"Sounds yummy," Serena said. All her acting experience made it easy to sound genuine.

Ruby laughed. "Actually, I'm going for the one with baked-in hash browns and sour cream on top."

"Good. I think I still would have been able to be friends with you if you were an extremely healthy eater, but it would have been a challenge."

"Their double-size mimosas each have a half a bottle of champagne. But mimosas are very healthy, all that orange juice, so you probably wouldn't want one."

"I would, but I want to get some work in on a couple monologues." Serena took a sip of iced tea out of the mason jar. "I have an agent meeting on Monday, and I might need to pull one out."

"It's only your third day and you already have a meeting. You work fast!" Ruby waved to a very pregnant woman and a handsome dark-haired man, who were walking across the patio, trying to keep a big dog with a really big head from eating off the tables they passed. The woman waved back. The man just smiled and nodded, keeping both hands on the leash.

"That's Jamie and David. They live at Storybook, too. I'll introduce you on the way out," Ruby said. "The beast is Diogee. The Waffle is known for being dog friendly, but I'm not sure they're *that* dog friendly. She winced as the dog managed to climb in a chair, which immediately began to tip over, threatening to take one of the bright yellow patio umbrellas with it. "They've been taking him to training classes in anticipation of the baby to be, but I guess he needs a few more lessons."

"Maybe one or two," Serena agreed as their waiter stepped up to their table. She liked his look—Hawaiian shirt, dreads piled high on his head, semi-elaborate facial hair.

"So, a meeting already," Ruby said after he'd taken their order and headed off. "Details, details!"

"I did all the usual stuff. Research. Sending out kits. But I actually got the meeting through this vlog I do, mostly acting tips. One of the people I ended up having some back-and-forth with was an assistant at Epitome for a few years, and she put in a good word for me with her boss. I reached out, and he agreed to meet."

"Epitome. Nice. Not too big, but with the connections they need," Ruby said. "You nervous?"

"I've been reconsidering one of those double mimosas," Serena admitted. "But I'm mostly the good kind of nervous, the kind that gets you pumped, but doesn't make you lose focus."

"I'm sure you've heard about LA traffic. It's all true. Make sure to leave lots of extra time."

Serena nodded. "I will, for sure."

"I didn't even think to ask how you're going to be getting around. We have some public transportation, but it's not exactly convenient."

"Rental car for now. I'm already looking for something to buy. Used. The car I had in Atlanta would probably have gotten me around the city for a few more years—with enough oil infusions—but I didn't trust it to get me out here."

"I'll keep an ear out," Ruby promised. "Did the former assistant of this agent tell you—"

Serena held up one hand, stopping her. "Nope. We have to talk about something else. If I think about the meeting much more, I'll definitely be tipping into the bad kind of nervous."

"Not a problem." Ruby smiled at the waiter as he set down their plates. "I'm nosy about everything, not just work stuff. Tell me what you thought of Erik, Storybook's own personal cop. I thought I saw a few sparks between you two."

What *did* she think of him? Flirty, in a nice, non-sleazy way. Easy to talk to. Crazy attractive. But also, possibly crazy crazy. One second, he was offering to make her dinner, the next, he practically sprinted away. As she'd stood there staring after him, she'd told herself to breathe it in. If she had to do a scene where she was rejected, she'd be able to pull up exactly how it felt.

"I thought I felt a few sparks at first," Serena admitted. "But nope. Nothing there."

CHAPTER 3

"What did you end up doing this weekend?" Kait asked Monday morning as she and Erik walked across the parking lot of the Gower Gulch strip mall, part of their new beat. "Or should I say whom?"

"Christ, Kait. You sound like Sean." Erik noticed that one of the tires on a fourteen-year-old Toyota was low. He leaned down and saw it had caught a nail.

"You're right. I now feel sort of sick," Kait answered. "But you know what's worse than sounding like Sean?" She looked over at Erik, waiting.

Erik finished writing a note to the Toyota's owner to give them a heads-up about the tire, then stuck it under the windshield. "What?"

"Acting like Sean."

He knew what she meant, but decided to play dumb. "Hey, I ordered the Fit Slam, not the Lumberjack," he protested. The first stop they'd made had been at the Denny's across the lot.

She responded with one of her exasperated huffs of air.

"Kait, what's the point of talking about this again? I know you disapprove of how many women I go out with. But I'm not making anybody any promises. It's all no harm, no foul."

"I'm more worried about you than about them. You're not that guy. You just aren't. And acting like one so much of the time can't feel too good. There was a study done at Tel Aviv University that showed authenticity is—"

Erik went for distraction again. Lately, Kait was on him about relationship stuff all the time. He nodded toward the Lucifers Pizza a few steps away. "Don't you think that should have an apostrophe?" Bad grammar usually got at least a fifteen-minute-long rant. She'd had about a six-month run when she was deep into grammar. It had gotten so bad he'd done some research, and told her that studies indicated she was suffering from Grammatical Pedantry Syndrome, a type of OCD. She didn't care. She thought everyone should be concerned with proper grammar. Kait only cared about psychological studies that backed up her point of view.

"Of course, it should have an apostrophe." Kait frowned, first at the sign, then at him. "And we both know that you know that." True. Being her partner meant he had acquired a lot of basically useless information. He could even use "whom" correctly and knew the difference between "affect" and "effect." "What I was trying to tell you, is that people who behave in an authentic way are hap—"

He didn't let her finish. "What percentage of people do you think don't know how to use apostrophes correctly?"

"I read a study that said more than half of Britons can't use the possessive apostrophe correctly. I don't know how many Americans," Kait answered. "And we were talking about you, about how I'm worried about you."

"I'm safe, if that's what you mean." He knew it wasn't, but he was still trying to avoid this whole conversation.

She let out another one of her huffs. "I assumed you knew how to use a prophylactic. What I'm worried about—other than how not being true to yourself is only going to keep making you unhappy—is that you're never going to let yourself have another real relationship. You won't let yourself even get close to one. You move from woman to woman too fast."

"Look, Lucifers now has cauliflower crusts as an option." Erik didn't bother to wait for Kait to tell him that wasn't what they were talking about. It had been a subpar effort at distraction on his part. "I'm fine. I like keeping things uncomplicated."

"Uncomplicated." She shook her head. "That's no way to—"

This time Erik abandoned distraction and went for turning the tables. "You're no different than I am. When's the last time you went on more than two dates with the same guy?" Her earlobes reddened. It wasn't that obvious with her brown skin, but he noticed, and he knew she was pissed off.

"That is completely different. I want to be in a relationship. You know that. I just don't see any point of continuing to go out with a man if I already know it's not going to work. Which is the opposite of what you do. Sometimes I think you stop going out with a woman if you get a hint it *might* work."

"I like being single, okay? Going out with the same person too many times means expectations, and expectations mean hurt feelings. This works for me. I go out maybe once a week, and the rest of the time, I get to hang out at home, read, watch crap TV, whatever I feel like." Kait drew in a deep breath. "Don't sigh at me," he warned.

She let out the breath quietly. "I just have a hard time believing you're really okay this way. I know you, Erik. You're not a casual guy."

"Okay, you've said what you have to say. Let's agree not to

have this conversation for another six months. I know you won't be able to keep quiet for longer than that." He waved her down the walkway. "Let's go introduce ourselves at the Supercuts."

"You are so aggravating."

"Let me aggravate you a little more," he said as they walked. "You need to be a little more casual. Can't you just have some fun? Does a guy really have to meet every item on that list you made back in college before you can go out with him?" He suspected the list had a lot to do with the brutal divorce her parents had had when she was in the eighth grade. There was some serious scar tissue there.

"Not every item. Just most of the items. I'd be happy with eight out of ten," Kait said.

"You like me and I probably only have about six of your perfect-man qualities."

"You wish you had six." Kait smiled at him, taking the sting out of the words. "You know I love you as a friend, and there's no one I'd rather have as a partner. You'd be perfect for some other woman. If you stop running away."

Erik groaned. "Enough."

"Fine. But I'm going to put a note in my calendar to let me know when the six-month ban on the topic is over." Then she took out her cell. He looked over her shoulder. She was actually doing it. Well, of course she was. She was Kait.

"Do you want—" Erik's radio interrupted him.

"6FB83. Code 2. 459 at 15 Charming Street. PR Lynne Quevas."

He radioed back to let dispatch know they were on the way. "And everyone kept telling us how safe Storybook Court was," he commented as he and Kait returned to their patrol car.

"Do you know the woman who was robbed?" Kait asked.

"Probably by sight, but I didn't recognize the name."

The drive to Storybook Court only took a few minutes, and since they didn't have to worry about the "no parking" regulation inside the community they arrived at the house—make that tree house—that had been robbed in less than five minutes.

Kait radioed in their arrival as they walked up to the place. The first floor was on ground level, but second and third floor were cradled in the branches of a large oak. Erik reached for the brass acorn-shaped door knocker, admiring the verdi patina on the leaf and acorn cap. He'd been thinking of trying a similar effect on a brass lighting fixture he'd found at a garage sale. Before he could actually use the knocker, the front door swung open.

Erik recognized the elegant sixty-something woman standing in the doorway. She'd been at the safety talk the day before, her silver hair in that same smooth twist, and he'd seen her around once in a while when he was with Tulip. "Mrs. Quevas?" he asked.

"Yes. Lynne. Call me Lynne." She fiddled with her pendant, a silver heart with two colored crystals dangling from it. He and his brother and sisters had given their mom one kind of like it, with one crystal in each of their birthstone colors.

"And we're Erik and Kait. I remember you from our talk," Kait said. "Lynne, the first thing we need to know is if you can give us a description of the burglar."

"No. I don't even know when the robbery happened." A faint crease formed between her brows. Very faint. Botox, maybe, Erik decided. If she'd had other work done, it was too subtle for him to pick up on. "I called as soon as I realized my necklace was missing, but it could have been gone for days. It's not something I wear often."

"Would you mind if we came in and asked you some more questions?" Erik asked.

"Oh! Of course. I'm sorry. I didn't think." She stepped back to let them inside. "Can I get you coffee or water or anything?"

"We're fine. But if you'd like anything feel free," Kait told Lynne as she led the way to the living room. There were windows everywhere. Potted plants and an area rug with a subtle leaf-and-flower pattern encouraged the feeling of being outdoors and indoors simultaneously.

A guy around Erik's age stood by one of two support beams carved into graceful tree branches. He looked like a jackass, dressed in hipster wear from head to toe—beanie, cardigan over ironic T-shirt, cuffed and lightly frayed jeans, some kind of high-cut vintage military boot.

"This is my son, Daniel," Lynne told them.

The extreme hipster pulled off his beanie, leaving his brown hair sticking up. "I just came back from an audition. The director's an Edgar Wright wannabe, so—" He gestured toward his outfit, then grinned. "Just so you don't think I'm a complete douche. If that's okay to say to cops."

"Not a problem," Erik told him. He'd had no idea who the director the guy name-checked was, but at least he knew he was dressed like a jackass, which meant he probably actually wasn't one. Erik wanted to ask him if he'd had any real acting jobs, but he knew that would make *him* the jackass, so he didn't.

"Please sit. Please," Lynne urged, her hand fluttered to her pendant again, then up to pat her hair. Erik wasn't sure if she was shaken by the robbery or if she was one of those people who got nervous around the police, whether or not they'd done anything wrong. "Can I get you tea? Or water? Or soda? Or ju—"

"Mom, stop." Daniel put his arm around his mother and gave her shoulders a squeeze. "Would you like anything to drink?" he asked.

"No thanks," Kait said, taking a seat on the long gray sofa.

Erik sat down next to her. "Some water would be great, thanks." He figured having a simple task might help Lynne calm down. She looked pleased as she hurried from the room.

Kait began gathering information for their report. "Daniel, can you tell us who lives in the household?"

He took the chair catty-corner to the sofa. "My dad, me, and my mom. I have a younger brother, too. He lives a few blocks from here, in that tower where the Old Spaghetti Factory used to be over on Sunset. I loved that place. They were supposed to at least keep the façade, but didn't happen. Did you know Max Reinhardt used to workshop his productions there? And give acting classes? Another piece of old Hollywood destroyed."

"Not to mention a place to get Mizithra cheese and browned butter spaghetti." Erik studied Daniel without being obvious about it. He was talking a lot. Nerves, or just his personality?

"Exactly!" Daniel exclaimed. "I love my brother, but it's people like him who are destroying this city. Rich bastards who have to have their luxury condos and don't care about the history and the personality of the city. I . . ." He let his words trail off when his mother returned with Erik's water. "Sorry. I get carried away."

"It's fine." Kait smiled at Lynne. "We were just starting to get some background information. Can you tell us the last time you saw the necklace?"

She began twisting her wedding ring around and around her finger as she perched on the edge of Daniel's chair. "A few weeks ago, my husband and I went to dinner at a friend's. I wore my black-and-white jacket dress, and I always wear the flower petal necklace my son Marcus gave me with that. I think I would have noticed if the necklace had already been taken from my jewelry box then."

"You should probably know the flower petal necklace was from Tiffany's. Lots of diamonds. My brother gave it to her the same birthday I gave her the one she has on. Thirty-five dollars.

And he knew I was giving her a necklace. I showed it to him."

O-kay. Clearly a little sibling rivalry there.

"You know I love them both," Lynne said. She was clearly the peacemaker type.

Kait raised her eyebrows. "The thief left the Tiffany's necklace behind?

"Nothing else was taken. I went through everything in the jewelry box, and Daniel helped me go over the house." Lynne started to pat her hair again, then seemed to realize how much she was fidgeting, and put her hands in her lap, fingers laced together.

"And the necklace that was missing? What can you tell us about that?" Erik asked. "If you have a picture, that would be helpful."

"It was a wedding gift from my husband's great aunt Maudie. It's—" She covered her mouth with her fingers, and whispered, "Hideous. The pendant is two mushrooms."

"I'd call it fabulously hideous," Daniel added. "And valuable. The pendant was originally a Van Cleef and Arpels brooch from the sixties. Red-and-white coral and diamond accents."

"I couldn't believe it when the insurance agent said we should cover it. I was only planning to insure the necklace from Marcus," Lynne explained. She gave Daniel an apologetic look.

"Is your insurance paid up?" Kait asked.

Someone knocked on the door before Lynne could answer. "Be right back. Kait, if you change your mind about wanting anything, tell Daniel."

"As far as I know the insurance is paid up. My mother is the type who pays the bills the day they arrive," Daniel told them. "My dad always says if he could he'd pay every bill a year in advance so she wouldn't have anything to worry about."

"Is money a worry?" Erik asked, glad Daniel had handed him the perfect opening.

"No. Not at all," Daniel told him. "My parents are in good financial shape. My mom is just a worrier, even when worry isn't necessary."

"I brought pound cake," Erik heard a woman announce. He grinned as Marie came into the room carrying a platter. She'd made good time. He and Kait had probably only been at the Quevas house for ten minutes.

"We're in the middle of preparing a police report," Kait told her. "Now isn't the best time for a visit." Marie ignored her, placing the tray on the coffee table, then beginning to transfer slices of cake and plastic forks to the napkins she'd also brought.

"Actually, it's the perfect time for Marie to visit." Marie handed Erik the first piece of cake without asking if he wanted it, which he definitely did. He'd had her cake before. "She knows everything that goes on at the Court. Have you seen anyone hanging around the last few weeks that didn't seem like they belonged?" he asked her.

"There's a new trash collector. He always leaves the lids up. When it rains, that swamps the cans." Marie handed Kait a piece of cake. Kait knew many horrifying statistics about what sugar did to brain function, but she didn't refuse to take it. Erik knew it was because she believed sacrifices had to be made to keep a potential witness happy. "I've spoken to him about it."

"Other than not following correct trash can protocol, is there anything suspicious about his behavior?" Erik asked.

Marie shot him a narrowed-eye look, trying to decide if he was making fun of her. Which he was, but only a little. He got a kick out of Marie. "No. And he's the only new person who's been at the Court," she said. "Well, Riley had a little friend from school over. Riley's only seven and her friend's right around there." Marie handed out the last piece of cake. "What did the person you're looking for do?"

"You mean you don't already know?" Erik teased. Marie scowled at him.

"My mom had a necklace stolen," Daniel explained.

"Not the one Marcus got you from Tiffany's!" Marie exclaimed.

"No, the one Kyle's great-aunt left me," Lynne answered.

"The one with the mushrooms?" Marie turned to Erik. "You're looking for someone blind. No one else would want it. You know it's true," she added to Lynne.

"They'd want it if they knew what it was worth," Kait said.

"That thing?" Marie gave a dismissive flip of her hand. "Impossible."

"When I was getting the anniversary necklace insured, the agent looked at the rest of my jewelry. He said it was worth—" Lynne hesitated, fiddling with her fork.

"Spit it out!" Marie ordered.

"Almost thirty thousand dollars."

For a moment, Marie was speechless. A first, as far as Erik knew. She picked up Erik's glass of water and took a long swallow, then asked, "Have you considered that cat?"

"Cat?" Kait repeated. "Erik, you said something about a cat yesterday, then you didn't explain."

Marie explained for him. "The cat's name is MacGyver. He went on a crime spree a few years ago. He belongs to Jamie Snyder. She's married now, but didn't change her name." Marie shook her head, lips pressed together in disapproval.

"Crime spree?" Kait repeated. "Crime spree?" she repeated again.

"Nothing valuable. It was mostly socks and underwear," Erik explained. "I was around a lot at the time. At Tulip's."

Marie clucked her tongue. "That silly girl." She turned to Lynne. "Aren't you going to give us something to drink with the cake?"

"I offered—" Lynne began, then headed for the kitchen without finishing her explanation. Marie was good at getting people to obey.

"And it wasn't just socks and underwear. He took two dolls, a plastic pony, a key chain, a diary, at least one earring, a Speedo—orange, and much too small for the owner—a T-shirt, and so many other things. You must have seen everything laid out on the fountain, when we were trying to get things back to their owners," Marie told Erik.

Kait's eyes had grown wider as Marie's list of stolen items had grown longer. "You really think this cat, this MacGyver, could actually be our perp? I apologize, but I must say it. That's bat-guano crazy."

"Would you like cold or room temperature?" Micah Jarvis's assistant asked her.

"Cold, please," Serena answered. She'd never been asked that in an Atlanta meeting. Although it had been a while since she'd gone to a meeting. Years, actually. Those years teaching and doing her vlog, wow, they'd gone by so fast.

"You got it." The assistant sauntered away.

Serena crossed her legs, admiring the geometric pattern on the inverted-heel orange pumps she'd chosen to give her outfit a pop of color. She'd gone for a black sleeveless turtleneck and dark wash J Brand jeans. Good jeans, jeans that *fit*, were an essential part of an actor's wardrobe, and she'd scoured eBay until she'd found two perfect pairs in her price range. She didn't really care about brand names, but it was important to look like, although you wanted a job, you didn't *need* a job. The J Brands, almost two hundred bucks new, sent that message, as did the shoes, Fendi, on loan from Bethany, one of her besties back in "The A."

A girl, probably only a couple years out of her teens, sat

down at the other end of the white semi-circular sofa that dominated the lobby. A few seconds later, the assistant returned with Serena's water. "Micah needs about ten more minutes," he said. Serena thanked him, then took a sip of water. She glanced over at the girl—young woman. Although she sat still, no fidgeting, Serena could almost see the nerves vibrating under her skin.

"Are you a cold-water person or a room-temperature-water person?" Serena asked, thinking some small talk might calm the girl down. She didn't answer. Serena repeated the question a bit more loudly.

The girl startled. "Huh?"

Serena smiled. "When I got here, they asked if I wanted cold water or room-temperature water. I'd never been asked that before. I was just curious what you get."

"Cold." She didn't turn toward Serena as she answered.

"Are you from LA?"

"Bakersfield."

The small talk was not working. Maybe the girl just wanted to be left alone so she could get focused before they called her in. But that's not the vibe Serena was getting. She was getting a scared-spitless vibe. She stood up. "I'm going to go Wonder Woman in the bathroom. It's this thing I do to get a confidence boost before meetings."

She'd only taken a few steps before the girl asked, "What is it?"

"It's kind of goofy. You just stand in a Wonder Woman pose." Serena illustrated by spreading her feet apart, planting her hands on her hips, and throwing her shoulders back. She glanced at the receptionist, who showed no reaction to her going superhero in the lobby. "I saw a TED talk about it," Serena continued. "When your body takes up more space, your stress hormones go down, and your testosterone goes up."

"I don't think I want more testosterone," she said, but she sounded intrigued.

"I'm not talking enough testosterone to grow a beard," Serena answered. "Testosterone's the dominance hormone. And I want to go into my meeting ready to dominate! By which I mean present my best natural self in a way that will make an agent want to represent me."

The girl laughed. "You know how many times I've read articles that say something like that? I'm not sure I even know what my natural self is."

"Sometimes I feel like mine depends on how much sugar and caffeine I've had," Serena confessed. "So, Wonder Woman? I'm Serena by the way."

"Juliet." She rolled her eyes. "I don't think you should name a girl after a suicidal teenager, but my mom loves it. And it's not that common, which is good for acting. And yes. I want to Wonder Woman."

"Bathroom?" Serena asked the receptionist, who jerked her chin toward a hall to the left in response.

"I'm insanely nervous," Juliet said once the door of the empty bathroom was shut behind them. "This is only my second meeting. And I tanked at the first one."

Serena got back in the Wonder Woman position. "Let the pose work its magic. I mean its scientific hormone adjusting. We're supposed to hold it for two minutes." Juliet set the timer on her cell, and joined Serena in the pose.

"I actually feel better," Juliet said when the timer went off. "I don't know if it's just my imagination, but—"

"Don't analyze it. Just accept it," Serena advised. "I've gotta get back out there."

"I'm going to stay a little longer. I'm a half an hour early!"

"Try doing a few minutes of this." Serena widened her feet again and held her arms up in a wide V, her chin raised. "It's another power pose."

"Thanks," Juliet said. "I wasn't expecting anyone to be nice to me here."

"If people don't treat you well at an agency, you're at the wrong agency," Serena answered. "I'm sure you're heard this a million times, too, but remember that the meeting is like a first date. The agent isn't the only one evaluating. You are too. You should be trying to decide if he or she is good enough for you!"

"Have a good first date, then." Juliet got into the new pose.

"You too." Serena left the bathroom, trying to remember the last time she'd had a first date. It had been . . . a while. After she split up with Jonathan, she'd had a couple, then she'd just sort of . . . taken a break, without really deciding to. That dinner with Erik would have ended the break. But he'd turned out to be—She searched for the right word. Fickle? Moody? He'd been flirting with her. It might have been a while since she'd had a date, but she still knew what it felt like when a man was flirting, and he was flirting. Then *pffft*.

Not the time to be thinking about Erik, Wonder Woman, she told herself as she returned to her spot on the couch. Actually, she shouldn't be thinking of him at any time. Because of the *pffft*.

A few minutes later, a tall man a few—make that at least four—years younger than she strode into the lobby. "Serena?" he said.

"Yes." She stood and shook his hand. "Thanks for meeting with me."

"My pleasure. Come on back." He led the way up a wide set of stairs.

If this was really a date, she'd be severely underdressed. Micah could have walked off a runway. He clearly used a bespoke tailor. His three-piece suit—Serena thought the color probably had a name like sangria—fit too perfectly to be off the rack. She was sure his textured leather shoes were from an impressive designer, but she had no idea who.

I'm the talent, she reminded herself. *If I showed up in a suit, they'd think I wasn't creative.* Once she'd asked an agent friend how a meeting with one of her acting students had gone. "He wore a suit," was the answer, and her friend had sounded bewildered, bordering on appalled.

Micah opened the door and ushered her to a chair that looked a little like patio furniture to Serena. She was sure the black strips that formed the seat and back weren't made of the same kind of plastic as her mom's deck chairs, but they looked identical.

"Nice shoes," he commented as he sat down behind his desk.

Bless you, Bethany. She'd have to shoot her friend a text and tell her that the borrowed shoes had been a big success. Except, now what? An agent meeting was supposed to be a chance to show your personality. The best ones really were like a good date, where you had a conversation with natural back and forth. She knew an actress who got an agent because the two of them had gotten into a conversation about hip dysplasia in golden retrievers. It had started with the actress admiring the picture of the dog the agent had on her desk. But Serena knew she couldn't hold up her end of a conversation about shoes. Or fashion. Micah was way out of her league.

She glanced around the room, hoping for inspiration. Nothing. Except . . . Yes, that was the corner of a Big Hunk candy bar sticking out from under a folder. She'd recognize that white *B* on that deep brown background anywhere. "That's my personal crack." Serena slid the folder over to reveal the candy. "My aunt would always bring me a couple when she came to visit. She lived in San Jose. Do they sell them around here? I have to order from Amazon!"

Micah laughed. "Around here, you can get them at pretty much every drug store or grocery store."

"Do you ever microwave them? Just for maybe ten seconds?

They get so gooey. It makes them even more yumtastic." Yes, she had just said "yumtastic." That was a little much. It's not like she was trying to get cast as the next Rachael Ray. Which was good, because of the not-cooking.

"Sacrilege! They have to be hard. Too hard to even break without whacking them on a counter." Micah pointed at her, face getting stern. "You can't repeat any of this conversation. If you do, I'll deny it. I'll call you a liar. Everyone knows sugar destroys every part of your body, and that is why I never eat sugar. Or Big Hunks."

Serena shook her head. "Big Hunks are completely fine. They're sweetened with honey. Honey is a phytonutrient." She lowered her voice to a whisper. "Except the first ingredient on the label is corn syrup, which everyone knows is even worse than sugar. And the second ingredient is sugar." She raised her voice again. "But honey, with the wonderful, wonderful phytonutrients is the fourth ingredient. So, eat on!"

Micah picked up the candy bar, slammed it down on the edge of his surely very expensive desk, and handed her a piece. She immediately popped it into her mouth. " 'Louis, I think this is the beginning of a beautiful friendship,' " Micah said, then popped his own piece.

"Impressive," Serena managed to say, even though the Big Hunk had partially cemented her back teeth together. "You got it exactly right. Not 'I think this is the start' or 'This could be the beginning,' "

"Attention to detail," Micah mumbled around the sticky candy. "It's one of my finest qualities as an agent."

Breathe it in, Serena told herself. This is you about to get an agent. Probably. Maybe.

Make that definitely. An hour later, Micah was outlining his plan for Serena. He was going to hook her up with a colleague who handled commercials, and start setting up auditions, probably just small parts. "Although there's one role." His eyes glinted as he smiled at her. "I shouldn't say anything yet."

"Oh, no, no, no." Serena shook her finger at him. "You can't keep anything from me. I don't want to resort to blackmail, but I do know about—the suuugaaar."

"Okay. I'll tell. The director of the remake of *Creature from the Black Lagoon*—"

"Norberto Foster! I love him. I loved that movie. He managed to make the Creature sexy, sexy and tragic. Not an easy task. Is he doing something with a part for me? Is he?" Serena knew she sounded like a five-year-old, but she didn't care. "I'd take anything. I'd work for free."

"Don't ever say that again," Micah warned. "He's starting up a project about a cat burglar. The twist is that the cat burglar is actually really a cat part of the time, a werecat. It probably sounds silly—"

"Norberto won't let it be silly," Serena interrupted. "He'll make it mysterious and beautiful and deep."

"Rumor is that he's looking for an unknown to play the werecat."

Serena felt her eyes widen and her breathing pick up. "The werecat is a woman?"

Micah nodded.

"And you think you might, possibly, maybe, get me in there to audition?"

He nodded again.

Serena reached out to shake his hand. "Louis, this is definitely the beginning of a beautiful friendship."

Mac slid a package of tuna from the cupboard. Jamie hadn't called him a bad kitty after he took the last one. It was like she hadn't noticed it was gone. With the package held between his teeth, he jumped up to the countertop. His ears flicked, listening for the sound of Jamie or David's footsteps. Even though he was extremely stealthy, sometimes they seemed to sense he was doing something against one of their human rules.

But no one came.

He walked down to the treat jars and opened the bonehead's with a couple flicks of the paw. He fished out one of what the humans called bones—although they didn't smell like any bone Mac had ever encountered—and let it fall onto the counter.

A second later he heard Diogee galloping toward the kitchen. The bonehead might be a bonehead, but he knew the sound a treat made when it hit the counter. The meatbrain gave a loud woof as he rounded the corner. Mac hissed back, one paw raised in warning, claws out. The bonehead knew what that meant, too. He snapped his jaws shut, not that that stopped the drool from sliding out of his mouth.

Mac looked down at the treat, took aim, and—*whap!*—sent it flying into the perfect position on the floor, just under the round window. The window that was too high for Mac to reach on his own. As soon as Diogee leaned down to grab the not-really-a-bone, Mac leaped onto his head.

Diogee gave a grunt of surprise—he'd never gotten over getting surprised during this maneuver. His stupidity could be useful. Useful to Mac anyway. The dog jerked his head up, giving Mac the assist he needed to reach the windowsill. He heard Diogee whining as Mac slipped outside. Usually when he whined, one of the humans would call to him to see what the problem was.

Mac listened, but no one called.

There was something going on with Mac's people. He'd have to figure it out, but later. He had hungry kittens waiting for him. He loped over to their hiding place, then squeezed into the tunnel, struggling to bring the package of tuna with him.

Before he'd gotten even halfway in, something grabbed him

by the tail! Something with sharp teeth. Mac abandoned the tuna and backed out fast. He spun toward his attacker, claws out, ready for a fight.

Sassy sat there staring at him with her sharp blue eyes. All the kits had blue eyes. Bittles' were the biggest, even though he was the littlest. Even though they were the same age, somehow Sassy's seemed like they'd seen a lot.

What was she doing out here? She was supposed to be safe inside with the others. Maybe he should start calling this kitten Trouble.

CHAPTER 4

"Before we get too much deeper in this case, do I need to look up how to Mirandize a cat?" Kait joked. She and Erik sat on the edge of the fountain. They'd just returned to Storybook Court. After they finished up at the Quevas house, they'd had to do a safety talk at The Gardens, the retirement home behind Storybook, and when they'd finished that, they'd headed over to Le Conte Middle to help out with soccer practice and meet some of the local kids. This was the first chance they'd had to talk about the robbery.

"I think you're good. When Mac was stealing stuff, he always left it someplace nearby. Sometimes at Jamie's, sometimes at other houses around the Court," Erik answered. "And while he's a clever cat, I'm doubtful he could pick the most valuable piece out of a jewelry box."

"Whoever the thief was, the Quevases made it way too easy for them. How can anyone routinely leave doors and windows unlocked?"

"Especially after we stood right here last week and gave

them safety advice." Erik shook his head. "I didn't think we needed to mention something as basic as locking up."

"I should have told them in the last six months there were one thousand nine hundred and seventy-three property crimes in Hollywood."

They'd been partners for almost four years, but Erik still marveled at Kait's ability to spew out statistics down to the last number, no rounding up or down. "How do you keep all those stats in your head? Where do you store stuff like plots of *Even Stevens* episodes and the multiplication tables?"

Kait shrugged. "Like I've told you, it's how my brain works. Actually, I thought everybody's worked that way until I was in high school."

"You're going to ace the detective's exam. I know for sure you have our policies and procedures and all the rest already stored in the database." He tapped her head.

"You'll do great, too. We're reviewing all the factual stuff in our group. And a chunk of the exam is problem solving, which you excel at," Kait reminded him. They were both planning to take the exam later that month, and had been studying together along with Jandro. Jandro had actually taken the exam almost a year ago, but hadn't passed and was prepping for a second run at it.

This month was the earliest Kait could take the exam. She'd just hit her four-year mark as a uniform cop. Erik was getting close to having six years under his belt. The only way to move up was to take the exam, and that's what pretty much everyone did. There were parts of a detective's job that intrigued him, but he'd miss being in uniform, especially now that he'd been assigned to a beat.

"You're not really worried about passing, are you?" Kait asked. "The psych evaluation might be a little bit of a challenge, but you can usually give the appearance of decent mental health."

Erik gave his best fake laugh, which turned into the real thing when Kait cracked up. "Let's focus on what we've got in front of us right now. What'd you think of the son Daniel?" Erik asked.

"Seemed to have a solid relationship with mom. Definitely some sibling rivalry going."

Erik nodded. "Same as what I thought."

"He also doesn't have much money. It's not like his mom, or I assume his dad, who is still working, need him at home. He has to be doing it to save on rent," Kait added. "If they're making him pay anything, I bet it's only a token amount."

"If he needs money badly enough to steal, it would have been easy for him to take the necklace. He also knew exactly how much the necklace was worth. It's hard to come up with a reason for another thief to take only one thing."

"Unless they got interrupted and had to run for it when they heard someone coming back into the house." Kait stood. "Let's ask around. See if anyone saw anything. Although if Mrs. Quevas was right about the time frame of the theft, we're looking at two weeks ago."

Erik scrambled to come up with a reason not to go to the lighthouse. But since it was almost directly across the street from the Quevas house, there was no acceptable excuse. He was just being, as Kait would say, a chicken-guano. "Let's go to the lighthouse first," he suggested. To show Kait that he had no problem with it.

"Rip the Band-Aid off. Best choice."

"There's no Band-Aid, because there's nothing to be Band-Aided anymore," Erik protested. Kait gave him a yeah-right sniff, but didn't say anything. It really wasn't like he walked around moping about Tulip all the time. He hardly ever thought of her anymore.

"It's hard to imagine living here," Kait said as they walked down the winding street. The Court wasn't a right-angle kind of place. "It's extremely adorable, but it's a little too make-believe for real life. For example, that house." She gestured to a cottage with a thatched roof and an artfully crooked chimney. It looked like a big version of one of those fairy houses his youngest niece loved. "I couldn't read over case notes in there. It's like I'd be corrupting it."

"Truth." Erik led the way over the crushed seashells that made the pathway to the lighthouse, tension building with every step. He was a cop, fer chrissake. A building shouldn't be able to do this to him.

He was sure Kait had picked up on his reaction, but she didn't comment. She didn't even sigh, or sniff. She was probably thinking of their deal not to talk about relationship stuff for six months. Kait took promises very seriously.

Erik gave two sharp raps on the door, ignoring the mermaid door knocker. "What are you doing here?" Serena blurted out when she opened the door. "Sorry," she immediately added. "I just . . . wasn't expecting you."

"We're here to ask you a couple questions about a robbery in the neighborhood," Kait told her.

"A robbery?" Serena's brows drew together. "Sure. Do you want to come in?"

Erik would rather talk to her right there, but Kait again took the lead. "That would be great."

Serena swung the door wider and stepped back so they could go inside. His eyes flicked over her. He couldn't stop himself from taking in the fit of those jeans of hers. And that sleeveless top . . . It wasn't low. At all. It had a turtleneck. A turtleneck! But it was sexy as hell, the soft material clinging to her breasts. His gaze moved lower, finally snagging on her toes. She had cute toes. There was a little chip in the orange polish on one nail and it made him—

Was he staring? He might have been staring. He forced his attention to the room. He hadn't been expecting it to look the same. He'd forgotten that the lighthouse came furnished. Everything brought back moments with Tulip.

"Have a seat." Serena gestured them to the big kitchen table. He'd had Tulip right there. He tried to force the mental image to go dark, but every detail stayed clear. He needed to go stick his head under the tap or hit it with a hammer. Since those weren't options, he sat down and took out the little notebook he always carried. He could at least give the appearance of a professional here to do a professional job in a professional way. Even though his brain was now showing him having Tulip up against that blue fridge over there. And bent over that counter.

"Who was robbed?" Serena asked, taking the seat across from Kait. She probably didn't want to have to look directly at Erik. He'd been an a-hole the last time they'd been together, asking her over for dinner, then uninviting her in basically the rudest way possible.

This time Erik didn't let Kait do the talking. "The Quevases across the street." Okay, okay, good. He'd sounded completely normal, not like he was in mid-meltdown.

"I love that place. I wanted a tree house so bad when I was a kid," Serena said.

"Didn't everybody?" Kait asked.

"I didn't," Erik told them. "I had one, and I hated it."

"You have to explain. You can't just say something like that and drop it." Serena gave the lazy Susan in the middle of the table a spin.

Erik hesitated. Before he could decide how he wanted to answer, Kait jumped in. "I bet it was the babysitter from hell." She turned to Kait. "Erik had the worst babysitter. She'd tell him and his brother and sisters these horrible stories. There was one about a bloody hand coming out of the toilet that had him sneaking outside to pee and—"

"And we get the picture," Erik interrupted. "She really was

evil." The lazy Susan had stopped and he impulsively set it spinning again. "She'd always say that the disembodied hand monster, or whatever, wouldn't come and get us as long as we were with someone older, like her. It kept us in line."

"And traumatized, I bet. If I'd had her as a babysitter, I'd still be sleeping with the lights on!" Serena exclaimed.

"I did until I was about twelve," Erik admitted. "She had a truly nightmare-inducing story about a kid-eater who lived in the tree house. It was really detailed. How it sliced the flesh of the kids while they were still alive. Although, of course, not if we were with her." He shook his head. "I wonder what she grew up to be?"

"Mascot. Definitely," Serena answered.

"Mascot. Like the San Diego Chicken?" Kait sounded puzzled.

"Exactly. They are all extremely creepy." She looked over at Erik, and he felt that same electric snap he had when he'd taken her hand to help her up on the edge of the fountain the other day. "Your former babysitter is now routinely creeping out thousands of people in a creepy mascot suit."

Erik laughed.

"I forgot to ask if either of you wanted water or anything." Serena stood. "I have some iced tea, some soda . . ."

"Iced tea would be great," Kait answered.

"I'm good," Erik told her. His eyes followed Serena as she started across the room. She was wearing the hell out of those jeans.

"I'm too new to know who's usual. I moved in not even a week ago. I haven't even ordered off the secret menu of In-N-Out Burger." Serena filled a glass with tea.

Erik suddenly realized that the Tulip erotica had stopped playing at some point during the visit. She was so warm, even though he'd been a jerk to her. And funny. He had a weakness for funny women. But he was not getting involved with another Lighthouse Award recipient. He knew how it would go. She'd throw everything into her Hollywood Dreams, all her passion and intelligence, and talent. And her heart would break into too many pieces to be repaired when she didn't make it. All his love wouldn't be enough to—

And in mid-thought he'd switched from Serena to Tulip. They were two different women. One was his ex. One was a casual acquaintance. Who'd created enough of a spark within minutes that he'd invited her over to his home. He hardly ever invited women over. Definitely not women he'd barely met. He usually suggested their place.

Serena returned with Kait's iced tea. Erik stood up before she could take a sip.

"Let's try the Quevases' next-door neighbor. The one with the curtains open. Didn't look like anyone was home on the other side yet."

Kait started to put her glass down. "Take it with you," Serena urged. "You'll be around on your beat. Just leave it on the porch if I'm not home.

"Thanks." Kait stood. "I recently read a study about brain function and dehydration. Test subjects who were dehydrated made as many errors as drivers who were at the legal limit for alcohol."

"I didn't know that. I knew it was good for you to drink a lot of water, good for your skin, but I didn't realize it had a big effect on the brain."

Kait smiled. "You should also know that the Lakers don't have a mascot. You—"

"We need to get going," Erik interrupted. He kept noticing things he liked about Serena. She'd sounded genuinely interested in Kait's dehydration PSA. Not everyone bothered to listen when Kait started spouting facts.

Kait ignored him and continued with what she'd been saying. "You can go to a game without fear."

"Aww, thanks, Kait." Serena smiled, a smile that made crinkles at the corners of her eyes. "You may have just changed my life!"

Erik started for the door, relieved to hear Kait's footsteps behind him. He'd been sure she'd have a few remarks for him about his rudeness, but she must have decided to give him a break. Which meant he was in worse shape than he thought.

They headed to the house next door to the Quevases'. "I love the wavy roof," Erik commented when they reached the gate, wanting to break the silence and get things back to normal between him and Kait. "It looks ramshackle, but was obviously designed that way." She didn't reply. "And that waterwheel. Beautiful touch. And the pond."

"Someone's outside," Kait said. Erik had been too busy yammering away to notice the Asian guy, late twenties/early thirties, sitting on a rustic bench on the side of the house opposite the waterwheel. When he saw Erik looking his way, he stood and gave a wave, but looked wary. Erik wished that was more unusual, but people usually looked wary when he and Kait showed up. Maybe going back to beats would change that. People would see them often enough they'd just be Erik and Kait, not those two cops who couldn't be here for any good reason.

"Hi, we're your new neighborhood beat cops!" Erik called as he and Kait walked through the gate. He didn't recognize the guy. He hadn't been at the safety talk the other day.

"Not to be confused with your friendly neighborhood Spider-Man," Kait added as they approached him. Spider-Man was her favorite superhero, partly because he was a regular guy, not someone born with superpowers, but mostly because he really cared about people, about individual people. He'd stay and chat with them. He was interested in their lives. He was kind of like a beat cop actually, a neighborhood superhero.

"Then it won't be a problem that I've been trying to recreate

Osborn's formula in the basement." He glanced over at the house. "The basement that I have managed to make invisible."

"Impressive. Not even Venom can pull that off. He can camouflage himself, but, unless I'm wrong, not objects."

"She's never wrong," Erik said. The superhero conversation seemed to have gotten rid of the guy's nerves. Good. Although his nervousness seemed to have been transferred to his partner. Kait shifted her weight slightly from foot to foot, then pushed one of her braids away from her face. And Kait wasn't a fidgeter.

She's attracted to him, Erik realized. He tried to look at the guy through Kait's eyes. Short black hair, the front left long enough to fall over his forehead. Straight dark eyebrows. Narrow eyes—brown. Pronounced cheekbones.

If he were looking through Kait's eyes, he was looking through her cop eyes. He tried to switch to her woman eyes, he guessed he should call them. And trying to think that way, yeah, the man was good-looking. And he liked Spider-Man. Liking Spider-Man wasn't on Kait's list of perfect-guy qualities, but it should be. It was a lot more important than texting or calling or otherwise communicating daily, which was, he thought, number six on the list.

Erik tuned back into the conversation. They'd moved on to someone who sounded like another Spidey villain. He waited for a lull, then asked, "Are you related to Grace Imura?" He figured this visit could be part interview about the robbery, and part getting to know someone on the beat. "I used to go out with the woman who lived across the street, and I got to know the neighbors."

"She's my aunt. I'm Charlie Imura." He shook hands with them both, then asked, "You want to sit?" He dropped down onto the bench and gestured to the wooden chairs across from it.

"Grace is great. Once my girlfriend, former girlfriend," Erik quickly amended, "posted on Facebook that she had a killer migraine, and your aunt showed up at the door about half an hour later with a bottle of Aleve.

"Sounds like her." Charlie smiled. "When I was a kid, every time she came over, we'd play Crazy Eights for pennies. I mean, we'd play game after game after game. Any other adult would have gone, well, crazy. But she never said it was time to stop."

"It's great that you're still close to her," Kait said. "At least I'm assuming you are, since you're here." Having a good relationship with family was absolutely on Kait's list. Charlie might actually be someone Kait could go out with more than a couple times.

"So, what's up?" Charlie shifted in his chair. His pant leg rode up, and that's when Erik saw it—the black ankle bracelet. He could tell from Kait's stiffening posture that she'd seen it, too. Charlie was on house arrest, and that meant he'd done something hardcore.

"We want to introduce ourselves to everyone in the neighborhood," Erik told him. They'd get to the bracelet. "And we want to know if you've seen anyone in the neighborhood these last few weeks that didn't belong. There's been a robbery."

"But first why don't you tell us about that ankle bracelet." Kait's voice had gone cool, all business, none of that sparkle it had had when they were talking Aunt Grace and Spiderman.

"I wasn't trying to hide it, exactly. I just usually don't bring it up, at least not right away. Maybe I should have, since you're cops. But if there's a rule about it, I didn't know." Kait had gone cop, and Charlie had gone perp, sounding nervous and defensive.

"Just answer the question, please," Kait said.

"Drug trafficking." He didn't give details or excuses.

"You're staying with your aunt as part of your house arrest, then." The muscles in her shoulders had gone tight. A criminal charge was nowhere on Kait's list of must-haves.

"Yes." Charlie didn't lower his gaze from hers.

Erik decided it was time to redirect the conversation. "Have you noticed anything suspicious, Charlie?"

"Nope," he answered. "And when I'm not at work, I'm here. You know the drill."

"You didn't take much time to think about the question," Kait challenged.

"If I'd noticed something suspicious around my aunt's place, I'd remember."

"If you think of anything, or if you see anything in the neighborhood you think we should be aware of, please get in touch." Erik stood and handed Charlie his card.

Charlie stood too. "I will." He looked over at Kait. "Remember that time Spider-Man robbed a jewelry store?"

" 'Amazing Spider-Man' number eighty-seven," she shot back. "But he was sick. He was delusional. I hope you weren't attempting to compare his actions to yours." She turned and walked away, without giving him a chance to answer.

"Friendly, neighborhood drug trafficker in our neighborhood. Nice," Kait muttered when they reached the sidewalk.

"And I'd actually started thinking he might be the guy who could meet enough of your requirements to get at least one date. Before we found out his deal."

Kait stared at him. "What? Why?"

"He was flirting with you. And you were flirting back. That's mutual attraction. Number nine on the list."

"It was just a conversation about a mutual interest. Not mutual attraction. Mutual attraction is what you had with Serena when we were just at her house."

"You know she's the last person I'd be interested in."

"That's not what it looked like when you were looking at her. And vice-versa. You weren't quite ogling, but it was close."

Erik couldn't argue.

"Seeing that, I might reconsider the not-eating-where-you-defecate rule," Kait told him. "But you have to treat her right."

The kittens were finally asleep. Even Sassy. Mac stood and stretched, his back curving, then he took in a deep breath of air. The scent of his urine was still strong, almost masking the scent of the kittens. He'd carefully buried their scat, not wanting anything out there in the dark to detect their existence. They were too weak to protect themselves. He'd never thought he'd be burying waste that wasn't his, but he did what had to be done. As always. It's not as if anyone else was stepping up.

After a final glance at the kits, Mac crawled through the tunnel and out into the darkening night. He needed to start investigating humans, so he'd know which ones deserved to share their home with one of his family. Yes, somehow, like it or not, they'd become his family, just the way Jamie had, then David and Diogee. He hadn't wanted to take on the bonehead, but David was Diogee's person and that meant the two of them had to stay together. And it had been obvious that David couldn't really handle the mutt without an assist.

Now instead of enjoying himself, he had to scout for four worthy humans. There were a bunch he liked in his neighborhood, but liking them wasn't enough. He needed to be sure they would understand a kitten's needs—food, water, cloth mousies who smelled so good they could make an adult cat dizzy, sardines . . . Mac knew where he could get some sardinesies. He could be crunching the little bones in minutes. But he was not a dog. He was not ruled by his stomach.

Ears forward, whiskers pushing forward, too, he trotted down the street to Zachary's house. When he got to the porch, he reared up on his back legs and slapped one paw down on the ding-dong. Zachary opened the door right away, but he didn't lean down to give Mac a scratch under the chin. He didn't head toward the kitchen to get Mac a treat.

Mac had trained Zachary better than that! Tail bristling, he followed the naughty human into the living room where Addison was waiting, as Mac knew she would be. It was almost impossible to surprise a cat. "We should just break up now," she blah-blahed. Her voice was high and shrill. It felt like a bee sting in Mac's ear.

"This was supposed to be a celebration," Zachary blah-blahed back. His voice was quiet, but Mac could smell that things weren't right with him. That other smell, the sharp, sweet smell that made Mac's nose itch, couldn't cover the odor of the human's emotions. "Was it stupid of me to think my girl-friend would be happy I got a full scholarship? For track, something I love."

"I thought you loved me," Addison blah-blahed. She smelled angry the way Zachary did, but also sad, the way Zachary did. And Addison wasn't paying any more attention to Mac than Zachary was. Mac had known these two should be packmates, and he'd made it happen. He didn't understand why they were always hissing and growling at each other.

"I hate talking to you when you're like this." Zachary shoved his fingers through the fur on his head. Poor humansies. They only had patches of fur, not even enough to stay warm. They had to wear clothes. Even if Mac went bald, he would not lower himself to wearing outfits. "It's not like Cal Poly is that far away. It's not like we'll never see each other. It's not like we're breaking up."

"That's what everybody says. And it always happens. No one stays together if they don't go to the same school."

Something warm and wet plopped down onto Mac's head. She was crying on him, and she hadn't even bothered to give him anything, not even one little bite of cat kibble.

"It's not going to happen to us."

Mac turned and headed back to the door as Zachary pulled Addison toward him, then started slobbering on her. He had to smack the door with both paws five times in a row before Zachary came and opened it for him.

With a huff of annoyance, Mac slipped outside. They had just completely disrespected him. They had ignored him completely. He couldn't trust either of them with one of his kittens. A kitten could starve to death while they blah-blahed and dribbled.

He turned in the direction of the home he and Jamie'd shared before they became packmates with David and Diogee. There was another old friend who might know the correct way to treat a kitten. Mac had thought she would be good for Riley, the young one who was one of Addison's pack, and, of course, he'd been correct. Ruby took good care of Riley when they were together. Taking care of a kitten would require more effort, but Ruby might be able to handle it.

Mac couldn't quite reach the ding-dong next to Ruby's door, so he meowed, and meowed, and meowed. He knew Ruby was inside, Ruby and Riley. He decided he'd try one more meow, and if they didn't respond, he'd tear a hole in a screen or climb down the chimney. The only reason he hadn't done that in the first place, was that he'd noticed it made humans agitated. Unlike cats, humans were very easy to surprise. Their noses hardly functioned, and their ears and eyes weren't much better.

He opened his mouth and let out a long meow that turned into a yowl. "There's a kitty outside!" Riley blah-blahed, then the door swung open. "Mac! It's you!" He took the time to rub himself against her leg in greeting, then sauntered into the house. He'd never been inside before. Ruby came to his house so often that he didn't need to go and visit her.

The smell of the place got his approval. Something in the cooking area had a scent similar to his Mousie's. It made him feel like running over to the curtains and climbing straight up!

But he wasn't here to play. He did have time for a little snack, though, and the odor of one of his favorite treats was mixed with the Mousie smell.

Ruby stood by the stove. "Will you pick a few basil leaves off that there plant, pardner?" she blah-blahed without turning around.

"We're not cowboys. We're princesses," Riley answered.

Ruby nodded. "Princesses from a planet where everyone is a princess. I just miss being a cowboy sometimes. Remember when I'd make purple flapjacks?" She gave a sigh. "At least you still love ponies."

"Princesses always have ponies," Riley blah-blahed. "Except when they have unicorns."

"Well, Princess Riley Pom-Pom, please set the table for our feast of regal salad and royal mac and cheese, with majestic cupcakes to follow."

"We request that we set a place for MacGyver, even though he isn't a princess. He could be a prince from a planet of royal cats."

"Mac's here?" Ruby turned and looked down at him. "How did you get in here, you glorious creature?"

"I let him in. Can Prince MacGyver stay?" Riley asked.

"Sorry, sweetie. You can give him a few blueberries from the salad. Jamie feeds them to him sometimes, and he loves them. But he can't stay. He'll get hair everywhere, and I'm allergic to cats. Whenever I get close to one—" Ruby gave a loud sneeze. "I sneeze."

She swept Mac up in her arms and gave him a cuddle, then hurried toward the door. "I love you, Mac. And I'm happy to sneeze whenever I'm at your house. But I can't have you in here." Ruby opened the door, put Mac outside, then quickly shut it.

Mac didn't get it. Ruby had been happy to see him. She'd

snuggled with him. Then she put him out. Put *him* out. It was much worse than being disrespected and ignored. It was—The door swung open, and Riley fed him three blueberries. They weren't fishies of any kind, but they were an acceptable offering. "You're a good kitty-cat. I'll see you soon." She shut the door.

If Riley were older, she might be an acceptable person for one of his kittens. But she still smelled mostly like a kitten herself. And Ruby—Humans could be so hard to understand. He liked Ruby, and he knew she liked him. He could always smell when a human didn't. But, still, she couldn't be trusted with a kitten, not after what she'd just done.

He trotted down the street, around the corner, past his old house, and over to the place where the humans called Al and Marie lived. Al was pawing around in the ground in the yard. Mac didn't see any reason for the digging. Al didn't have any waste to bury. No claws to sharpen, either. Al didn't sleep outside, so he couldn't be trying to make a comfy bed. Mac didn't smell any tasties in the hole, so Al couldn't be attempting to hunt.

Why bother to try to understand humans? Mac had figured out back when he was a kitten himself that they made no sense. They could be trained to do a few things, like deliver food and water and toys, but they didn't have the capacity for much more than that. Which is why they needed cats to look out for them. When they grew up, his kittens would end up doing much more for their humans than their humans did for them. Basic law of nature.

Mac didn't have time to visit with Al right now. Marie was the alpha of the pack, that had always been easy to smell. She was the one he needed to evaluate. He started toward her front door, and before he reached it, it swung open, like Marie had known he was there before he ding-donged. She was more observant than any other human Mac had encountered. It's like she was part cat.

"Well, if you're coming in, come in," Marie blah-blahed. "Although we both know you're supposed to be safe at home."

Mac trotted inside. Marie shut the door behind him, then disappeared into one of the other rooms. Mac jumped onto the chair that looked the coziest. There was no reason he shouldn't evaluate Marie in comfort.

She returned a moment later and narrowed her eyes at him. "No, sir." She picked him up and dumped him on the floor. Dumped! Him! She put the folded towel she carried on the chair, then scooped Mac up again and plopped him—Plopped! Him!—down on the towel. "Don't move!" she blah-blahed sternly. Then she left again.

This time when she returned, she carried a small plate. Mac's nostrils twitched as he smelled the turkey. Marie held the plate out in front of him. Mac didn't need to be asked twice. He quickly ate the treat, then licked the plate to make sure he'd gotten every delicious drop of the warm gravy. Points for Marie. Big points. Maybe enough to cancel out the dumping and plopping.

Until she began wiping Mac's mouth with a small, damp cloth. She wiped his mouth! With water! Did he look dirty to her? No. Impossible. Mac was a cat, and unlike humans, cats knew the purpose of their tongues—to keep themselves clean. Humans didn't have the capacity to understand this basic fact. They were always submerging themselves in water or spraying themselves with water, or wiping themselves with water.

Marie reached for one of Mac's front paws. It was clear she intended to get it wet! He sprang off the chair, raced to the chimney, and jumped inside. Bracing his paws on either side of the brick tunnel, he climbed straight up, then out into the fresh air. He was absolutely not going to put one of his kittens in the care of Marie. She might have good intentions, but she had no idea what a cat needed. Well, she knew a cat needed turkey, but the wet. The wet! No, he had to keep looking for homes.

Mac opened his mouth and used his tongue to flick air inside. He evaluated the odors, then chose a group of smells he thought had possibilities. He leapt onto the trunk of a nearby palm tree, digging his claws in hard, then he scrambled down to the ground and followed the scent trail he'd chosen. It took him to a house not too far from where he put the kittens. Only a screen door blocked his entrance, and one good paw-flick took care of that.

Three humans, two male and one female, sat in the living room blah-blahing. They smelled like a pack.

"Marie actually told me she *hoped* someone would steal a ring that's been in Al's family for generations. She thinks it's hideous, and—" The woman dropped her voice to a near whisper. "I'm afraid it is."

"Don't sound so scandalized," one of the males blah-blahed. "Admit it, Mom. You're happy the mushroom monstrosity got stolen. Now you can buy yourself something you'll actually want to wear with the insurance dough."

"Daniel! That's a horrible thing to say." Mac wandered over to her. She smelled a little agitated, but there was nothing in her scent that made him think she might be unsafe. He jumped in her lap as a test. "Well, hello!" she exclaimed. She gently ran her hand over his head and down his neck, and her agitation lessened. She was happy that he'd come close. Mac couldn't help purring with contentment. He wondered if she might make a good person for Bittles. He was a kit who needed lots of attention. "How did you get in here?" she asked, continuing to stroke Mac.

"Probably through the screen door. It never latches completely and you and Daniel didn't bother to shut the other one," the other male in the pack blah-blahed.

"It's such a beautiful night. I thought we should let the air in." The woman began rubbing Mac under the chin. She knew all the best spots. "I wonder if our visitor would like something to eat or drink."

"He's a cat, Mother. You don't need to put on the company manners." The man laughed. The sound came from deep in his chest and reminded Mac of a purr.

"Mom's not humanocentric, Marcus," the first male who'd spoken—Daniel—said.

The woman was Mom, and the other male was Marcus. Mac thought Mom and Daniel lived here, but not Marcus. The smells of the house weren't nearly as strong on him.

Mom gently moved Mac from her lap to Marcus's. "Take care of our friend," she blah-blahed. Mac realized that the woman wasn't the only human in the room who was agitated. It felt like there was a low thrum of anxiety running through Marcus. He had it so tightly under control that Mac hadn't noticed it immediately. But it was strong, and Mac thought it must be something the man had been feeling for a long time. It would have taken practice to keep it hidden so well even a cat didn't notice it.

This man might not be worthy of a kitten. Mac didn't have enough information to make that call yet, but Marcus definitely needed the help of a cat. Especially if the cat was MacGyver. Mac rubbed his head against Marcus's shoulder, committing to finding out what was wrong and fixing it. He already had way too much to do, but he couldn't leave the human in this state. It would be cruel, when Marcus clearly wasn't intelligent enough to solve whatever his problem was.

"I can't believe Dad didn't skip his dinner meeting. He must have known Mom would be upset after finding out about the robbery," Daniel said.

"He called me. I told him I'd come by."

"Of course." The pleasant smell that had been coming off

Daniel soured a little. "I'm the one that lives here, but he called you."

Did Daniel need Mac's help, too? Mac was resourceful, but he couldn't be expected to solve everyone's problems! He decided he'd just keep an eye on Daniel for now. Marcus was the one who needed immediate assistance.

"He probably thought you'd be out auditioning for some big job. How much did you get paid for the last one? That play?"

"Two-fifty," Daniel muttered.

"Two hundred and fifty. And you spent how many hours rehearsing, plus helping build the sets?" Marcus asked.

"Two dollars and fifty cents." That sour smell grew stronger. "We split the box office, and there was a really big cast. It was a musical, not that you'd know. You haven't seen anything I've been in for years."

"Two dollars and fifty cents." Marcus looked down at Mac. "Did you hear that? Two dollars and fifty cents."

"I didn't do it for money." Daniel's voice was harsh in Mac's ears. "I did it to be seen. Agents go to plays. Casting directors too. Managers. It's a lot better way to get work than sending out a million headshots."

"Oh, great! So, you got a job? What's the part?" Marcus exclaimed. Mac felt a charge in the atmosphere. Like it was about to storm. Or like the two humans were going to start fighting.

But before they could, Mom walked in. With tuna. Mac leapt down as she set the plate of yummy on the floor.

Marcus laughed that purring laugh again. "Tuna salad?"

"I'd already used the last of the tuna to make it," Mom blah-blahed. "I don't think he'll mind a little mayo and celery."

As Mac began to eat, he could feel that approaching-storm feeling fade. Maybe they'd only been going to kitten-fight. Sassy and Lox always growled when they wrestled, but they were just playing. The same way Mac was playing, mostly, when he'd give Diogee's ropey tail a little bite. He turned all his attention to the lovely tuna. How he'd missed it! He hadn't allowed himself even a bite of what he'd brought to the kittens.

"He doesn't look like he minds," Daniel said.

"I should head out." Marcus stood. "Early day tomorrow. Talk to Dad about letting me get a security system set up, okay, Mom? It would make me feel better."

"I'll talk to him," she promised.

At least lock the door before you go to bed, all right, Daniel?" Marcus said.

Mac got another whiff of the sour smell, but then it melted away. "I will," Daniel answered. "You don't have to worry. I'm not going to let anything happen to Mom."

Mac took the last bite of his tuna. He decided all three of these humans were possibilities for his kittens. He'd need to visit again, though. He needed more time to observe them.

With a meow of thanks, Mac trotted to the door and head-butted his way out, then jerked to a stop. He couldn't believe what he was seeing. Sassy stood on the bottom step of the porch, looking up at him.

That kitten had followed him!

She had *stalked* him!

And he hadn't even realized it!

CHAPTER 5

Serena had to read the barista's T-shirt twice, then she got it and laughed. He raised his eyebrows, smiling. "Delayed reaction to your shirt," she explained.

"I can't even remember which one I'm wearing." The guy looked down and read his T-shirt out loud, " 'Save a Cow. Tip your barista.' "

"I love it," Serena said. "And I love this place. It's so homey. I want to sit down and play Ants in Your Pants." The game was just one of the battered toys and board games on the big wooden bookshelf that separated an arrangement of cozy chairs and sofas from regular tables.

"I'll have to put you on the waiting list," the barista joked.

"Why aren't there more people in here?" There was only one customer, a middle-aged woman with a turquoise streak in her salt-and-pepper hair. "I guess that's rude to ask, but I can tell it's already going to be my favorite neighborhood place." She'd felt like she had, well ants in her pants, ever since Erik and Kait came over the day before. She'd tried to settle herself down. She'd paid some bills. She'd called her parents. She'd made sure all possible outfits were ready to wear. She'd continued to prep for the possible—not likely, but, still, possible—werecat audition by watching a billion cat videos and reading articles on cat behavior. But even the extreme cat cuteness couldn't hold her attention.

Eventually, she'd thrown herself into bed, but even her sleep had been restless. She'd woken with the sheets in a tangle and the comforter on the floor. She'd decided to try a walk, even though she'd already figured out that wasn't really done in LA. After only a few blocks, she'd found Yo, Joe! She'd fallen in love with the coffee place before she even stepped inside. It had a cheerful turquoise-and-white awning, and parked underneath was a red Huffy bike, big seat, big tires, the basket turned into a planter for a mix of orange, red, pink, white, and yellow gerbera daisies. She really didn't get why there weren't more people. It was almost quarter of eight.

"Where are the screenwriters with their laptops?" she asked the barista. "Even in Atlanta, you can't go into a coffee place without bumping into a couple, and this is actually Hollywood."

"You!" he exclaimed.

"What?"

His smile widened. "Delayed reaction to your face. I just realized I know you. Not know you, know you. But I watch your vlog. I'm giving you a free coffee."

"Don't you dare, Daniel!" The woman—Serena realized her turquoise streak matched the shop's awning—jumped up from her table.

"I meant free to her. Not free, free," the barista—Daniel—called back. "I'm paying for it." He made patting motions in the air, and the woman sat down. "My boss, Mrs. Trask. She owns the place."

"I was serious when I said I love it. What's the deal? Was there a murder in here recently or something?"

"What happened recently was a Coffee Emporium opening directly across the street," Daniel explained. He lowered his voice before continuing. "We still get some regulars, but not nearly enough. I don't know how long this place is going to last."

" 'You're never beaten until you admit it,' " Mrs. Trask offered. It seemed as if she were talking as much to herself as to them.

"General Patton quote," Daniel explained. "She's been reading bios about him. For inspiration, I guess."

"Ah." Serena couldn't think of anything else to say. "Please don't pay for my coffee," she added.

"Sorry, I'm paying. I owe you for all the times I watched your vlog. It reminded me that I actually love acting. Which is surprisingly hard to remember when I've overdosed on stuff like 'The Ten Things to Do at an Audition,' and 'The Ten Things Never to Do at an Audition,' and 'The Three Things to Get You a Callback,' and—"

"I've read hundreds of those articles," Serena jumped in. " 'How the Right Pair of Shoes Can Win You the Part.' "

" 'How the Wrong Tie Can Lose You the Part,' " Daniel shot back.

" 'How the Wrong Hair Can Lose You the Part.' "

" 'How a Cheap Pair of Jeans Can Lose You the Part.' "

" 'How Chitchatting Too Much Can Lose You the Part.' "

" 'How Forgetting to Wear Deodorant Can Lose You the Part.' "

It was Serena's turn, but she was laughing too hard to talk. She was almost laughing too hard to breathe. When she got control of herself, she said, "I had a student do that once. He was auditioning for a guy who'd basically been living in a cave for a couple years, extreme off the grid. He went in smelling so ripe he was asked to leave before he could say a line. I told him I didn't think it was the way to go, but—" She shrugged. "Who knows, maybe there's somebody out there who would have loved the commitment."

"What I like about your vlog, is that it's about the real stuff. Giving the right impression during an audition. Figuring out what makes a character tick, and how to show it. Understanding your character's purpose in a scene. You really do make me remember why I wanted to be an actor in the first place."

"That's . . . Thank you," Serena said. "I started out just making the vlogs for my students. Choosing different parts and showing some ways to prepare. It's still surreal that people I don't know watch it."

"And will buy you coffee because they do. Which reminds me. I am supposed to be making you coffee, specifically a . . . ?" he asked.

"Latte. I guess I should have skim milk, now that I'm back to going on auditions instead of just handing out advice."

"You mean you're still doing dairy?" Daniel exclaimed, eyes wide in mock horror. After he handed her the drink, he leaned over the counter and shouted across the almost empty room. "I'm sitting with my new friend while she has her coffee!"

"You can sit with every customer, as long as they keep coming back," his boss answered.

"I'll absolutely be back," she promised. "This is going to be my coffee shop. Daniel will be making my order before I've opened the door, because he'll know what I drink on each day of the week." She lowered her voice. "Except that won't happen too many times, because Daniel will soon be getting cast in his dream project."

"You're getting a free muffin, too." Daniel used tongs to pick one up and put it on a plate.

"You're eating half," Serena said when they sat down on the sofa.

"If you insist. I read an article online that said you should carbo-load before an audition. Or maybe it was fast. It might have been eat a hard-boiled egg with a Ritalin chaser."

Serena already felt like she'd been friends with this guy for years, just the way she did with Ruby. "You have an audition?"

"Yep. For a friend of a friend's play. Not my dream project, but a way to get out there and get seen."

"Should I ask what you're wearing?"

"Something that suggests character, but does not look too costume-y. Although I've also heard if you're going for a lawyer, wear a T-shirt and jeans because it will make you stand out from all the people wearing suits." Daniel put his face in his hands and groaned. "I've been doing this for more than a decade and I still don't know this stuff."

"Nobody does. Otherwise there wouldn't be all that contradictory advice out there. Are you feeling ready?"

"Uhhhh. Yeah, I guess."

"Convincing." Serena tore her muffin in half and handed him a piece. "Want me to run lines with you or anything?"

"I've got it memorized. Even though some people say you shouldn't be off book. I read Holly Hunter likes to keep the script in her hand to remind everyone she isn't giving a finished performance."

"I read that, too! She said she likes them to know that what she's doing at the audition is only part of what she'll ultimately be able to bring to the part." Serena leaned her head on the back of the sofa and stared up at the pressed-tin ceiling. "I adore Holly Hunter."

Daniel dropped his head back next to hers. "Who doesn't?"

They sat in silence for a few moments, then Daniel straightened up. "There is something you could help me with, if you don't mind." Serena sat up and turned to him. "There's this one part where it says Brian—my character—gets tears in his eyes. And I can't do it. At least not every time. I've tried every painful thing I can remember, and nothing works consistently."

"Don't worry about it," Serena told him. "The writer's just indicating the kind of emotion that Brian's feeling. But I don't think it matters if you express it exactly as it is on the page. Find your own way to show his emotions."

Daniel pulled a script out of his backpack and opened it to a scene near the end. "You're Sheila."

Serena grinned. "Doing what we love!" *Breathe it in*, she told herself. "Remember, it's playtime! And during playtime, nothing is too silly or weird to try."

She could see some of the stress pour out of him. "Playtime. I like that. Okay, let's play!"

Some of her twitchy energy subsided. A good scene, that would hold her attention. When she was acting, only the world of the script existed. That meant her cell didn't exist, so she didn't have to worry about whether or not her agent would call. And way too cute, way too moody Officer Erik? He didn't exist, either.

Kait reached over and rapped Erik on the forehead. He jerked away. "What?"

"What?" she repeated. " 'What' is you haven't even attempted to answer one of the last five questions. This is a study *group*. Participation is not an option."

"Sorry," Erik muttered to Jandro and Angie. Angie wouldn't be able to take the detective's exam for a couple more years. She needed more time in uniform. But she asked to come to the study sessions so she'd be completely prepared when her time to take the test came. She was kind of like Kait in her desire to be prepared.

"It didn't seem as if that apology included me," Kait commented. She'd been testy the last few days. Pretty much since she'd seen that bracelet on Charlie Imura's ankle. Coincidence? Unlikely. Although he knew for sure Kait would say it was.

"You're my partner. I don't have to apologize to you," he told her.

She opened her mouth—probably to shoot back an angry reply—then shut it. "Next question. What four reasons will the DOJ accept to release information?"

Erik stood up and headed to the Mr. Coffee on the table against the wall. No one was using their makeshift office right now, so they'd taken it over for the study session. He glanced at his cheap digital watch. Almost seven thirty. They'd barely been at it an hour. It felt like three.

"Erik! Are you going to answer?"

He had to think for a minute to remember what she'd asked, then said, "Record check. Background information. Investigation." He hesitated, trying to think of the fourth. After a second, it clicked into place in his mind. "Adoptions where there are absent parents."

"Right," Kait said.

Erik wasn't really too worried about the test. He knew his stuff, and he could pull from what he'd learned as a uniformed cop to answer the more theoretical questions. It wasn't that he thought studying was a waste of time. . . . He just—

He just wasn't sure if he wanted to become a detective. He'd never even told Kait that. You worked as a uniform for five or so years, then you went for detective. That's just how it was. He knew one cop who'd been in uniform for almost twenty years. Everyone liked him, but there was the occasional joke, like it was a given he didn't have what it took. Erik knew he had what it took, but didn't mean it was what he wanted.

Crap. Erik had poured himself a cup of coffee on autopilot, and when he took a sip, he realized that while on autopilot he must have added at least five spoons of sugar. He could pour it out, start over, but decided just to drink it.

Kait asked another question. Erik gave the answer so fast no one else had the chance, and she gave him an approving nod. What would Kait think if he—Jandro's cell interrupted Erik's thoughts.

"We said no cells," Kait reminded him.

"There's an automatic exception for the spouse," Angie explained as Jandro picked up the call. "Could be something wrong with one of the kids. Could be there's no bread in the house." She sighed. "I need someone to call when there's no bread in the house."

"Why would there ever be no bread in the house?" Kait asked, sounding genuinely baffled. "You keep a magnetic pad on the fridge and keep a running grocery list."

"Kait's all about the lists," Erik told Angie. In response, Kait stepped on his foot under the table. Hard. Did she think he was going to bring up her perfect guy list? She should know him better than that. He knew what was just between them and what wasn't.

"Look at this." Jandro held up his cell and a video of his littlest daughter, Sofia, who was about four.

"Okay, do your routine for Daddy," Jandro's wife said, off screen.

"She has her first dance recital this weekend," Jandro explained, as on-screen Sofia pressed her hands over her face and began to dance. "Lucy is going crazy because of the—" He put his own hands over his face. "She's afraid Sofia is going to fall off the stage."

"No matter what she does, she'd going to be adorable," Angie said.

Jandro smiled, then shook his head. "Not if she breaks her leg, though."

"My niece almost didn't perform in her recital at all when she was Sofia's age," Erik said. "I got the idea for her to teach me the dance. She loved being able to boss me around. She made me do the dance about fifty times. And by that time, she wasn't nervous about it anymore. You should try it with Sofia. She won't be able to show you the dance and make sure you're doing it right with her hands over her eyes."

"You're a genius." Jandro stood up, typing a text. "I gotta go. The recital's in two days."

"We've barely started," Kait protested.

"It would work just as well if Sofia taught Lucy the dance," Angie said.

"But Lucy also has to help Becks with her homework. And her parents are coming for the recital and she's panicking about the house not being clean enough. I can't stay. You can say it. I suck," Jandro added as he started out the door. "But I'm a dad."

"A good dad," Angie commented. She looked over at Erik. "You'd be a good dad, too. Sounds like you saved the day for your niece."

It had been fun. Maybe not all fifty-plus times they'd done the routine, but mostly. And even when it wasn't, it had been worth it when he'd seen her up there on stage, grinning and waving to him—when she was supposed to be turning and clapping.

"I have twenty-three more questions for tonight," Kait said.

"Let's wait for Jandro." Erik was already on his feet. "We don't want him to get behind."

"It sounds like Erik is eager to hit counterpart.com," Angie observed. "Which is fine with me. I can't take the test for two more years."

"Erik doesn't need to hit counterpart," Kait told her. "He met someone out in the real world." That was definitely something that was supposed to be between him and Kait. And, anyway, it wasn't true.

"I have a big night planned for myself. I got a couple old wooden ladders that I'm going to turn into bookshelves. I'm going for a distressed look. I painted them, but now I need to do some sanding. And I want to try out Miss Mustard Seed's Antiquing Wax. I read great stuff about it."

Kait got up. "I'm still going to study. But at home. It has much better coffee, and it doesn't smell like pizza and feet."

They walked out of the station together. When Angie peeled off toward her car, parked at the other end of the lot, Kait put her hand on Erik's arm. "I was serious. You should ask out Serena. You're ready to get serious. If you could have seen your face when you were talking about your niece, you'd know that."

"Since I didn't have a mirror, it would have been difficult," he answered.

She didn't let him derail her. "Angie was right. You'd be a good dad. And you want it. You have the house and the yard, and you want the wife and the kids. Probably the dog, too. I don't know why you pretend that you don't."

"We agreed we—"

"Cheese and rice, Erik, I know what we agreed. I'm sorry, but I can't wait six months. Serena isn't Tulip. I knew Tulip, remember. And you like Serena. You haven't even liked anyone for years."

"That's not—"

"Of course, it's true," Kait interrupted. "If you liked someone, you would stick with them for more than a couple dates."

Erik could say the same thing about her dating record. But he already had. And he didn't want to go round and round again. "Look, I appreciate your concern. And maybe you're right. Maybe I do want everything that goes with the house and yard. But I don't see settling down with a wannabe actress. You're all about the stats. What percentage of people who come out here to make it big in Hollywood end up staying?"

She didn't answer. And that said a lot. "I've got that bookshelf I want to start working on. I'll see you tomorrow," Erik said.

"Yep. Okay."

He watched Kait until she got into her car, even though the station parking lot had to be one of the safest places in the city, then he got behind the wheel of his Honda. He turned on the ignition, then hesitated. Suddenly, he didn't feel like a quiet night on a DIY project. Too quiet. Too much opportunity for thinking, and he didn't want to think right now.

He opened the counterpart app on his cell.

"Long day?"

Erik realized he hadn't been holding up his end of the conversation. Worse, he'd only been half listening to Amber's. He leapt on the excuse she'd handed him. "Yeah. But good. We just switched things around at work so that my partner and I are working a beat. We're just starting out, but we'll be able to really get to know the people in our neighborhoods."

He focused all his attention on her. She was striking, her makeup dramatic, her dark hair in one of those asymmetrical cuts with the edges sharp as blades, nothing like Serena's strawberry-blond waves.

Serena? Why was he thinking about Serena, especially now? It's just that when he looked at her hair, all he wanted to do was plunge his fingers into it. When he looked at Amber's, all he thought about was that he'd mess up the perfection.

"What's the career path for you? Beat cop, then, what? Detective? Or is there something in between?" Amber leaned a little forward. She seemed genuinely interested, not like she was just going through the usual Internet first meet-up questions.

It's just that everybody seemed to want to think about a career path. Except him. "I was actually studying for the detective's exam with a few other people earlier tonight." Erik took a swallow of his coffee. Another few minutes and it would be cold. He didn't want it anyway. What he'd already drank felt like it had coated the inside of his mouth, turning it sticky.

"That's great!" Amber exclaimed. "What'll it be like? How wrong does TV get it? Of course, I know a crime isn't solved in an hour, but what about the other stuff?"

As she spoke, Erik caught one of the waiters giving Amber an appreciative look. She was definitely sexy. Serena was, too, but in a different way. He tried to define the difference. Serena was—And here he was, thinking about Serena again. Not acceptable.

"Well, for one thing, there's a lot more paperwork. Mountains of paperwork. But that wouldn't make exciting TV," Erik began. "And a lot more of a detective's time is spent inside the office. Witnesses are brought in to be interviewed, instead of them going out. And witnesses pretty much never confess, no matter how good the detective is at interrogation."

"Huh, that's—"

"There's this other thing that TV gets wrong most of the time. Patrol officers like me do investigation, too. We're the first on the scene. The suspect might even still be there. We do initial interviews with witnesses, and we look for additional witnesses. We can also respond back to the scene to gather more information." He realized he was talking faster, his enthusiasm growing. "Uniforms know their area better than detectives. Detectives can't start investigating until a crime happens, but a lot of times uniforms can, at least in a way. We can get a sense that something's about to happen, because we know the community so well." He made himself stop. Amber hadn't asked for a lecture.

"I like your passion." She reached out and briefly touched his arm, sending him a subtle signal that she was interested.

"What about you? What's up next for you as a fund-raiser?" He hoped he had that right. She had said fund-raiser, hadn't she?

"Dangerous question. I could end up talking all night. I have a hundred-step plan for world domination. But I'll refrain. At least until our second date." Another signal, not as subtle. "The short version is there's not really a clear-cut path, but it's a career that's really growing. I'm aiming toward being a manager of a team, where I get to set the goals, sniff out the big donors, oversee big, fabulous events. All to benefit a cause I'm deeply committed to, of course."

She wrapped both hands around her huge coffee cup and raised it to her lips. Erik's eyes landed on her perfect nails, painted a classy beige. They made him think of the bright orange polish on Serena's toes, and that one little chip. And how he'd wanted to pull off her shoe and lick that toe, suck on it. It's not like he was some kind of foot guy. But the crazy impulse had just grabbed him. He wasn't getting any impulses sitting there with Amber.

"Are you from LA originally?" Erik asked, forcing his attention away from his foot fantasies and back to the woman sitting across from him, the attractive, attentive woman with a job in a growing field, a job that helped people the way his did.

"Yep, I'm a native. Grew up in Glendale, but now I'm in Frogtown."

Didn't sound like someone who'd ever leave. Unlike Serena, who wasn't going to be around for more than this year. Not that he was assuming she didn't have talent. She probably did. And she had that quality, that inner spark, charisma, whatever it should be called. Maybe just capital *I* It. But lots of people did. And only a few actually made it.

And he wasn't paying attention to Amber. Again. He had to focus. Focus! Except should he really have to focus so hard on a date? Focus so he'd make a good impression, maybe. But focus so he would actually listen to the woman he was with, look at her without thinking of someone else?

He gave a fake yawn, hoping it didn't look fake. "I'm fading. I guess I'm more tired than I thought. Long day, like we were saying. It was that study group on top of work. When I was in college, just drinking a few gallons of coffee would do it. But now?" He gave a shrug. "Mind if we call it a night?"

"Of course not," she answered. The way he'd put it, what else could she say.

They stood, and he walked her out and over to her car. Now was the tricky part. He always wanted to say "I'll call you." But Kait had hammered it into him that a guy should never say "I'll call you" if he knew he was never going to call you. "Thanks for coming out. It was good to meet you." He gave her a fast, friendly kiss on the cheek.

"Good to meet you, too," she answered. He could tell she was trying not to sound disappointed. He wanted to say something else—but there was nothing else to say. He gave a wave as he walked toward his car. He got in and cranked the radio, hoping for some distraction, and headed for home.

Except, somehow, he ended up driving down Sunset in the opposite direction he needed to go. And all he had to do was glance to the left to see the lighthouse in the glow of the old-fashioned streetlights of Storybook Court. He spotted an empty parking spot, and with a muttered curse pulled into it.

He was here. He might as well do a fast patrol of the place, before he headed home. He got out of the car, crossed the street, and started down Gower. The walk would be good for him. The coffee had made him edgy, and he needed to wind down a little. It's not like he was going to be going to sleep any time soon. If it had been a normal night, he and Amber might have ended up at her place, and he'd have had plenty to use his coffee high on. But that hadn't been an option, not when he kept thinking about someone else when he was sitting a few feet away from her.

It was probably just that thing where if someone told you not to think about pink elephants, all you could do was think about pink elephants. He'd told himself not to think about Serena—for a very good reason—so now all he could do was think about Serena. It's not that she was so special. Okay, she was hot. And she was funny. And she was smart. But lots of women were hot, and funny, and smart. Or if not a lot, then some. He'd just made her forbidden, and now he couldn't stop thinking about her.

Did that mean he should spend a little more time with her? He was supposed to be spending some time getting to know everyone at the Court. Would that get rid of the whole forbidden thing?

His feet seemed to have decided for him, just the way his car had, because he was walking toward the lighthouse. He stopped, trying to decide if this was actually a good idea or him being really stupid. It had been more than three years since Tulip, and if he was really honest with himself, which a lot of the time he avoided being, he was still getting over her. She'd broken his heart. Kait had been right about that. He'd never say it out loud, but it was true. It was the first time he'd really been in love, and when she walked away, it was devastating.

Sometimes, when he was feeling really sorry for himself, he thought it would be easier if she'd died. Not that he wanted her dead, just that it would be easier. The fact that he wasn't enough to keep her here—not just here, anywhere, he would have gone anywhere she wanted if she'd let him—it meant her feelings for him weren't anything close to his for her.

His gut feeling had been to stay away from Serena. Odds were that she'd end up destroyed by Hollywood, the same way Tulip had been. Then she'd want to get far away from LA and from anything that reminded her of her failure. Which would include him. It wasn't worth it. He should stick with what his gut had told him as soon as he realized she was living in the lighthouse.

He started walking again. In the direction of the lighthouse. But that was because he'd decided to patrol, and if he was going to patrol, he needed to patrol the whole place. Especially the street where a robbery had recently occurred. He snorted. *Yeah, right. Keep on telling yourself that, bud.*

A flash of movement to his right jerked his attention away from his thoughts. A cat. Gold-and-tan stripes. MacGyver. Moving fast. Something flashed between his teeth. He was carrying something! The Quevas woman's necklace?

He took off after the cat, almost reaching him just as he wriggled through a hole that led under the miniature lighthouse that was the big lighthouse's shed. Erik tried the door. Locked. The decision about whether or not he should seek out Serena was now moot. He needed the key.

It wasn't much after nine, and the lights were still on at her place, so he rang the bell. She answered wearing a silky pair of blue-and-white-striped pajamas with little pineapples scattered over them. "It's you."

"It's me." He noticed that the words "juicy fruit" were written around some of the pineapples. "Cute pajamas." Someday, maybe, he would actually think before he spoke, and he'd stop saying inane things like "cute pajamas."

Serena gave him a long, steady look, then said, "Did you have more questions? You left pretty fast the other day." He felt his face flush, remembering how he'd bolted without even drinking the tea she'd brought him. "Or did something else happen?"

"No. No to both. Everything's fine. I just need to get the key to your shed." He couldn't stop himself from looking down to check on her toenail polish, raspberry-colored tonight.

"Everything's fine, but you need the keys to my shed? That makes no sense."

"It's going to make even less sense when I explain," Erik told her. "I was doing a patrol. With the robbery, I just wanted to have more of a presence. And I saw a cat disappear through a hole that runs under your shed."

"Still not quite following." Serena smoothed the collar of her pajama top. "You're worried the cat can't get back out? Or you want to arrest him for trespassing?"

"This cat has a history of stealing things. I don't think it's all that likely that he somehow got into a jewelry box and managed to grab the most valuable thing in it, but I thought I saw something shiny in his mouth. I want to check it out, see what he's up to."

"I'm coming with! I need to see this cat burglar!" Serena slipped on a pair of flip-flops and grabbed a key off a row of hooks beside the door.

"I don't think that's a good idea."

"Why? What could happen?" Serena protested. "You're a cop. And we're talking about a cat."

He didn't have an argument for that. "Fine. Come on." He led the way back to the shed. He heard a soft cry as he slid the key into the lock.

"What's that?" Serena asked.

"I'm not sure. Maybe another animal? Stay back until I have a look." Erik took out the compact flashlight he always carried and shone it inside the shed as he pulled open the door.

"Kittens!" Serena exclaimed, pushing past him. "Look at these sweet little babies." Erik grabbed her arm before she could rush over to the spot where the kittens were gathered around what looked like an open pouch of tuna. Mac stood between them and Serena and Erik. He'd always been a friendly cat, but his stance was, not aggressive, but protective.

"You're right. Their mother might not like me getting close. She looks suspicious of us," Serena said. She took a step back, bumping into Erik. "We're not going to hurt your precious kittens," she cooed.

"That's not their mother. That's Mac—MacGyver—the cat I was telling you about. He's a male."

"The father, then? They all look so much like him. Are protective fathers even a cat thing?" Serena asked. "I've never had one."

"When I was a kid, a tomcat killed part of a litter of kittens a neighbor's cat had," Erik answered, keeping his eyes on Mac-Gyver, who was staring back at him. He seemed calm, not hissing or anything, although his tail was low and slowly waving back and forth. "I'm not sure if that's typical or not."

Erik crouched down, laying his flashlight on the ground, pointing away from the cat. As soon as he did, he heard a hiss, and one of the kittens ran up to Mac's side. It looked right at Erik and hissed again. Mac reached out one paw and gently batted the kitten back. The kitten immediately came forward again. Mac gave what sounded like a growl of frustration and stepped in front of the kitten. A few seconds later, the kitten popped through Mac's front paws.

Serena laughed. "That's one determined little guy or girl." She crouched down next to Erik.

"Hey, there, Mac. Remember me? Want to come say hi, kitty, kitty." He held out his hand. Mac studied him a moment longer, then sauntered over and rubbed his head against Erik's knee. The kitten stayed where it was, positioned between Erik and Serena and the other kittens.

"It looks like Mac remembers you," Serena said softly. "But that's not making that kitten feel like making friends with us."

Erik began to scratch the side of Mac's head, and Mac began to purr. "There's my buddy," Erik said. "It looks like you've got your paws full here. I'm pretty sure you aren't physically able to be the father. Just stepping up, huh?"

"I was wrong about them looking exactly like him. That one looks like he's wearing a little white bib." She pointed toward the littlest kitten, then leaned a little closer. The guard kitten hissed, then gave a growl that was ridiculously non-threatening. "Sorry. Sorry." Serena straightened up. "Do you think that tuna pouch is what you saw in Mac's mouth? It's silver."

"Makes sense. Makes sense it's what I saw anyway. I'm not sure it makes sense that he could analyze the situation and go get tuna. But he's always been an unusual cat."

"How do you know him anyway? You just started having this beat, right?"

"Yeah, but I . . . had a friend who lived in the Court a few years ago. That's how I knew about his stealing," Erik answered. He didn't want to get into the whole Tulip story.

"I want to get them some water," Serena said. "They don't have any. They must be thirsty. Look at how they're lapping up the oil left inside the pouch."

"Good idea."

She stood and slipped around him, the cool, slick material of her pajama bottoms brushing against his arm. Erik gave Mac a couple more scratches, then picked up his flashlight and looked around the shed, careful not to point the beam directly at the kittens.

The guard kitten launched himself at Erik, landed on his butt, scrambled up, and started for Erik again. He pounced, landing on Erik's shoe.

Mac seemed to have had enough. He picked the kitten up by the nape of his neck and carried him back over to his littermates. He gave guard kitten a gentle shake before he deposited it on the ground. The kitten gave Mac a half-hearted hiss, but stayed where he—she?—was.

Erik returned to playing the flashlight beam around the room, without moving from his spot. He didn't see a necklace or anything else that looked out of place. There was some furniture, some gardening tools, a few boxes, maybe stuff left by other Lighthouse Award recipients.

"Here you go, kiddos." Serena came back inside and set a large bowl of water a few feet away from the kittens, then returned to her spot next to Erik. The kittens hurried over, mew-ing. One moved so fast he couldn't stop in time and ended up with two wet feet. He gave a tiny sneeze.

"That might be the most adorable thing I've ever seen." Serena smiled as the kitten shook off one foot then the other, then sneezed again. "What should we do with them? I'm happy to leave them here for a while. I can bring them food and water. I hate to move them when they're so little."

"It seems as good a place as any to keep them. It's warm and dry, and they have an honorary big brother or whatever Mac thinks he is. And a small but feisty protector," Erik answered. "I can bring some food, too. Check up on them. If it's okay." He looked over at her, and she smiled, that slow smile she'd given him when he'd helped her up on the edge of the fountain after Ruby had volunteered her to assist him.

"We can have co-custody," she answered. "You, me, and MacGyver. I'll just leave the door unlocked. I don't think anyone is going to want to go rummaging in the shed." She stood. "I don't want to leave them. But I don't think the feisty one is going to take a drink while we're here. Too busy making sure we don't make one false move."

Erik stood too, and used the flashlight to guide Serena back outside. "I guess you better get back to patrol. With that recent robbery and all," she said, looking up at him. "That's why you're here, you said."

That's not why he was there. He'd known he'd been lying to her when he said it, and to himself. "I came over here because all I can think about is kissing you," he answered, again not thinking before he spoke. "You have the most perfect mouth." He traced the outline of her top lip with one finger. She didn't move away.

Then she swayed toward him. He wasn't sure if she'd intended to, or if her body was calling the shots, the way his had when it walked him over to her door. Either way . . . He leaned down, and brushed his lips against hers. He felt them part slightly, and that was all he needed. He deepened the kiss, her mouth so warm, slick, soft, so welcoming.

Erik did something else he'd been wanting to do. He slid his fingers into her silky hair. She wrapped her arms around his neck in response. Then she jerked away. "Ow!"

"What's wrong?"

"Something bit my toe."

They both looked down, and saw the feisty kitten staring up at them. There was a soft scrabbling sound, then Mac appeared. He let out a huff of air, picked the kitten up by the back of the neck, and carried her back toward the shed.

"When that kitten gets a little bigger, I think Mac will have met his match. And that's saying something." He turned back to Serena, and she took a half step away.

"This has been . . . an unusual night," she said. Was she regretting kissing him? It sure as hell hadn't felt like it when it was happening. "Maybe we should . . . Do you want to come inside?"

"Yes." It didn't matter that it was the lighthouse. It was going to be impossible to think of another woman, any other woman, when he was with Serena.

She took his hand and they started across the grass of the backyard. "You know what, this is a lucky twist of fate."

"Me needing to patrol?"

"Well that." Her fingers tightened on his. "But also, I'm going to be auditioning for, if you can believe this, a werecat burglar. My character—well, the character I'm going in for—changes back and forth between cat and human. I think she'd still have some catlike characteristics in human form. Watching the kittens, and Mac, will give me some great ideas. The director is one of my absolute favorites. I would love, love, love to work with him."

Erik heard the raw hope in her voice. She wanted this badly. Did she even consider how many other actors would be going for the part? Did she think she really had a chance? He stopped walking. So did she. He slid his hand away from hers.

"Sorry. I guess I was kind of babbling. Sometimes when I'm nervous I just talk. Talk, talk, talk. Not that I'm nervous exactly, just that . . ." The sentence faded away as she looked at him in the moonlight. "Is everything okay?"

"Yeah. But I actually do need to patrol."

"You could come back."

"No. Sorry. I forgot I set up a late drink with a woman I met on counterpart.com. It's too late to cancel." He thrust his flashlight at her. "Take this to get back inside safely. I'll bring cat food tomorrow."

Right now, he had to get out of there. He'd felt himself being pulled toward her, like she was some kind of tractor beam. But he'd heard that yearning, that ambition, that desire, when she'd talked about that part. It sounded like it was everything to her. She was just like Tulip, and he wasn't going through all that again. Not for anyone.

CHAPTER 6

"The part is a shigella. I got the call about the audition just before you got here," Serena told Ruby Friday morning during their first official check-in. They stood on the widow's walk of the lighthouse, looking down at Storybook Court as they talked and had their coffee.

"Shigella. Isn't that—" Ruby began.

"It's a bacteria," Serena said. "It causes a disease with symptoms that include fever, abdominal pain, and diarrhea, usually with blood or mucus." This was exciting. She should be excited about this. She had an audition, not a cattle call, an audition with an assigned time and everything, and she'd only been here a week and a half. She flashed jazz hands at Ruby to show that she was thrilled. She was theoretically thrilled, but what she felt was weary.

"That's great. A commercial credit would be a very nice addition to your resume. And playing something non-human. It'll show you've got range," Ruby said when she'd stopped laughing.

Serena took a long pull on her coffee. She felt like she'd only gotten about fourteen minutes of sleep, but knew it had to be at least fifteen.

"Tired?" Ruby asked.

Serena groaned. "Does it show? The audition is in less than a week. I need to start sleeping better. I can't turn up looking haggard. Unless maybe shigella would look bad. But I picture them energetic, enjoying getting into people's bodies and causing havoc. They mostly infect kids."

"Here's all you have to do. Throw some mint leaves in the blender. Get the juice. Mix in a pinch of turmeric. Smear it under your eyes. After it dries, wash it off—use room temperature water."

"Never heard that one. Thanks." Serena smiled. It took more effort than it should. Was she so tired she couldn't even lift the corners of her mouth without strain?

Ruby studied her for a long moment. "It's more than just being tired, isn't it?"

Serena sighed, then shook her finger at Ruby. "You're one of those perceptive kinds of friends, aren't you?"

"Guilty. What's going on? You don't have to say," she added quickly. "No pressure here."

Maybe talking about it would help her figure out what had happened. That's what had kept her up last night. Trying to figure out what in the hell had happened. They'd been kissing, then they were about to go inside for presumably more kissing and maybe more than that, then he was outta there. "Erik came over last night."

"Oooh. Was I right? Were there sparks?"

"Big sparks. So big they actually wouldn't be called sparks. More like a—" Serena made the sound of an explosion.

"I knew it. I could see it that first day by the fountain. It might be weird for me to say this, but this makes me really happy. He's so great, and you're so great. Except . . . except you're not so great right now."

"I'm okay. I mean, I barely know the guy, so it's no big deal. But I'm confused," Serena admitted. Actually, she was more than confused. She was hurt, but she was embarrassed to admit it. Erik shouldn't have the ability to hurt her. They'd seen each other for a combined total of how many minutes? Probably less than two hours' worth.

"Confused about . . ." Ruby prompted.

"We kissed. We"—she made the explosion sound again—"*kissed.* My knees actually went weak. Literally. If I wasn't holding on to him, I'm not sure I could have stayed upright. And I asked if he wanted to go inside—"

"Wait. Where were you?" Ruby interrupted. "You said he came over."

"He came to the door because he wanted to get keys to the shed. He'd seen a cat go inside with something shiny in its mouth. He thought maybe it was the necklace that got stolen from across the street."

"Don't tell me. Gold-and-tan-striped cat, name of Mac-Gyver?" Ruby asked, eyes sparkling.

"That's the one."

Ruby grinned. "Oh, Mac, Mac, Mac."

"He didn't take it, though. It wasn't the necklace in his mouth, it was a pouch of tuna. And there was a litter of kittens inside. It's like he'd brought it to feed them, but I don't think a cat can strategize like that. Or can they? I've never had one."

"Me either. But I think most people who know him would say Mac is unique. Did Erik tell you Mac's a matchmaker?" Ruby asked.

"He said MacGyver had stolen things before, but that's it."

"Maybe he didn't know the rest of the story. What happened was, Mac really seemed like he was trying to find a guy for Jamie. He kept stealing men's socks and underwear and leaving them on her door. A lot of the stuff came from David."

"Who is now her husband."

Ruby nodded. "They met through Mac's thieving. And they aren't the only couple he got together. When Jamie and David were on their honeymoon, Jamie's cousin Briony pet sat for them. Mac ran off, and Briony got a call from Nate, the man who found him. He manages The Gardens, the assisted living community that backs up on the Court. Now they're married, too. Also, four people who live at The Gardens paired off and got married after Mac started paying visits over there."

"And you think Mac planned all that?"

Ruby shrugged. "All I know for sure is four couples who met because of Mac got married. Maybe five. Mac sort of had a hand, paw rather, in Nate's sister meeting Briony's ex-fiancé, and the two of them are now engaged. Very long story. Tell you later." She smiled. "And now something Mac did brought Erik to your door. I can't wait to see what happens next!"

"I'll tell you what happened next. We're holding hands, walking toward my house, and then he says he has to go. And why? Because he just remembered he had a late drinks date with some woman he met through an Internet dating site. He didn't want to cancel so late."

"That's . . . polite."

"But he didn't say he would just have a quick drink and come back. He didn't say he'd call me. And he didn't call me." Serena could hear the hurt in her own voice. *Breathe it in*, she told herself. *You can use this.* "Plus, he practically sprinted away from me. It's like he'd just found out I had the clap. Or asked to see his credit score." Ruby usually had something to say about everything, but that silenced her. "Hence the confusion," Serena added.

"Well, yeah." Ruby took another swallow of coffee. "Although, it wasn't like the other couples Mac got together had a smooth time of it. They all had some rocky patches."

"We won't be getting to the point where we have a rocky patch. It ended before it started."

"Except for the kiss."

Except for that damn kiss. Erik couldn't have felt anything close to what she had. If he had, he wouldn't have been able to walk away.

"You want a coffee refill?" Serena asked Ruby. She'd drained her own cup, and was hoping if she had another, she'd start feeling somewhat alive, instead of half dead.

"Can't. I need to go over to Vintage Junction. I'm looking for the perfect grandfather clock for my moldy old mansion," Ruby answered. "You want to come? There are always amazing things, although sometimes you have to dig a little to find them."

"Usually, yes. But I need to spend some time getting into the head of shigellae. Even though shigellae don't have heads," Serena said. "Do you need anything else for your report to the Mulcahys?"

"Not a thing. You're doing so great. Got an agent, got an audition, and you've barely unpacked." Ruby gave Serena's arm an affectionate pat.

Serena nodded. "Right. You're right. And that's what the Lighthouse Award is for. To give me time to focus on acting. I'm not spending any more time trying to figure out what was going on in Erik's head last night. There are a lot more important things to think about." She headed into the cupola and started down the winding staircase, Ruby right behind her. Before she reached the first floor, she heard the *ohhhhh-waaaaah* of the doorbell.

Erik?

The thought slammed into her head before she could stop it. There was no reason to think Erik would be at her door. Unless he wanted to drop off cat food. She told herself if it was him out there, she'd be polite and friendly, the way she'd be with the UPS man. Yeah, that's what she told herself as she began taking the steps two at a time.

When she reached the first floor, she sucked in a deep breath, straightened her shoulders, then walked without rushing to the front door. When she opened it, the first thing she saw was a huge bouquet of flowers—orange lilies, sunflowers, hot-pink gerbera daisies, peach roses—so huge it obscured the face of the man holding it. "Wow," she heard Ruby whisper from behind her.

"Wow," Serena repeated.

"That's the reaction I was hoping for." Daniel lowered the bouquet and grinned at her. "For you." He handed Serena the flowers. "I got the part! Thanks to your coaching!"

"Daniel, congratulations!" Serena exclaimed. "But you didn't have to do this." She gave the bouquet a little shake. "It's gorgeous, but it's way too much."

"It's not nearly enough," Daniel answered. "Hey, Ruby."

"Congrats from me, too, Daniel. What's the part?"

"It's in a new play. Never performed before," he explained. "We're doing it at the Lankershim Playhouse in November."

"I'll be there," Ruby promised.

"Me too," Serena added.

"Tell him your news," Ruby urged Serena.

"Okay, are you ready for this, Daniel?" Serena asked.

"Hit me." Daniel slapped his chest.

"I have an audition to play a shigella bacteria in a commercial for a new bathroom cleaner."

"That's the way to do it!" Daniel cried.

"She's on fire," Ruby jumped in.

They were right. Things were going great. She had a Hollywood agent and an acting job.

"Feel like playing bacteria with me for a while, Daniel?" That's what she needed, some rehearsal time with a man who wasn't at all confusing. Or crazy.

*   *   *

"The ring was the only thing stolen, is that right?" Kait asked.

"I want you to search Jamie and David's house. That cat is to blame. He was over here last week, sitting right where you're sitting"—Marie pointed to Erik—"eating turkey with gravy. I even warmed it up for him."

Al gave a grunt. Erik wasn't sure if it was in approval or disapproval of Marie warming up food for a cat.

"Maybe he grabbed the ring while I was in the kitchen!" Marie continued. "Why are you two still sitting here. You should be going through that cat's house, looking for his hiding places."

"We'll go to Jamie and David's," Erik reassured her. "We just want to make sure we have all the information we need first."

"I don't see why you need more information," Marie began, speaking very slowly. "The cat is a thief. The cat was in this house. My ring is gone."

"We just have a few more questions. Was the ring insured?" Kait asked.

"It's covered by our homeowner's insurance. If you do your job, we won't need the insurance," Marie told her. Al grunted, and this time Erik was almost positive it was a grunt of agreement.

"And when was the last time you remember seeing the ring?"

Erik was happy to let Kait ask the questions. He felt like crap. Because he'd slept like crap. Half the time, when he'd started to drift off, he'd get a flash of that insanely hot kiss. He'd been with other women since Tulip, too many of them, according to Kait, but none of those women had melted his body the way just kissing Serena had.

The other half of the time, when he was getting close to

sleep, he'd seen Serena's expression when he told her he was going off to meet another woman for drinks. He didn't regret lying to her, though. It had to be done. He absolutely couldn't let himself get close to her. If he did, he wouldn't be able to keep it casual. The kiss had told him that much.

Then when she ran away from Hollywood, he'd have to put himself back together again. He was finally okay after Tulip, and he planned to keep it that way. With the way he'd acted last night, he was sure Serena had zero interest in seeing him again. So, mission accomplished.

"We'll let you know what we find out," Kait was saying when Erik managed to return his attention to the interview. He hadn't heard any of the answers—or the questions—Kait had just asked. Great. Not only did he feel like crap, he was doing a crap job. He reminded himself that he didn't need to spend any more time thinking about Serena. He'd solved that problem.

"If you can get us a picture of the ring, that would be helpful," Erik said as he and Kait stood to go.

Al gave an extra-loud snort. "I just said I would." Marie's tone was snippy. "I know I have some pictures with me or one of Al's relatives wearing it. I'll let you know as soon as I find it." She walked them to the door, and surprised Erik by stepping outside with them. "I have something to tell you two," she announced. "I hate that ring. It's ugly as sin. I'd just as soon have the money. I'd buy a new toaster oven, for starters. But it's been in Al's family for generations. He'll be miserable if it's gone for good. So, you go find it."

Without waiting for a reply, she returned to the house. "Well, we've got our orders," Kait said. "What do you want to do first? Talk to witnesses or go see the cat's owners? She's not going to be satisfied if we don't check out the cat."

"Let's do the cat first, then," Erik answered. "You know what would be really helpful?" he asked as they started for the hobbit hole of a house where Jamie and David lived. "It would be really helpful if someone in this complex had a security camera. Especially since no one locks their doors."

"Marie seems much too practical to leave a door unlocked, but she really believes being a light sleeper is all the security she needs. I don't know what she thinks a frail eighty-something woman is going to do if she hears someone breaking in."

Erik grunted in reply, and realized he sounded like Al.

Kait gave a loud sigh. "Are you going to give it up, or am I going to have to interrogate you?"

He didn't try to pretend he didn't know what she was talking about. "Like I said, it's irritating that no one in Storybook Court bothers with even minimal security." He doubted she'd accept that, but it was worth trying. He wasn't going to talk to her about Serena. His goal was not even to think about Serena.

"Bullpucky."

"I had a bad night's sleep, that's all."

Kait gave a softer sigh. "You'll tell me eventually."

"This is it." Erik stopped in front of the artfully crooked gate that led to Jamie and David's.

"You do the talking this time," Kait told him. "I don't speak meow."

"Fine." Erik knocked.

"Coming! Not fast, but I'm coming." A few moments later, Jamie opened the door, face flushed. "The pregnancy books say there's supposed to be this thing called 'lightening' that happens in the ninth month, where the baby's position changes and it gets easier to breathe. I guess my baby is comfy where it is." She rested one hand on her belly. "And that was probably too much information."

"Nope. It's been a while, but we're still friends. Say whatever you want." Erik and Tulip had met Jamie and David at Ruby's annual Christmas blowout, and they'd hung out a few times after that.

"It's good to see you again, Erik." Jamie's smile was warm.

"You too." He hesitated a second, then gave her a gingerly hug. "This is my partner, Kait. I don't know if you heard, but we've been assigned Storybook Court as part of our beat."

"Ruby told me. That's great! Sorry I didn't show up for the security talk. The pregnancy books also say that I might get a burst of energy around now. But, no again. Which is why I was napping when I'd been planning to be over at the courtyard."

"We can go over everything with you," Erik said. "But there's something else we need to talk to you about."

"Sure. Come on in. Would you like a cupcake?" she offered as she ushered them into the living room. "David has been stress baking."

"David does all the baking for the Mix It Up Bakery in Los Feliz," Erik told Kait.

"Maybe I could take one to go? We were just over at the Defranciscos' and Marie—"

"Say no more. I know the way Marie feeds her guests. I'll bag you up an assortment before you leave." Jamie slowly lowered herself to the couch.

Erik sat down next to her and Kait took the armchair. "Hey, where's Diogee?" The dog was usually the first one to the door. And talking about Diogee would create a natural opening to bring up Mac.

"At the groomers. David decided he had to have a bath. The pregnancy books say 'nesting impulses' are common during the ninth month. My husband is definitely experiencing them. He wants everything spotless, including the dog."

"What about Mac? Will he be spared?"

"I told David that it would be better to greet the baby with his skin intact. He thought about it, and decided the number of tongue baths Mac gives himself are sufficient."

"Sounds like a wise decision. Actually, it's Mac we wanted to talk to you about."

"Uh-oh. What did he do?"

"He may not have done anything," Erik told her. "But we were over at Al and Marie's because a ring of Marie's was stolen. There was a necklace stolen from another house in the Court last week. Marie wanted us to check—"

"And make sure Mac wasn't the thief," Jamie finished for him. "I get it. A few years ago he went on a cat crime spree and stole something from half the people in the neighborhood. But he just took things from one house and left them in front of another house. Everyone eventually got everything back."

"Nothing that doesn't belong to you has turned up in your place?" Kait asked.

Jamie shook her head. "I can check with Mr. Clean, just to be sure. But if he found jewelry that wasn't mine, I'm sure he would have mentioned it."

"A friend's dog had a hiding spot," Erik said. Actually, it was more of a hookup than a friend, but that wasn't necessary information. "He was little enough to squeeze under the couch, and he made a tear in the lining and stashed tennis balls and squeaky toys up there. And he'd bury rawhide bones in her bed."

Jamie laughed. "Poor Diogee. He doesn't really have any toys to call his own. Mac always commandeers them. I know he doesn't really want them, but he doesn't want Diogee to have them."

Kait leaned forward. "Where does he put them?"

"He doesn't put them anywhere. It's just that if Diogee heads toward one, Mac blocks him. Diogee isn't exactly afraid of Mac—but if Mac wants something, Diogee lets him have it," Jamie answered. "Mac can be sweet to him, too, though. I'm almost positive Mac gets into Diogee's treat jar and gives Diogee treats. I've never caught him at it, but I've seen evidence."

"Would you and David keep an eye out for the jewelry? I know it's a longshot, but we want to cover all our bases."

"Absolutely," Jamie promised. "But Mac's really an indoor cat. He manages to slip out every once in a while, but not often.

When I moved in here, David permanently closed the dog door, and we blocked the chimney, because we found out he could get in and out that way. It's nice to have a fire, but it's nicer to know the kitty is safe at home."

"Actually, I saw him out the other night. He seems to be playing nanny to a litter of kittens," Erik told her.

Jamie's brow furrowed. He hated worrying her when she had so much else on her mind. "Kittens? Who do they belong to?" Jamie asked.

"The woman who is living in the lighthouse found them in her shed." Erik didn't think there was any reason to say he knew her. Wasn't pertinent. "She's taking care of them until they're a little older."

"And you saw Mac over there?" Jamie asked. Erik nodded. "I don't even know how that's possible," she continued. "We must have missed one of his escape routes. David and I will go over the place when he gets home. We can check for the stolen goods at the same time."

Erik stood. "Thanks for taking the time to talk to us. Congratulations on the baby."

"Just give me a minute to bag up those cupcakes."

Mac slipped into the small room, and easily spotted Erik and the human called Kait. He'd wanted a little more time to evaluate them as possible people for his kittens, so he'd followed their scent trails. They'd led him about four blocks from home, and that was fine with Mac. He liked to explore.

"This cupcake just gave me a foodgasm," a man blah-blahed, spitting something that looked like a bug onto the floor. Mac strolled under the table to investigate. Not a bug. A piece of a cupcake. Sometimes David made cupcakes just for Mac, tuna and cheese with a shrimp on top. But this piece of cupcake was not that kind, so he left it alone. Diogee would have eaten it, but Diogee was a dog.

The man continued to blah-blah, spraying crumbs onto the floor. Diogee would love this human. "I think this has tequila in it. Yeah, definitely. And a touch of lime zest."

"Pass them on," a female human blah-blahed.

"I don't know if you should have taken these, *buey*. What does the Law Enforcement Code of Ethics say about gifts?" a different male blah-blahed

" 'Gratuities or favors of any kind, which might reasonably be interpreted as an attempt to influence their actions,' " Erik began blah-blahing. Mac wandered over and sat by his chair.

Now Kait was blah-blahing. "No one is going to be influenced by a cupcake, except possibly Tom."

"I don't know. They were baked by a person who doesn't want your top suspect to go to jail."

"The Big Cat House!" The man laughed, spraying even more crumbs.

Cat? Was the man talking about Mac?

Suddenly, all the humans were blah-blahing at once.

"Not top suspect. The cat's the only suspect!"

"That's a cat-lamity!"

"You gotta be kitten me!"

"His owner doesn't have to worry. The cat must have a get out of jail fur-ee card. All cats do."

It seemed like they were blah-blahing about him. He was the only cat in the room. And they were *laughing*.

Mac's whiskers twitched, and the fur along his spine rose. There was nothing amusing about MacGyver! At least Erik wasn't laughing. Erik was a good human. Mac gave Erik's leg a head-butt to show his appreciation.

Erik looked down, and his leg jerked when he saw Mac. A few seconds later, something he'd heard David call a windbreaker dropped down on Mac. David had said that word a lot of times after Mac had used the windbreaker to help remove a piece of old claw.

Before Mac could get free of the windbreaker, Erik was picking him up. "Kait," he blah-blahed. "We have to get back to the Court."

As Mac was rushed out of the room in Erik's arms, one of the humans blah-blahed, "Has something cat-astrophic happened?" And everyone laughed again.

They laughed at The Cat.

CHAPTER 7

"I hate the idea of Mac in a cage," Jamie blah-blahed.

Mac watched her and David from the third step of the staircase. David was banging and clanging. Changing things.

"I do too, Jam. As soon as I get this crib together, I'll start work on a catio for Mac," David blah-blahed. "Adam promised to come over and help me." He made another bang. "I didn't think Mac could jump from the bathroom window to the tree, but that's obviously what he's been doing."

"I have to keep reminding myself it won't even be for a whole day." Jamie took a bite of cupcake, then a bite of carrot. "This one bite healthy, one bite junk plan is genius."

"It won't even be for a whole day. And when we're done, Mac's going to have a great outdoor space to hang out in. He'll still be able to go out that window, and even down to the ground. It won't be as great as roaming free, but it will be a lot safer, for him and the neighbors."

"You don't think he really stole that jewelry, do you?" Jamie blah-blahed.

David made a bang and two clangs. "We looked everywhere,

and he usually brings things home or gives them to someone nearby. The ring and necklace haven't turned up. I don't think he's the thief. This time. Although he's been antsy lately. Like a cat on a hot tin roof half the time.

"A Mac on a hot tin roof, you mean." Jamie rested her hand on her tummy. "I think he knows something's up."

David gave a bang, then a shout. "Got my thumb!"

Mac couldn't take the loud sounds anymore. He turned and creeped upstairs, then slunk under David and Jamie's bed. He took a breath, wanting the comforting smells of Jamie. But the scent that filled his nose was the new, strange odor his person had been producing. It didn't soothe him.

He needed to check in on the kittens, but not yet. He needed a little more time in the dim, cozy space. He was the only one in the house who could fit there, and knowing that helped him deal with all the changes in his home. The completely unnecessary changes. Mac felt the vibrations in the floor that meant Jamie was coming into the room, then the bed sank down, and he knew she was sitting above him. "Hey, my Mac-Mac. How's the best kitty in the world?" she blah-blahed. Her smell had changed. So had the vibrations she made when she walked. But her meow was still the same, and it still made him feel her love for him.

"Do you think you could come up here with me? I'm not exactly shaped correctly for laying on the floor. I might be able to get down there, but not up. What do you think, kitty, kitty, kitty?"

Jamie's "kitty, kitty" let Mac know she wanted him. The bangs, and clangs, and shouts, had stopped, so he cautiously crept out from under the bed. Even though she smelled strange, Mac wanted to be near Jamie, just the way she wanted to be near him. He leapt up onto the bed and curled up on her pillow. She started scratching him in his best spot for scratching. Humans learned slowly, but they could learn.

"Macs, here's the thing. People think you might have been taking things from them," Jamie blah-blahed, continuing to scratch the side of his jaw. "And it's kind of your fault because you did take all those things when we first moved here. You're going to have to stay in a ca—You're going to have to stay out of trouble. But you're going to get an amazing present tomorrow. It's almost going to make up for the ca—For everything. I know you can't understand me. But I'm sorry. I really am."

She sat up and scooped him into her arms. He would rather be scratched some more, but he knew sometimes Jamie needed to hold him. It made her feel better, and he could smell that she wasn't feeling as good as usual.

His body got tense as she carried him out of the bedroom and down the stairs to the kitchen. Something with bars sat on the floor. More changes. Everything was changing.

David came in and touched the thing. It had a door, but the door had bars.

"Look what we got here, Mac. A super-size catnip mouse, buddy." He didn't smell very happy, either. Mac needed to figure out what was happening in his pack. He knew it wasn't good.

"Sardines, too. And your litter box," Jamie blah-blahed. "Think of it as a luxury hotel room." She carried Mac right up to the thing, then leaned down and set him inside. No! He wasn't staying in—

Clang! David closed the door.

Mac was trapped.

"You're not going to like this idea," Erik told Kait. They were having an early dinner at Lucifers, partly because they wanted to make their faces familiar everywhere on the beat, partly because of the excellent pizza.

"I'm going to loan you a book on the psychology of persuasion." Kait started to move the mushrooms from her pizza slice to her side salad. "You will find the opening 'you're not going to like this idea' is not recommended."

"We're friends. When you were talking to me about that book—which you did every day until you finished reading it—you said that if you like someone, there's a much higher chance you'll say yes when they ask you for something. You like me, so I'm in. I don't need anything else."

She beamed at him. "You know one of the reasons I like you? You listen to me. And you don't just listen, you remember."

"Yep. I do," Erik told her. She was a great partner. They didn't socialize a lot after work, but she made him laugh—sometimes even when she meant to—and she was decent, all the way down to the bone. "Now, can I tell you the idea you won't like?"

She gave a snort of laughter. He took that as a yes. "I think we should talk to Charlie Imura again. We've got to try something." Jamie had called that morning and said David had torn apart the house looking for the ring and necklace—while she'd supervised from the sofa—and hadn't found anything.

"I don't have a problem talking to him again."

About six months ago, Kait had watched some webinars on the Rigidity Effect. She'd filled him in on how when people are lying, they can freeze up because they're trying too hard to control their facial expressions and body language. It wasn't an obvious thing. It could be something as small as a lowered number of blinks. Kait had been intrigued with how the concept might be used in interrogations. And maybe it could be. But right now, he didn't need any help to know Kait was lying.

He didn't call her on it. "Let's head over when we're done. He should be off work by then, and he has to go straight home."

"Sure. I don't even know why you'd think I'd have a problem with it."

"You know. Just because you two kind of hit it off, then you found out he had the drug trafficking charge."

"I talked to him for about a minute before I saw the ankle bracelet. It's not like we were engaged." Kait picked up her mushroom-stripped slice and took a bite.

"You're right." She *was* right. He was probably more disappointed than she was. He knew Kait would like to have a boyfriend, and she deserved that. Charlie had seemed like a good candidate for about a minute.

Kait took another bite of pizza, then dropped the rest of the slice back on her plate. "Ready when you are."

"You're not eating the salad?" She'd picked off every mushroom of her pizza so her salad would have at least one per bite.

"I'm feeling itchy. We just started this beat. I'd like to wrap the jewelry case fast, show everyone in the neighborhood that we can take care of business."

Erik finished his slice in a couple big bites, then stood. "Ready."

They walked over to the Court, and when they reached Charlie's street—which was also Serena's street—he immediately looked for Serena. She wasn't in the yard or up on the widow's walk. Good. Leaving when he had—saying what he'd said about meeting a woman for drinks—had been the right call. But he didn't especially want to have Serena look at him like he was the biggest—he tried to decide how Kait would say it—like he was the biggest weeweehead she'd ever met.

"He's out there." While Erik had been looking for Serena, Kait had obviously been looking for Charlie. "Same place as last time."

"I'd probably try to stay outside as much as possible if I were on house arrest," Erik commented.

"You would never be on house arrest," Kait shot back. "You're not that kind of person."

"You really do like me, don't you?"

She socked him on the arm in reply. By the time they reached Charlie's gate, he was there to meet them. The anxiety he'd displayed when they initially talked to him was gone. "Remember when Peter's parents tried to kill him?" he asked, not bothering with a greeting.

Kait didn't hesitate. "Amazing Spider-Man two hundred eighty-eight. But they weren't his parents. They were androids. And droid-mom didn't try to kill him. She fought against her programming. Is there a reason you're referencing one of the five worst storylines in Spider-Man history?" she demanded. "Are you trying to suggest an evil android was in fact the drug trafficker, and that you're innocent?"

"No. I was guilty. I am guilty," Charlie answered. His tone was matter-of-fact, and he met Kait's gaze directly.

Kait gave one of her "you're telling me" snorts. Then got down to taking care of business. "There was another robbery in the Court."

"Where?" Charlie didn't open the gate. Instead, he propped his arms on top of it, and leaned toward her.

"Over on Glass Slipper Street." Erik told him.

"I still haven't noticed anything strange around the neighborhood," Charlie answered.

Kait took a step closer to the gate, to Charlie. "Did you know that the average burglar lives within two miles of the victim?"

Charlie's dark eyebrows rose. "Am I a suspect?" He gave a harsh laugh. "Of course, I am. I'm the known felon in the neighborhood."

"I was just asking if you were aware burglars usually live near the victims," Kait answered.

"Which I do. And why not just assume I'm responsible. I have a record," Charlie said. "There's only one problem. When it's not work hours, I'm not allowed to be more than seventy-five feet away from my monitoring equipment. Going over to Glass Slipper would put me out of range. Going next door to the Quevases' would put me out of range." One corner of his mouth rose.

"Have you had any interrupted signals?" Kait asked.

Charlie's amused smile faded. "Once. The sim card got knocked loose. I didn't even know it until my parole officer told me I had to get a new monitor."

Kait continued to shoot questions. "And when was this?"

"About six weeks ago."

"And how long was the monitor inoperable?"

"I don't know exactly. I assume my parole officer got on it pretty quickly. Like I said, I didn't know the signal wasn't going out until she contacted me."

"It wouldn't take long to get from here to the Quevases' or the Defranciscos' and back," Kait stated.

"The Defranciscos are the ones who were robbed?" Kait nodded, and Charlie pushed away from the gate, straightening up. "No. It wouldn't take long to get to either place."

"Did you know eighteen percent of those in federal prison committed their crimes to get money for drugs?"

"Did you know that four percent of lost TV remotes are found in the fridge or freezer?"

Kait looked intrigued for a moment, then frowned. "That has nothing to do with what we're talking about."

"Oh. I thought we had segued into an enjoyable conversation about statistics." His eyes flicked over her face. "I'm a royalty calculation analyst, but I enjoy statistics of all types."

"We're here to question you, not chitchat," Kait shot back.

"Oh. My bad. I thought the questioning part was over. Marie was over visiting my aunt a few days ago, and, of course, they were talking about Lynne Quevas's necklace being stolen. Marie mentioned Lynne wearing the necklace to a party three weeks ago. Which makes it after the day my signal was interrupted. Also, my signal was interrupted once, not twice. Both of which mean I couldn't be the thief. But I'm always up for some chitchat. I don't get a lot of company."

Kait opened her mouth, shut it, then opened it again, but didn't manage to get any words out. Erik had never seen her in that state before. "Thanks for your time," he told Charlie.

As he and Kait started away, Charlie called, "I don't agree that the droid parents was one of the five worst Spidey stories ever. One of the worst ten, absolutely. But I can think of five that top it. Or I guess it should be bottom it. Starting with Gwen Stacy having the Green Goblin's kids. If you want to try to prove me wrong, you know where I am."

He knew Kait. He knew she was bursting with the desire to give Charlie all the reasons he was wrong about where the droids fell in the list of worst storylines. She wouldn't be happy until she had pounded any arguments he could come up with into the ground by her indisputable logic. But she kept walking.

"Well, it was worth paying him a second visit. At least we can eliminate him," Erik said.

"If you're going to pass the detective's exam, you need to remember that people are able to lie, even to the police," Kait snapped.

"Hey, hey. Be nice. I'm not the one who questioned your Spider-Man analysis." Erik knocked his shoulder lightly against hers.

"Sorry," she muttered. Kait hated to apologize. He thought it was because she didn't have much experience at it. The amount of facts crammed in her head kept her from being factually wrong very often, and her basic goodness kept her from treating people badly.

"S'okay." Erik's gaze flicked to the lighthouse. He couldn't stop it. Still no sign of Serena. "And it goes without saying that we'll check Charlie's story with his parole officer."

Kait gave one of the longest sighs Erik had ever heard from her, which was saying something. "It'll probably turn out that he was telling the truth. He wouldn't have been able to have that smug look on his face if he knew we would find evidence that made him a solid suspect. But there's something off about him. He's hiding something. And I'm going to find out what it is."

"We'll keep looking for other possibilities, too." The detectives on the case were good about letting him and Kait stay involved. Some wanted uniforms out of the way; some realized how useful they would be. Erik knew he'd like the crime-solving part of a detective's job. He liked working a crime now, but he liked it as part of a mix. He'd miss all the interaction with regular citizens, like Al and Marie, once he passed the exam.

"He doesn't have anything to look smug about anyway," Kait muttered. "If he's not guilty of the robberies, that doesn't make him innocent. He's a convicted felon. Him, not some evil android version of him."

Neither he nor Kait usually let talking to suspects get to them. And if one of them did get pissed off, it was usually Erik. Charlie had managed to get under Kait's skin, at least a little, not something easy to do, either in a good way or a bad way.

Serena set the electric hurricane lamp on one of the boxes in the shed, threw a clean blanket over the beat-up sofa, then settled in for some kitten time. Watching them was good prep for the werecat audition—if she got the werecat audition. But who was she kidding? She didn't need a reason to visit. They were kittens!

One kitten, the one with the roundest tummy, was stalking a bug. He pounced on it, and gobbled it down. Maybe that's why he was the plumpest. All that extra protein.

Another kitten tore around the couch twice, scrambled up the arm, leapt from there to Serena's shoulder, then did a double jump to get back down again. He raced halfway across the room, then dropped. Motionless. Was he okay? Serena leaned closer, then smiled. The crazy kitten had fallen asleep, pretty much in mid-step.

A tiny mew drew her attention to the spot in front of her feet. The tiniest kitten stood there, looking up at her with big blue eyes. He gave another mew. Serena gently picked him up and put him in her lap. He turned around two times, then he went to sleep, too.

The feisty kitten moved closer. He gave a little hiss at Serena, as if he was warning her she'd be in trouble if she did anything to hurt the tiny kitten she held. "You don't have to worry," she promised. The kitten gave her another hiss.

She heard the door of the shed slowly open, and her body went tight. *Don't show him anything*, she ordered herself. *Act like it's all good. Like you haven't given him a thought since he took off.* She could do it. Because she was a kick-ass actress.

"Your turn for kitten time," she said cheerfully. She put her arms over head and gave a big stretch. She was probably pushing her acting into overacting, but whatever. Carefully, she transferred the kitten to the cushion next to her, then stood. "I'll leave the lamp."

"I have a flashlight," he said, almost, but not quite, meeting her gaze. He was focusing on her temple and probably hoping she'd think he was looking right at her. Was he too embarrassed to look her in the eye? He should be, especially if he'd had a great time with that woman he met for drinks, and they'd had hot, hot sex.

"I only see three kittens. Where's the feisty one?" he asked.

"She was here a minute ago." Serena grabbed the lamp and began slowly searching the shed, not wanting to miss any tiny place a tiny kitten could squeeze itself into. Not there, not there, not there.

"Do you see her?"

"If I saw her, I'd tell you I saw her," Serena snapped. Her sharp tone didn't go with the it's-all-good attitude she was supposed to be projecting, but it went with the situation. She returned to the search. Not there, not there, not there. "You must have let her get out when you came in. You didn't shut the door fast enough."

"Maybe you're the one who let her escape. Did you see her in here?"

"Obviously. That's what I meant when I said she was here a minute ago. I'm going to look outside." The amount of junk crammed into the small space forced Serena to brush against Erik as she moved toward the door. An electric tingle rippled through her body. Somehow it had not received the message from her brain that Erik's behavior completely negated his attractiveness.

"I'll come with you," Erik said.

"Sure," she replied. There. That was better. Casual. A you-can-if-you-want-to vibe. "I don't think she'd be able to get far on her little legs." She held the lantern up, and began to croon, "Here, kitty, kitty, kitty," as she slowly walked across the backyard. A dog barked in response. It was close. "People don't let their dogs roam around free, do they?"

"Not in the Court," Erik answered. "For one thing, Marie wouldn't stand for it. Once a mastiff jumped a fence and was running around loose. Everyone was calling him and chasing him. He wouldn't stop. He was having too much fun. Then Marie showed up. All she had to do was say, 'Malarkey, you go home,' and off he went. Even though he outweighed her by probably a hundred pounds."

He was talking way faster than he usually did. Nervous? Serena wondered. Uncomfortable? Well if he was, good for him. It showed he had at least a little scrap of a conscience.

"I haven't met her," Serena told him.

"You will. She knows everyone. She sees everything. I can't believe someone managed to rob her and Al's house, even though they never bother to lock the door."

"There was another robbery?"

"On Friday. A ring of Marie's. Kait and I have been trying to get—"

"Wait," Serena interrupted. "I think I hear something." They both froze, listening. Then she heard the sound again, a soft mew.

"That way." Erik began circling the house, Serena right behind him. Another mew. Closer. They were heading in the right direction.

"Kitty, kitty, kitty!" Serena called. A mew came in response. So close. She paused, searching, letting the lamplight play slowly over the grass.

"Up there!" Erik pointed to a tree to Serena's right. She'd had to stop and breathe in that tree every day. It exploded with round clusters of yellow flowers, bigger than cantaloupes. And next to one of the clusters near the top of the tree, Serena spotted the striped gold-and-tan face of the kitten.

"Nice camouflage, baby!" Serena called up to it. "But we found you. It's time to come down now." She clucked her tongue. She wasn't sure if that was a cat thing or not. Her parents hadn't been animal people, and her apartment in Atlanta hadn't allowed pets. The kitten stared down at her and mewed again. "Is she stuck? She's a she, by the way."

"I hope not. She's got to be twenty feet up," Erik answered.

"You're a cop. You have experience with treed kittens, right?"

"You're thinking firemen. And even for them, that's not really a thing. They tell people to call an arborist. Some of them will handle treed cats." He stared at the kitten. "Maybe I could get Marie and she could order her down."

They both called and called to the kitten. All it did was mew back. "I think there was a ladder in the shed," Serena said.

"Let's give her a little time," Erik said. "She got up there. She should be able to get down."

Serena pulled out her phone and did a quick google. "It says a cat's claws make it easy for them to climb up trees, but it's a lot harder for them to climb down."

"That's a definite design flaw." Erik rubbed the back of his neck, continuing to look up at the kitten.

"I'm seeing a few things we can try. First, we can put a treat at the bottom of the tree. Then we move way back in case we're making her nervous, and give her time to try getting down on her own. We can also rest a ladder against the tree at an angle, to give her an easier way down to the food." Serena put her cell back in her pocket. "I have some tuna in the house."

"I'll get the ladder," Erik answered.

About five minutes later, they had the food and ladder in position. "Now we just give the kitten some space." Serena backed up almost to the lavender bushes that grew around the base of the lighthouse, and sat down on the grass. Erik sat down beside her. He left a good foot between them, but she could still could feel his body heat, even through his clothes and hers.

"Did it say how long it usually takes?" Erik asked.

"The article recommended waiting twenty-four hours before you attempt to bring the kitten down," Serena said. "I guess going after it can freak it out even more. It could even decide to jump. Poor little kitten."

"Twenty-four hours?" Erik repeated.

"You don't have to stay. I'm fine watching by myself." More than fine. The longer she was around Erik, the itchier and edgier she felt.

"I'm not leaving you out here."

"It's my own yard. Nothing's going to happen."

"I'm staying."

"Fine." And it was fine. What did it matter if he ran hot and cold? She barely knew him, and someone you barely knew shouldn't be able to have much effect on you. So, he'd rejected her a couple times. He didn't really know her, so what did it matter?

All that was really logical. But it didn't make that itchy, edgy feeling go away. It didn't help that with him sitting nearby, she'd started thinking about that kiss again. She could almost feel his mouth on hers. . . .

Serena shifted into a new position, sitting cross-legged, trying to get more comfortable. Didn't help. A few seconds later, she tried leaning back on her elbows, legs straight out. Didn't help. She wanted to try something else, but refused to let herself. She was still shooting for the it's-all-good attitude, and not being able to sit still for two seconds wasn't helping with that. *Think about something else*, she ordered herself. *You've had good kisses before. You'll have good kisses again.*

"How do you like LA so far?" Erik asked.

She could do this. She could make polite conversation until the kitten came down. No problem. "How was your date the other night?" Serena wanted to slap both hands over her mouth, but it was too late. The words were out there. Damn it. So much for it's all good. So much for polite conversation.

"It was nice. I guess. You know how those things are. A lot of the same questions, a lot of the same answers."

"Sounds fascinating." She couldn't keep the snark out of her tone. What had happened to her ability to act? That should have gotten her though this conversation. *Kitten, please just come down before I make even more of a fool of myself*, she thought.

Erik turned toward her. Serena didn't look at him, pretending to be fascinated by the night sky. "I'm sorry about that night. I should have said that before."

Serena pushed herself up into a seated position, and looked at him. "It was . . ." She struggled to come up with the right word. She didn't want to tell him he'd hurt her, even though he had. "It was surprising." There. That was true. Partly true, anyway.

"It was more than that. It was inexcusable. I just—There was no woman, okay?"

"Wait. What?" Serena exclaimed.

"I didn't have a drinks date."

"It was an excuse to get away from me?" It was better when she'd thought he was rude and possibly crazy. So much better.

"Yes. No. Sort of." Erik scrubbed his face with his fingers. "Look, I had a bad breakup. It's been a while, too long, but I guess I'm not completely over it. I started feeling . . . I panicked."

"How long are we talking about?"

"Three years," he admitted.

Three years. Whoever the woman was, she'd really hurt him. "You haven't been going out with anyone all that time?"

"No, I do. I actually go out a lot. Usually with women from counterpart.com. I guess that's why it came into my head as an excuse."

"I'm confused. That panicked feeling. Does it only happen once in a while?" Serena asked.

"It's never happened before. The woman I was with, she lived in the lighthouse. I've been in your place hundreds of times. I practically lived there. That's the difference. I was here, where I'd been with her, and I guess it brought up some stuff."

Serena nodded. "I get that. I'm glad you told me."

They were both silent for a moment, until a little mew came from the tree. "It's hard to have to wait without helping her," Erik said.

"Yeah," Serena agreed. "She's so little. She must be scared up there, even though she was brave enough to make the climb." Her itchy, edgy feeling was fading. Having an explanation for Erik's behavior made a huge difference.

"I don't want her to go wandering off if she does decide to come down. She could end up on a busy street. And she's part of my beat. I can't have that."

"Just doing your duty, is that it?" Serena asked.

"Yep." Erik stretched out on his side, his head propped on one hand. "I take my duties very seriously."

"Did you always want to be a cop?"

"I didn't put a lot of thought into what I wanted to do. Then suddenly I was a senior in high school. And I was like, oh shit. What do I do now?" Erik laughed, and Serena had to laugh, too. "The school had a job fair. I talked to a cop who was there. I liked the idea of being outside, not stuck in an office. I feel stupid admitting it, but that was enough for my teenage brain. Fortunately for me, it ended up being a good fit. And now getting assigned to a beat, where I can get to know a whole community, that's about a perfect assignment for me." He plucked a blade of grass out of the lawn and rubbed it between his fingers.

She stretched out on her side, facing him, so they could talk more easily. "I knew pretty early on I wanted to an actor. I was a wolf in a play about ecology in the fourth grade. I really got into it. I read books about wolf behavior and watched nature shows. I drove my teacher and the other kids crazy, because I was always stopping rehearsals to say a wolf would never do this or that," Serena answered. "I still really love that part of acting. Learning new stuff. Plus, you know actors, we want fame and adulation because there is something missing inside us."

He didn't say anything for a moment, just looked at her with an expression she couldn't read, and she was good at reading faces. "Yeah, I'm secretly power hungry," he told her. "I want the authority to make anyone do what I want them to."

"Ha! I knew it!" She smiled at him, no acting involved, then she heard a scrabbling sound. She grabbed Erik's arm. "No fast moves. I think our kitty has gotten up the courage to try coming down," she whispered. They both sat up slowly and watched as the kitten emerged from the leaves and flowers and backed down the trunk of the tree. When she reached the ground, she gave a yawn, then began eating the tuna.

"She doesn't look traumatized, does she?" Erik asked.

"How do you think we get her back into the shed? I'm afraid she'll run if we move toward her."

The kitten finished her treat, then, tail up, trotted across the lawn. Serena and Erik followed her, not getting too close. Without hesitation, the kitten trotted to the hole that led into the shed and climbed inside.

"Do you think we should close up that hole?" Serena asked.

"Mac will have a fit if he can't get in, and we don't want to leave the door open," Erik said. "Let's go back in and try to create a kind of playpen out of the boxes and stuff." She pushed herself to her feet. Erik stood too. "I invited you to dinner the day we met."

She looked up at him. "You did."

"Would you still like to come?"

She smiled. "I would."

That was—unexpected. And if that kitten hadn't gotten stuck up that tree, it probably never would have happened.

CHAPTER 8

"We could have just called Charlie Imura's parole officer. Or there's this new thing. E-mail," Erik told Kait on Tuesday morning. "It's measurably faster than the post office. Also—"

Kait waved him off before he could finish. "You know how hard it is to get those people on the phone. And e-mail is only faster if someone answers the e-mail."

Erik shrugged as he turned onto Vine. "You wanted to come, and here we are." He found a spot almost in front of the government office, which looked more like a not-all-that-nice apartment building.

Kait narrowed her eyes at him. "You're in a good mood this morning."

"You sound disappointed," Erik said.

"Of course not. That's ridiculous." Kait gave a huff, then got out of the car and slammed the door. "A study by a researcher at Wharton and one at the Fisher College of Business showed that if you're in a bad mood in the morning, you continue to stay in that state all day," she continued when Erik joined her on the sidewalk. "And there are many studies that show correlation between a good mood and high productivity. Why would I be disappointed that my partner is likely to have a highly productive day?"

She walked toward the building without waiting for him to answer. Erik followed. "Why are you in such a good mood?" she asked, without turning around. She sounded accusatory, but Erik didn't point it out. He didn't want another mini-lecture.

"Got better sleep is all." Apologizing to Serena had allowed him to get a good night's rest. They'd gotten friendly waiting for the kitten, and having her over to dinner would put things completely right between them. "And what can I do to help you be the best partner you can be? Should I get you some nuts? Weren't you telling me omega-3s improve mood?"

"You really do listen to me. Thanks." She knocked shoulders with him. "You know what would actually make me happy? If Charlie Imura's parole officer tells us that there was an issue with his monitor, something that would have made it possible for him to be the thief. Because there's something about him. I get the vibe that he's hiding something. If he's behind the robberies, I don't want him to be able to get out of it through a faulty alibi."

She led the way through the main door and over to the receptionist, who sat behind a security window. "Officers Tyson and Ross to see Ms. Ayala."

"Take a seat." The receptionist jerked his chin toward two black vinyl couches sitting back to back in the center of the room. More of the couches were scattered against the walls.

The few people in the room avoided looking at Erik and Kait when they sat down. Kait tilted her head from side to side, then lowered her shoulders, something she did to work her way out of a negative mood. He left her to it.

A fifty-something woman opened the door next to the reception window and walked over. "Hi, I'm Melissa Ayala. Melissa. Come on back. I don't have much time to talk, but I'll try to answer everything." She took them back to an office that was barely big enough to hold a desk with two chairs in front of it and one behind it. "You can see I don't have much space for us to talk in, either. But at least it's not a cube." She squeezed behind the desk and sat. "Ask away."

"We've had two robberies in the neighborhood where Charlie Imura lives. We wanted to confirm that he hasn't had issues with his monitor that would have allowed him to move freely without your knowledge."

"There was one instance about a month and a half ago," Melissa told them. "There was a problem with the sim card. We got him into a new bracelet within the hour. Other than that, he'd been where he's supposed to be. No more than seventy-five feet away from the house when he's not working or commuting to work."

"Does he have any associates that you know of? Anyone connected to his drug trafficking?" Kait asked.

Valid question. Erik should have thought of it.

"No," Melissa answered. "Nothing like that came out in court." She flipped through the file as she continued to speak.

"Mr. Imura is an interesting case. No priors. I mean squeaky clean. No possession charges. Not even a speeding ticket," Melissa told them. "He had people volunteering to be character witnesses coming out the wazoo. His lawyer made the call not to use them. You know how cross-examination goes. They bring in something negative to impeach the witness, and then everything the witness said seems tainted to the jury."

"Was there reason to think there was dirt on the witnesses?" Kait asked.

"I don't have any indication of that. But it wouldn't be in the file. A lot of lawyers don't use character witnesses. I don't think you should read anything into it." Melissa shut the file, and glanced at her watch. "Anything else?"

"What's your impression of him?" Erik asked.

Melissa gnawed on the cap of her pen, thinking. "Respectful.

Compliant. Easy to deal with." She smiled. "Funny. Not in a joke-telling way. More in the way he sees things. Honestly, I like the guy. But that and three bucks will get you a cup of coffee."

Kait leaned forward. "Did you get him enrolled in a substance abuse program?"

Melissa reopened the file and quickly found what she was looking for. "There was no history of drug use. Every random test has come up clean."

Erik looked over at Kait. She gave him a shrug and stood. "Thanks for your time," she told Melissa. Erik thanked her, too. He was grateful to get back outside to the mostly fresh air and the sunshine. He didn't think he could take spending every day in a cramped space without even a window.

"What next? Wanna check in on that lady over at The Gardens? Make sure she's not still worried about an intruder?" Erik asked.

Kait nodded. "My impression of the guy who runs the place—I'm blanking on his name."

She was really having a bad morning. Kait didn't forget things.

"Nate," Erik filled in.

"Right. I think between him, his wife, his sister, and his parents, all the residents feel really taken care of, but it can't hurt to show that we're there for everyone, too," she said. "Then I guess we should check the database again to see if the ring or necklace got pawned."

She didn't sound hopeful, and there was no reason for her to. Most thieves that sold to pawn shops used fake IDs, or they sold to a middleman who then sold to the pawn shop. "You think this is the end of it? Or do you think someone's still targeting Storybook Court?"

"If I were a thief, I don't think I'd walk away yet. We haven't even managed to convince everyone to lock their doors and windows."

* * *

"Look out!" Serena called to Daniel as she hurried into Yo, Joe! "A shigella bacteria is coming at ya!"

"You got it?" Daniel exclaimed.

"I got it!" Serena did a little drum solo on the countertop. She pulled a copy of John Sudol's *Acting Face to Face* out of her bag and handed it to him. "This is that book I was telling you about. A thank-you for helping me prep."

"Getting to perfect my E. coli was more than thanks enough. Every actor should have a bacterium in his repertoire. But thank you." Daniel leaned over the counter and kissed her on the cheek.

The string of demitasse spoons that made up the door chime jingled as two familiar-looking women in probably their seventies came in. "Helen, Nessie! What a pleasure." He glanced over at his boss, who was at her usual table, a stack of receipts at her elbow. She smiled and waved, but Serena was a professional people-watcher. The smile was fake. Was the business really about to go under? Serena hated the thought. It was such a perfect little coffee shop.

"What can I get started for you?" Daniel asked the women.

"Something with a lot of sugar," one of them said.

"Helen is mad because we ran out of sugar and Marie wouldn't loan us any," the other—had to be Nessie—explained. "Marie disapproves of the amount of sugar Helen eats."

"Which is none of her business," Helen declared.

Daniel laughed. "She thinks everyone and everything at Storybook Court is her business."

Storybook Court. Of course, that's why the women looked familiar. She'd seen them that day at the fountain. The day she'd met Erik and thought he was so cute. She still thought he was, but he clearly still had big issues with his ex. She needed to keep him in the friend zone. She was pretty sure he felt the same way about her. Dinner was just dinner. He liked to cook. She liked to eat.

"Don't hate me, but I get a kick out of Marie," Daniel was saying when she tuned back into the conversation.

"Me too. And she's one of Helen's best friends, even though Helen is too cranky to admit it right now," Nessie said. "I hope I'll still be swing dancing by the fountain when I'm Marie's age."

"You couldn't be swing dancing by the fountain now," Helen commented.

"Get her her sugar," Nessie begged Daniel. "She's getting crankier by the second."

"How about a frozen caramel macchiato? I can throw some chocolate chips on top."

Serena noticed Mrs. Trask's head jerk up. "The chips are on me," Daniel reassured her. Clearly, he'd noticed too.

"Perfect," Helen said.

" 'Accept the challenges, so that you may feel the exhilaration of victory,' " Mrs. Trask muttered as she returned to her paperwork.

"More General Patton," Daniel told Serena, then he took Nessie's order, a small mint tea.

Before he could start on the drinks, demitasse spoons gave their cheerful jangle. A twenty-something man in a suit as spiffy as her agent's came in. "Don't worry, Mrs. Trask!" Daniel called. "I remember the rule. No free coffee to relatives. I'm actually planning to charge him double. He's rich."

Mr. Spiffy Suit stepped up next to Serena. Daniel did the introductions. "Marcus, Serena. Serena, my brother Marcus. Serena's living in the lighthouse this year. And, of course, you know Nessie and Helen."

"Of course. How are you, ladies?" Marcus asked.

"We were so sorry—" Nessie began.

"—to hear about your mother's necklace being stolen," Helen finished, looking from him to Daniel.

"It wasn't one of her favorites," Marcus said.

"That would be the one from Tiffany's Marcus gave her." Marcus began to protest, but Daniel hit the blender, drowning him out.

"Marie already has a replacement for the ring she had stolen picked out." Helen held out a hand to stop Daniel from pouring her drink into a glass. Serena loved how the coffee shop used real glasses. "I want that to go. I want Marie to see me with it."

Nessie shook her head at her sister. "Don't forget. Marie is your best friend."

"I know," Helen answered. "Doesn't mean she isn't a bossy old woman. Lucky too. I wish someone would steal Sad Bunnies."

"Sad bunnies?" Serena asked.

"We think they look sad. Their ears are down and they're peering over a log. It's a porcelain figurine by Herend. The bunnies shouldn't look sad. They're very sparkly, all covered with diamond and sapphire chips," Nessie explained.

"It was a limited edition, and it's hard to find now. I saw one listed at a little over eight thousand," Helen added.

"Why don't you just sell it?" Daniel put a lid on Nessie's tea.

"It was given to us when we were babies. You can't sell a gift." Helen looked over at Nessie.

"Much as we'd like to," Nessie added.

They paid for the drinks. Helen took a long swallow on her way out and looked much happier than she had on the way in.

"The magic of sugar," Serena murmured.

"What variety of Lighthouse Award recipient are you? Actress, director, singer, costume designer, or?" Marcus asked with a smile that showed off dimples in both cheeks. Cute.

"You're dimple smitten. I can see it," Daniel told Serena. "Why do women love face dents so much? They're actually a birth defect. The zygomaticus major muscle is shorter than it is on normal people. That's the muscle that pulls your skin in when you smile."

Daniel's tone was light, but Serena could hear a streak of— Meanness seemed a little too harsh, but something like that. "I admit I find face dents attractive." She smiled at Marcus. "I'm an actor type. Your brother helped me prepare for a part in a commercial that I just got!"

"And Serena helped me prep for the part I got in the play. The part you don't think is worth anything."

"I didn't say that exactly," Marcus protested.

"Yeah, you actually did." Daniel shot Serena an apologetic look. "Sorry. My sibling rivalry is showing. Marcus is a big shot ad exec. I guess I get a little jealous sometimes." Ah, jealousy, that's what Serena'd heard. "Sorry, Marcus. I can be an asshole."

"Hey, it must run in the family," Marcus answered. "'Cause so can I."

"Our mom's the genuinely nice one," Daniel explained.

"She's extremely nice," Marcus agreed. "Is she doing okay? I wanted to check in on her while I was at lunch."

"She wasn't hurt during the robbery, was she?" Serena asked.

"A little shaken by the idea of someone being in the house, but she didn't see anyone," Daniel told her, then added to Marcus, "I'll tell her you tried to see her." He glanced at the clock. "Kind of late for lunch, isn't it?"

"Lunch at my job is pretty flexible," Marcus answered. "Although they do expect me back at some point. I should go."

"Wait. Let me make you an espresso."

"Americano, please." Marcus pulled out his wallet. When Daniel gave him the coffee, Marcus gave his brother a twenty. "Keep it," he said when Daniel started to make change.

"I was kidding about charging you double," Daniel told him.

"Keep it," Marcus said again.

"Thanks." Daniel watched Marcus leave. "That pissed me off," he admitted to Serena. "It shouldn't have. Marcus knows I'm always broke-actor broke. I'm sure he was just trying to be nice with the huge tip. But it felt patronizing. And patronizing from a younger brother . . ."

Serena gave his arm a pat. "But I could tell you two care about each other."

"Oh sure. It's just that there's some crap stirred in the mix. Maybe it's like that with all brothers."

"I have one, but he's a lot younger. The most annoying thing he did was follow me and my friends around like a puppy. Even that was fun some of the time. He was pretty cute," Serena said. "Brother-sister isn't the same dynamic as brother-brother, though."

"True dat." Daniel started making Serena her usual skinny latte.

"Is it okay if I tip you the amount I would tip someone I didn't know?" she asked when he gave it to her.

"Sure. I hope you don't think I'm a complete jerk now."

"Not possible," she assured to him. "I don't make friends with jerks." She felt lucky she'd met Daniel. He'd made her first weeks in LA lots more fun, and it was great having a rehearsal buddy.

Hearing him say he was broke-actor broke had given her a twinge of guilt. She hoped he hadn't thought he owed her something because she helped him prep for the audition. "Let's make a pact," she said. "Let's keep helping each other with our acting, but no more thank-you presents, agreed?"

"Agreed. As long as I get to keep my book."

She laughed. "And I get to keep my flowers." That bouquet had been huge. Truly excessive. She didn't know how he'd managed to afford it. He couldn't be earning much as a barista, especially because with so few customers the tips had to be abysmal. *If he couldn't afford it, he wouldn't have done it*, she thought. But she still wished he hadn't.

The house was quiet, except for the sounds of Diogee and David snoring. It was time to leave.

Mac stretched one paw through the bars.

Flick! Thwap!

The small metal rod slid over.

Click!

Mac gave the door a gentle head-butt. It swung free, and Mac stepped out. Easy as a sardine sliding down a cat's throat. But he didn't feel proud. He didn't feel happy. His packmates had locked him away. He didn't think he could forgive them, even if he could get out of any cage. He didn't think he'd ever be able to come back here.

He leapt up on the counter. For the last time, he unlatched Diogee's treat jar. He heard the bonebreath give a snort as he woke up. A minute later he was standing in front of the counter, whining for Mac to give him the treat.

Mac whapped the biscuit onto the floor, then jumped onto Diogee's head when he lowered it. Diogee jerked his head up, as always, and alley-oop, Mac was on the windowsill. A moment later he was down in the yard.

He took one look back, then slipped into the night.

CHAPTER 9

Mac headed straight for the kittens. That's what was important now, the kittens. They were his pack. The first thing he did after he climbed through the tunnel and into the shed was check their food and water. Both fresh. He could smell that the humans Erik and Serena had been there. They were more intelligent than many of their kind, and had done as much as they knew how. Mac buried the kittens' scat and remarked the place with his scent. Then he turned his attention to the babies.

First, he gave Bittles a few licks of greeting. He was getting stronger under Mac's care. Bittles purred and snugged up to him.

Sassy crept closer.

Zoomies ran straight over Mac's back, spun around, then charged back toward him. He didn't stop in time, and bammed straight into Mac's side. Mac gave him a little growl, just to let him know it wasn't acceptable to smash into adult cats. Zoomies gave Mac a lick and took off again.

Sassy crept closer.

Lox ambled over with a cricket between her teeth. She

dropped it between Mac's paws, then curled up next to Bittles and added her purr to his. Mac ate the bug. He liked crickets. They tasted a little like shrimp. Even if he hadn't cared for bugs, he would have eaten it. Unlike most humans, he knew the polite way to accept a gift. Half the time Jamie threw the ones Mac brought her in the trash.

Sassy crept closer.

Mac continued to pretend that he didn't notice her sneaking up on him. She made her move, leaping into the air, and landing on Mac's neck. He felt her little teeth bite into his skin. He gave a shake that sent her tumbling to the ground, then he gently pressed his teeth against her neck. She needed to learn a little respect.

After a moment he released her, and rubbed his cheek against the length of her. She was a little troublemaker, and if she got into trouble when he wasn't around, everybody needed to know she was under his protection.

Mac curled back up, and Lox and Bittles returned to their spots at his side. Sassy joined them. Zoomies made one more loop around the shed, then dropped down on top of his siblings and fell asleep almost instantly.

Mac allowed himself a short nap, then got up, stretched, and headed for the tunnel. The kittens mewed in protest, even Sassy. It would be nice to stay and play with them, but there was no time. Mac had important things to do.

As soon as he'd crawled out of the tunnel, he took a deep breath, whiskers twitching. There were so many odors, but he quickly found one that he wanted to follow. It belonged to a human he needed to investigate, someone who might deserve a kitten and be able to supply him or her with all the necessities.

Mac launched into a lope, following the scent trail he'd chosen. It didn't take long to catch up to the human he was tracking. He slowed to a walk and followed from a distance. He expected the human to get in a vroom-vroom, but the male continued down the sidewalk.

After a few blocks, he stopped. Mac crept closer, close enough that when the man opened a door, Mac was able to slip inside before it swung closed. The human walked over to a wall and pushed on it. When the wall slid open, Mac realized it was an elevator! He hadn't been on one in years, not since he and Jamie moved to his neighborhood.

Mac walked onto the elevator with the human. He didn't even notice. Most of the time, they didn't seem to see things that were completely obvious to Mac. Well, it made them easier to stalk. When the man got off the elevator and opened another door, Mac was again able to slip inside without being seen.

The male headed toward what smelled like the kitchen. Mac stayed where he was, surveying. The room was big, and almost empty. It had plenty of room for a kitten to run when it got the crazies. There were no drapes on the windows, but there was a chair with a high back that would be good for climbing practice. The place seemed acceptable, but what about the human? He lived there alone, that was clear from the smell. Was he capable of caring for a kitten by himself?

The man came back in the room and flopped down in the room's only chair. On occasion, Mac enjoyed a nap on a comfy sofa, but a sofa wasn't an essential for a kitten. He watched as the human flicked on the blah-blah machine. Mac liked it when things in the machine moved fast, like they were right now. His eyes followed the motion of a vroom-vroom, his muscles tensing. He wanted to chase!

Mac reminded himself he was here to observe the male, not the machine. It had gotten boring already anyway. It was only fun when things were going, going, going, otherwise, it was the same old human blah-blah.

The man opened a jar of the goop Diogee loved. The bonehead acted like is was creamed sardines. It seemed like it glued his tongue to the top of his mouth, but he always asked for more. Diogee had actually drooled on Mac's head once when David was eating what he called peanut butter. It had been necessary for Mac to give him a one-two paw whap—claws in. Diogee couldn't be punished too harshly, because he was too stupid to know better.

The human smeared some goop on a cracker. Mac didn't understand why people and dogs liked crackers, either. There were much more tasty things available. Mac kept trying to interest Jamie or David in a special treat, but when he brought one home for them, they didn't understand what to do with it. They threw it away. He gave them a gift, and they threw it away. He had to remind himself that they simply weren't that intelligent, but sometimes it was hard not to feel unappreciated.

It wouldn't happen anymore. Mac wasn't ever going home. He couldn't. Not after what Jamie and David had done to him.

Time for a test. Mac walked over to the man and meowed. Finally, the human realized Mac was there! He meowed again, keeping his eyes on the snack in the male's hand. Would he understand? Would he hand over Mac's share? Mac would not let one of the kittens live with a human who wouldn't share.

Mac didn't want any goop. It didn't smell like anything that he wanted in his mouth. But he needed to see how the human would react to the request. "How did you get in here?" the human blah-blahed. Mac meowed again, not moving his gaze.

The man let out a breath. "I could use some company, if I'm honest. I actually went to see my brother—voluntarily. Not that Daniel's not a good guy. He's just unbelievably unambitious. I don't get it. He's older than I am and is working handing out coffee. He actually admitted he's jealous of me. I knew it, but I never thought he'd say it. But he apologized. Didn't expect that, either."

Oh, the blah-blah! Did he not see that Mac wanted a bite of his snack? He leapt onto the human's lap and leaned toward the hand that held the goop. "Do you want some?" the human asked. Mac meowed. They might be getting somewhere. "I don't know if it would be good for you." Mac meowed again. "I guess a tiny bite won't hurt." The human broke off a piece of cracker and held it out to Mac. He took it. He wasn't going to be rude. The goop tasted the way it smelled. He forced himself to swallow, then jumped down so the human wouldn't offer him more.

He'd seen enough for now. He trotted to the front door and meowed. The human let him out. Now he'd proved twice that he possessed basic intelligence. Mac would need to observe him again before he made a decision. Possibly this would be a good place for Zoomies, since there was lots of space for him to run, and hardly anything for him to crash into.

"Blah, blah, blah. Blahblahblah, Blah! Blah! Blah!" Serena was glad she'd gotten her new used car, a ridiculously big, but reasonably cheap Cadillac, before the commercial shot. She always told her students to get to an acting job at least a half an hour early, which is what she'd always done before she slid into teaching full time. Having a car made that much easier. LA had public transportation the way Atlanta had a public transportation. Good for getting to the airport, okay to get across town, and that was about it.

A car was also great as a private rehearsal studio. Serena had done all possible prep in the two days since she'd found out she got the part, but she liked to do vocalizations as close as possible to performing. She'd done a few commercials in Atlanta. One had a trailer for her, one had one room for all the actors. She had no idea what to expect today.

She moved on from the *blah-blah*s to some *hmmmm*s, *gah*s, and *mm-mmm*s, then launched into a tongue twister that always made her giggle, which was probably as beneficial as the exercises. "Freshly fried flying fish, freshly fried flesh." Yep, by the time she'd reached the eighth repetition she was laughing so hard she had to stop. She checked the watch. Time to go.

The security guard had given her a map of the Paramount lot. Serena took another look at it, then climbed out of the car and headed toward the iconic water tower. She paused to take a pic of the Blue Sky Tank. It was being used as a parking lot, but Serena knew sometimes it was filled with water, and that one of those times had been for the whale scenes in *Star Trek IV*. Even though she knew it made her look like a tourist, she had to take the picture for her father who owned Betamax, VHS, Blu-ray, and digital versions of the movie, of all the *Star Trek*s.

She also took a picture of the Rodenberry building, since she was walking right past it. Who was she kidding? She would have sought it out—after the shoot—for her dad. However, when she spotted Jessica Lange, who was probably there shooting another piece of the *American Horror Story* anthology series, she shoved her cell into her pocket. She was such an admirer of her technique, which is why she'd never go all fan girl over the woman. Not respectful. Not professional. Still, it had been a thrill to get a peek at her.

With only one wrong turn, where she ended up walking past a subway stop in the New York backlot, she found the studio. Now she just had to find someone to tell her where she was supposed to be. She glanced around until she spotted a young woman wearing a headset. When in doubt, go for the headset, that's what she always told students.

Serena walked directly over to the woman. "Hi. Serena Perry. Talent for the Scrubby Doo commercial."

"Great. You're early. I love early. First thing is to get to wardrobe." The woman took the map out of Serena's hand, then she frowned. "Pen. Pen, pen. I always expect everyone to be prepared and then—" Serena gently plucked a pen from behind the woman's ear and handed it to her. "Thanks. I'm Tori, by the way." She circled something on the map and handed it back. "Just in case you need it. But all you need to do is go out the way you came in, turn right, and go down two doors."

"Thanks." Serena smiled at her before she headed off. Her goal, one of her goals, was to make a positive impression on everyone she met today, no matter who. So she put another smile on her face as she stepped into wardrobe. "Hi, I'm Serena Perry—"

"Shigella," a middle-aged man with a shaved head said. "And I'm Tom, but everyone calls me Tater. Please don't ask." He wore battered jeans and a gray T-shirt with a smiling bowl of Ramen on it. Tater with Ramen. That would help her remember his name. Serena wondered if it took a long time for someone who dressed other people for a living to get ready in the morning. Maybe she'd ask if the two of them got friendly.

"That's me. I can't wait to see what you came up with for the costume."

Tater flipped through a rack crammed with clothes and pulled free a purple jumpsuit. Next, he took a pair of purple sneakers and matching purple socks off a shelf, and handed everything to her. "You can change behind the rack. I know it's not much privacy, but—"

"Not a problem." Serena ducked behind the rack, slid off her jeans and simple button-down shirt, then wriggled into the snug, really quite snug, jumpsuit. She always reminded students not to knock off a few pounds or inches. Going to a fitting, and not fitting? Not professional. She was sure she'd given accurate weight and measurements when she was asked for them, so the jumpsuit must be meant to fit this way. *I'm a bacteria*, she told herself. *This isn't clothing. This is my body.*

She quickly put on the shoes and socks and stepped back

into view. "The hem is a little long. I'll get them taken up. You can change back now. Then it's off to hair and makeup."

Forty-five minutes later, Serena was escorted to her half of a small trailer by a production assistant. "There's no bathroom in here," he told her. "If you need to go, walk up that ramp and through the big doors of the building that we just walked past. The bathrooms will be to the left."

"Got it!" Serena said cheerfully. She knew cheerfulness was a valuable commodity, but she was truly feeling cheerful. She had an acting job! Once the PA left her alone, she took a long look at herself in the small mirror on the wall. Getting her hair done had been fast, because all it involved was fitting her with a metallic purple bob. Her false eyelashes were also metallic purple, and her face was lavender with accents in a deep plum around her eyes. She hadn't needed to worry about having bags or dark circles. Her lipstick was almost black. It was likely that no one would actually recognize her when they saw the commercial. But she was going to be in a national commercial. The others had just been regional.

Breathe it in, she told herself. But when she took in a deep breath, the smell of the makeup made her sneeze. A big sneeze. She pulled a tissue out of her purse, and began gently blotting away the evidence, then she sat down on the tan corduroy sofa and waited. And waited. And waited. She'd downloaded an audiobook onto her phone, because she'd known a lot of waiting was typical, but she didn't feel like listening to it. Bacteria didn't care about the new David Sedaris collection, and laughing as hard as Sedaris always made her laugh might put unwanted lines on her purple face.

When a knock finally came at the door, Serena's pulse picked up. She was nervous, but she could use that. Her shigella was high energy. When she answered, she found the same PA who had brought her over. And she couldn't remember his name. Had he told her his name? Didn't matter. All she had to do was be friendly and upbeat. That's what would make the best impression.

Serena and What's-his-name walked to the other end of the trailer and knocked on that door. A tall, skinny guy in a bright blue jumpsuit answered. His metallic hair was in a buzzcut, but his makeup was the same style as Serena's except in shades of blue. She noticed that his jumpsuit had a half-dozen metallic ropey things dangling from the waist to the floor. The man saw her looking at them. "Flagellum," he explained. "I'm E. coli. Cal."

Serena shook his hand, giving her bacteria and real name. "They decided to add a scene, and we're going to be shooting it first," What's-his-name told them as they started back to the studio.

Serena and Cal exchanged looks. His expression was hard to read under all the blue. She hadn't thought about how her facial expressions would be muted by the makeup. But she'd studied mime and dance, and could do some basic gymnastic moves. Face wasn't her only tool. "What do we need to know?" she asked.

"We're going to start with the last shot. You two getting squirted with Scrubby Doo."

"Green screen?" Cal asked.

"Nope," What's-his-name answered. "Foam cannon. The kind they use at frat parties."

"I went to one of those once. Getting blasted was fun! Everyone loved it." Cheerful and true.

As soon as they entered the building, Serena and Cal were ushered over into an area with a white tiled floor and three matching tiled walls. The shower, Serena realized. That had been in the script she'd been given.

The director, Aidan, rushed over. "Serena. Cal. Welcome. We're going to be moving fast. We had to make some changes based on last-minute client notes, so we need to make up some time. You were both great at improv during your commercials. That's what I want to see here. You're going to be blasted with foam representing the Scrubby Doo. I want you to do your best death scene. No such thing as too big. And when I give the signal, I need you to shout, 'I hate you, Scrubby Doo!' Getting the words out should last seven seconds. Got it?"

"I'm ready to give you an epic death," Serena answered, giving a completely unforced, very cheerful smile. A death scene? What actor didn't want to deliver at least one all-out death scene. "Ready for some scenery chewing?" she asked when she and Cal were in their places.

"He wants big. Let's give him big!" Cal's eyes were gleaming.

"Action!" Aidan called.

Whomp! The foam exploded out of the cannon, obliterating her and Cal. Serena still launched into her death, moaning and writhing and wailing. She couldn't see Aidan, but when she heard Cal start the Scrubby Doo line, she joined in. When Aidan didn't call cut, she kept on dying. You weren't ever supposed to stop until you got that word, no matter what. Cal kept up with her, groaning and shrieking.

Finally, Aiden called "cut!" Serena reached up to wipe the foam off her face, then remembered her makeup and let her hands drop to her sides. "Obviously way too much foam. Cut it by a quarter. Get Serena and Cal into fresh costumes, hair, and makeup."

Almost six and a half hours later, Serena hustled into a clean jumpsuit, got a new wig and eyelashes, and had her makeup pretty much redone—for the fifth time. The second time they'd done the death scene, there wasn't enough foam. Then there were two more takes with too much again. Then one more with too little. In take five, the foam was perfect, but Cal had screamed out "I hate you, Scooby Doo!" instead of "Scrubby Doo." The line could be dubbed, but since it had the name of the product Aidan wanted it to be perfect.

Each time, Serena and Cal had to be prepped again, and the foam had to be cleaned from the giant shower set. "This is the one! I can feel it!" she told Cal as they got into their places again. She bounced on her toes a few times to rev herself up, trying to ignore her stinging eyes and itchy skin.

"Sorry I flubbed it last time." Cal wrapped his arms across his chest. The cool foam had felt good at first, but Serena was feeling chilly now, and it looked like Cal was, too.

"*Pffft.* No worries. Happens to everyone."

"All right, let's do this thing!" Aidan called. "Action!"

Serena threw her head back and screamed, using some of her built-up frustration as fuel. She shuddered and flailed, then cried, "I hate you, Scrubby Doo!"

"Cut! That's the one!" Aiden told them.

"That's dinner," Lizzie announced. "Prepare yourselves for a long night. We're going to have to go into overtime."

Serena had gotten so wrapped up in dying—again, and again, and again—that she'd almost forgotten she and Cal had a scene where they played with a couple kids, trying to infect them with shigella and E. coli. *How many takes for that one?* she wondered.

Didn't matter. She was making a commercial! This would really improve her teaching. It had been too long since she'd been on set. Now she'd be able to really prepare her students for the hurry up and wait, the tedium, the feeling of being a tiny cog in a huge machine.

Serena headed for the craft services table. Before she could think about eating, she needed a big bottle of water. She didn't know how much of that foam she'd ingested, but enough to make her feel faintly nauseous.

"Didn't you tell me something once about fluorescent lights making people nauseous?" Erik asked Kait as they waited for Jandro and Angie to show up for the study group.

"Hmmm?" Kait murmured, her attention on the file in front of her.

"Fluorescent lights. Some study about negative effects on people." Erik looked up at the long tubes that ran the length of the makeshift office. He could hear the bulbs buzzing softly. The sound was starting to put his teeth on edge, just the way a knife scraping against glass did.

Kait didn't look up. "What?"

Erik slapped his hand down over the page she was reading. "I wanted to know if it's true that fluorescent lights can make you nauseous. Because I think that's what's happening right now. We're spending too much time in here. It was a lot better when we could just do paperwork in the car. And now we're here even more time to prep for the detective's exam. Which we could do anywhere. We could do it at my place."

"We decided to meet here, because it's a central location," Kait reminded him. "And, yes, fluorescent light can cause nausea, headaches, anxiety, all kinds of negative effects. Maybe since we're spending more time indoors, we should bring in a desk lamp and turn off the overheads."

She slid his hand off her papers.

"What are you reading anyway?" he asked her. "You're not already studying, are you?" She hesitated, and Erik thought he saw a flash of guilt or maybe embarrassment cross her face.

He scooted his chair closer to hers, trying to get a look.

Kait shut the folder, then sighed, one of her long ones. "If you must know, it's Charlie Imura's file. There's something off with him. It's going to keep nagging at me until I figure out what it is."

"You really think he could be our perp?"

"All I know, is that I have the feeling I'm missing something, that he's hiding something," Kait told him. "I read a study, and there are lots of them, that says following your gut leads to better decision making. We all have unconscious information, and that's where intuition comes from. There's something with Charlie I need to figure out."

"Anything popping out at you from the file?"

Kait opened the file again and flipped a few pages. "This is from his boss, and it's typical 'I find it impossible to believe that Charlie committed this crime. I would trust him with my money and belongings. He has babysat for my kids on occasion, and I would still trust him to do that.' "

"Trusting Charlie with his kids, that says a lot," Erik commented. His own intuition told him Charlie was a good guy. "He pled guilty, didn't he?"

"Yep. Cops stopped him for a broken taillight. He opened the glove box to get his registration, and there was a baggie of tablets. No excessive amounts of cash or paraphernalia for distributing. But it was his car. That makes unwitting possession a tough defense."

"He could have gone for it. But if he did and he lost, that might have taken house arrest off the table." It made sense to Erik that Charlie didn't want to risk actual jail time. "Are you still thinking he might be working with an accomplice, giving somebody info on where they'd find the most valuable stuff?"

"I don't know anything anymore," she admitted. "Except that my intuition is telling me to look closer."

"It still doesn't make sense that the thief, whoever it is, didn't take the Tiffany's—"

Erik was interrupted by Jandro coming into the room. "You're both gonna be loving my ass. I had to go to Pasadena, so I stopped at Maquina Taco. I got fish. I got chicken, bacon, and jalapeño. I got mushroom and asada. I got oxtail and lengua, but only for me, because the rest of you people are too white to know better."

"Got a potato one?" Maybe Jandro would have been able to convince him to try a tongue taco on another day. But the lights already had his stomach feeling unhappy, and now he was starting to get a headache.

CHAPTER 10

Mac wanted to go home. He'd checked on the kittens, and they had everything they needed. Now he wanted someone to take care of him. He wanted his own dinner in his own bowl. And later he wanted to curl up on top of Jamie's head, and fall asleep to the sound of David—and Diogee—snoring.

But Jamie wasn't really his Jamie anymore. She didn't even smell like herself. What had happened to her? How could his person have locked him away? If Jamie wasn't Jamie, then home wasn't home. There was no reason to go back.

He didn't have time to spare anyway. It was time to do another investigation of a possible person for one of his kittens. He could smell a male human nearby. He liked the odor. It soothed him. It might be good for Zoomies to have a calm person. He couldn't race around all the time. Every once in a while, he would need a place to nap, and a human could make a comfortable nap spot.

Mac trotted across the street and slipped through the fence. There was a lot of rushing water by the house. Mac didn't like the sound. It reminded him of the time Jamie had given him a bath. She kept blah-blahing about fleas. But there was plenty of dry ground in the yard. It was easy to reach the human sitting outside without getting his paws wet. The human's eyes were closed, and he had his face lifted up to the sun. Mac approved. Dozing in the sun was one of his favorite activities.

He decided to take a snooze. When the human got up, Mac would follow him. Maybe he liked sardinesies, too. He found the perfect patch of sunshine, turned around three times, then decided he needed two more turns. Ahh. Now he could nap. He lay down in the warm grass and closed his eyes.

Mac's sunny spot had become partially shady when the sound of the gate opening and closing woke him up. A human female was heading his way. Mac stood, and the human male stood, too. "Shelby! I wasn't expecting you," the man blah-blahed.

Mac's nose twitched. The female's scent had a sharp tang that irritated him. Not sadness or anger. It was kind of like she'd been rolling in flowers and kind of like she'd been spraying herself with the stuff Jamie sprayed in the trash can to cover up all the good smellsies.

"You know I like to be unpredictable." The woman kissed the man, then handed him a bag of what Mac knew was fried chicken. It wasn't sardinesies or tuna, but his tummy was saying "get me that." He knew he'd have to wait for one of the humans to take the food out of the bag. Humans sometimes liked to give, but they did the loud blah-blahs if you decided to take what you wanted. Mac wouldn't mind grabbing and running. It didn't matter to him what humans liked or didn't like. But he needed more observation time. "How have you been?"

"Let me see. I need to recap, what's it been, about three weeks?" the man blah-blahed.

"Oh, Charlie, you know I can't come as much as I want to. It takes so long to drive here."

The man's scent began to change. It smelled like he might

need some help after all. Was there any human who could manage their own life? "Highland Park is about eight miles from here. You run ten miles on the treadmill every day."

"I started staying with a friend in Santa Monica. Our place is just too empty. Without you. And you know what the 10 is like." Her odor was changing, too. Now it was making Mac's whiskers twitch when he took a deep breath.

The male opened the bag and took out a piece of chicken. "Who's the friend?" He took a bite. His voice wasn't getting louder, but his smell was the kind that went with loud blah-blahs.

"Someone new at work. Her roommate moved out unexpectedly, and she doesn't like being alone, especially at night."

"Don't you want to sit down? Or would you rather go inside to eat?"

"I actually can't stay." The woman shifted slightly from foot to foot, the way Mac did that time he hurt one of his paws.

"Oh." The man took another bite. "Well. Thanks for the food. Don't be a stranger. Write if you get work."

"Don't be like that." She shifted her weight again. Mac decided her paw wasn't hurt. She looked more like she wanted to do a zoomies.

"I kinda don't have a choice." The man dropped the piece of chicken back in the bag. Did he think it was trash? That wasn't trash. "I gotta be me. I gotta be free," the human yowled. "But I can't do that second part, as you know."

"I can't talk to you when you're like this. I'll visit again, when you're in a better mood." The woman didn't zoom, but she walked away fast.

Yes, this human needed Mac's help. He'd smelled good before the woman arrived. Now he smelled almost as bad as David had, before Mac made sure he became Jamie's packmate. Had David and Jamie forgotten everything Mac had done for them? How could they treat him so badly?

This wasn't the time to think about those humans. Mac strolled over to the man, then leapt up onto the bench beside him.

"Chewie? Is that you? Better go find Captain Marvel. She needs her copilot." The man gently stroked Mac's head. "I amuse myself," he blah-blahed. "If no one else."

Mac reached out one paw and tapped the bag that held the chicken. It would be valuable to see how the male responded. He turned out to be quick—for a human. He reached into the bag, pulled out a small piece of chicken, and handed it to Mac. As soon as Mac swallowed, the man handed him another piece. Mac hadn't even had to give him a hint.

This could be the perfect person for one of the kittens. Mac just needed a little more time to decide. A little more time, and a little more chicken.

Remember what Kait said about going with your gut, Erik told himself. His brain was starting to have doubts about inviting Serena over for dinner. But his gut was what had prompted him to ask in the first place. The words had just come tumbling out of his mouth.

It was too late for doubts anyway. It was Friday night. He glanced at the clock. She should be here in about a half an hour—and there was nothing left to do. He'd cleaned the place and gone shopping yesterday, and he'd prepped everything for dinner that could be done in advance when he got home.

He decided to go out in the backyard. He'd been indoors too much lately. He and Kait spent a lot of time on their beat, but with the extra paperwork for the new assignment, and the study sessions, he was sunlight deprived. He stretched out on one of the loungers and opened the new Marquis de Lafayette biography. He read a couple paragraphs, then wondered if he'd hear the doorbell from out there. Usually he did. But he didn't want to leave Serena standing on the doorstep, thinking he wasn't home. He'd been enough of a jerk already. He could take the book out to the front porch, but that might look a little too—

Too what? What was he even thinking? It's like he'd turned into a high school kid going on a first date. He went out with women all the time, and he pretty much always had a good time and thought they did, too. Although Kait always pointed out that if he had such a good time, he'd want to continue to have a great time by going out with the same woman more than a few times in a row.

Anyway, this wasn't a date. It was just a friendly dinner. He flopped down onto the couch and started to read again. He had to keep reading the same page over and over, though, because he'd get to the bottom and not be able to remember anything.

Maybe he should grab a beer, take the edge off. He heard a car pull up. From his spot on the couch, he could see out the window. It was her. Thank Christ. He'd been making himself nuts. But why wasn't she getting out? Was she having second thoughts?

He had to get a grip. This was ridiculous. He sat up, tossed his book on the coffee table, then picked it back up. He'd read a little more. He wasn't just going to sit there, poised to answer when Serena rang the doorbell. She was probably making a call or something.

Erik read the same page three times in a row. How long was she going to sit out there? He wandered over to the door, hesitated for half a second, then stepped outside. He saw Serena look toward him and waved. She waved back and got out of the car.

"Everything okay?" he asked when she reached him.

"Sure. Why?" She answered her own question before he could. "Oh, because I was sitting in the car? I don't like to be early. I actually like to be a little bit late. Sometimes people are still getting ready."

"Not me." He opened the door and stepped back to let her

inside. She was wearing that flowy green dress she'd had on the first time he saw her. As she passed him, the soft cloth brushed against him and he could smell her perfume, flowery, but with a little spice.

"You coming in, too?" Serena smiled at him.

Wow, he'd been standing out there, so caught up in his thoughts he hadn't even followed her inside. He quickly joined her.

"Your place is amazing." Serena looked around with appreciation. She walked over to a set of shadow boxes made out of dresser drawers mounted over the sofa. "Did you make these?"

He nodded. "I found this beat-up dresser at a yard sale. I liked the shape of it, and the hardware, so I bought it. It sat in the garage for months before I figured out what to do with it. I probably do that too much, buy something with no actual idea what I want it for."

"Having seen one of the results, I say trust your instincts." Serena leaned forward to study one of the shelves more closely. "That's one of the Cottingley fairy photos, isn't it?"

"Most of the things in the boxes are family mementos, and in a way, that one is, too. A new family memento. My niece was over one day—Harper, she's eleven—and she said I should make one with all fairies. She had a picture book about the Cottingley fairies that she loved, and we used to read it together. That's why I used that."

Serena reached out and gently touched one of the fairies suspended from a gold thread that ran across the front of the box. "We made those together," Erik explained. They'd created the fairies out of pinecones and acorn caps and lots of glitter.

She turned to him and smiled. "You are one amazing uncle. DIY fairies. I love them."

"I tried to give Harper the box, but she wanted it hanging here, with the others."

"I agree with Harper." She took a step back. "Hey, I brought dessert!" She reached into her purse and pulled out four Big Hunk candy bars. "I just found out you can buy these all over the place here. Not where I come from. Have you ever had one?"

"I'm not much of a taffy guy. I think I had one back when I was about ten. I almost pulled out one of my back molars," he answered.

"I don't want to bring up old trauma. Fortunately, I also brought this." She handed him a bag. "Chocolate tarts from Bestia. Daniel gave me a tour of the Arts District today, and he said it's the best dessert to be found in the city."

He felt a little stab of jealousy and ignored it because he had nothing to be jealous about. He barely knew Serena. And this dinner was as much a welcome-to-town thing as anything. "Daniel?" he couldn't stop himself from asking.

"Daniel Quevas. The son of the woman with the stolen necklace. Have you met him?"

"Yeah." The hipster who wasn't really a hipster. Was he gay? He might be. Obviously, Erik couldn't ask, especially because the only reason he wanted to know was jealousy. "Kait and I met him when we went over to get Mrs. Quevas's statement."

"I met him at the Yo, Joe! coffee shop before I even knew we were neighbors. He works there."

That answered the question about if he'd had real, paying acting jobs. He can't have had many if he still had to work as a barista. Erik wondered if he could somehow use Daniel as an example of one of the thousands of people who were trying and failing to make it. He wanted Serena to know that was the norm. If she did, maybe it would hurt less when she didn't get the Hollywood dream.

"You know, some of my friends warned me that LA would be really unfriendly," Serena continued, "but I haven't found it that way. Daniel brought me an enormous bouquet of flowers just because I gave him a couple acting tips that helped him get a part in a play."

The cop part of Erik's brain immediately picked up on the incongruity. Barista giving enormous, meaning hugely expensive, bouquet of flowers. He filed it away as something to discuss with Kait.

"Let me stick these in the kitchen." He held up the bag with the tarts. "And get us drinks. I made sangria because I decided to do dinner tapas style. I realized I didn't ask if you were vegetarian, or pescatarian, or beegan or anything, so this way you'll almost definitely have something you can eat."

"First, did you say beegan?" Serena followed him out of the living room. "Second, that's so thoughtful of you. Third, I'm up for pretty much anything, food-wise."

"Great. And I did say beegan. I knew someone"—he didn't want to say it was a woman he'd briefly gone out with—"who was one. It's vegan, but you still eat honey." He set the tarts on the counter.

"Beegan. That's cute." Serena laughed. "I didn't even know regular vegans didn't eat honey. Why don't they eat honey?"

"It's because it takes a lot of effort for bees to make it, and I think millions of flowers for one pound." He was pretty sure she'd said millions. "Basically, the bees need it for themselves."

Serena dropped her head. "I now feel like a horrible person."

"I encounter horrible people regularly. You are not a horrible person. Remember, you were willing to sit outside for twenty-four hours, waiting for a kitten to come down from a tree."

"And so were you. So, we're both non-horrible."

"We need to drink to how much we have in common. The sangria? Or I have beer, wine—"

She didn't let him finish the list. "Sangria, please."

Erik poured them glasses and set out a bowl of large black

olives he'd been marinating in red wine vinegar and spices. He added a plate with slices from a baguette he'd picked up after work, then sat down at the table with Serena. He'd decided the kitchen was a better way to go for dinner. The dining room table was too big for two people, and he would have had to keep leaving her alone to stick things in the oven.

Serena spooned a few olives onto her little plate, then popped one into her mouth. "So good."

Erik let himself take a few moments just to look at her. She really was beautiful. Just looking at her hair made him want to bury his hands in it. *Okay, enough looking. Say something*, he told himself. But his mind went blank. The last thing she'd said had been about the olives. He couldn't build on that. "I'm going to put the peppers out, too." He'd made them the night before, but had taken them out when he got home to let them warm up to room temperature. He jumped up, got them from the counter, and brought them back to the table. Okay, that had taken a few seconds, now what—

Serena saved him with a question. "How'd you get interested in cooking? Because I'm getting the feeling you *cook* cook."

"I was at a garage sale, and I found this cookbook of really, really basic stuff, like how to boil an egg. I was maybe a year out of college, and I was almost tired of living on pizza. Almost. Cold pizza is still my favorite breakfast food." Serena offered her hand for a high five, and he slapped her palm. "I decided to give it a shot. Just started at page one. I like how there are specific steps. I'm not one of those people who experiments."

Serena tried one of the peppers. It was low effort on his part—some olive oil, some capers, some balsamic vinegar, and a couple spices—but she nodded as she chewed, and he could tell she was really enjoying it.

He wanted to ask her something about herself, but he didn't

want to hear her get all excited and passionate about acting. He couldn't ask how she ended up here, because that went straight back to acting. "You ever hit yard sales?" Not an especially insightful question, but it was something.

"Sometimes. But I'm not like you. I don't buy useful things like cookbooks or things I can transform like the dresser you used to make the shadow boxes. I buy weird things."

He raised his eyebrows. "Weird things?"

"Actually, I did buy a cookbook once! It was a cooking with Crisco cookbook. I never made anything in it. I don't think I even read any of the recipes. I just found it so odd, I felt compelled to get it. It's the same way I felt about my Madonna troll doll. It was from the Madonna era of the pointy bra cones. That's what the troll was wearing. It had her mole, and the thing that was the clincher for me was that it had troll pubic hair. That's what pushed it into the weird-thing-I-must-have zone. And now you're thinking I'm weird, right? You're thinking I'm weird and also that I talk too much. Do not get me started on weird things again, okay?"

"I just have to know one other thing. What do you do with all these weird things?"

"Mostly I kept them stuffed in boxes in my closet. Sometimes I would bring an assortment in and use it to kick off an improv exercise. Every few minutes, I'd toss the group something new that they'd have to work into the scene. You know what? I just realized I could have taken all of that stuff off my taxes! Totally work related."

He swerved past the acting part of what she'd said. "Sounds like you were a good teacher. Creative."

"Thanks. I hope so."

His gaze followed her hand as she took another olive and raised it to her lips. He had an obsession with that mouth of hers. And he didn't really know if this was still the welcome-to-town dinner. It had been the first time he'd invited her. But then there had been that insanely hot kiss. If he'd asked her right after that kiss, this would definitely be a date, a date that, if he were lucky, would end up in the bedroom. But he'd been a jerk after the kiss, and teaming up to save the kitten had brought them to a kind of friend vibe. Which meant she probably wasn't thinking of this as a date. And he shouldn't be.

"Should we move on to something slightly more substantial?" he asked, as much to escape his thoughts as anything. "I was thinking Spanish omelets."

"Sounds perfect. Can I help? And 'can I' is exactly the way I should ask it. Because whether I am actually capable of helping very much depends on what you want me to do."

"Sit. Drink your wine. I got this." He'd already peeled and thinly sliced the potatoes and chopped the onion. He stuck them in a skillet with some olive oil and fried them for a few minutes, then lowered the heat and put on a lid. "They need to cook for about twenty minutes. But while we wait . . ." He took a plate of honeydew and Serrano ham toothpicked together out of the fridge and placed it on the table when he rejoined Serena.

"You went to so much trouble. Thank you, thank you." She sounded so pleased and appreciative.

"None of it is very hard," he answered, but it meant something to him that she was enjoying it. He didn't cook for people too often. Mostly just when he'd bring something to a family gathering. He used to cook for Tulip, when she'd let him. She liked to go out, usually with a group of friends. He pushed the thought away. He didn't want to think about Tulip when he was with Serena.

"What?" she asked.

He shook his head. "I don't know what you're asking."

"You suddenly looked, I don't know, stressed, maybe. Worried."

He wasn't going to tell her about Tulip, but, what the hell, maybe he could prepare her for what would probably happen. It might make the blow softer when it came. "I was thinking about you."

"Me. That's what got that look on your face?"

"You're great. It's not that," he said quickly, then added, "I was thinking about you coming out here for a year, trying to break into acting."

"Not break in exactly. I was acting in Atlanta, even though I'd been focusing on teaching for the last few years. And I got a commercial! Did I tell you that? I just finished shooting it. It's national too. I play a shigella bacteria. And I rocked it. Even though I did have to get sprayed with foam about a billion times, and the shoot didn't end until about two in the morning."

He hadn't been expecting that. "That's great! Congratulations!"

She grinned, then her expression turned serious. "You were explaining the face. You were thinking about me coming out here to act, and—"

"And I was just wondering if you'd thought about how many people are doing exactly the same thing. You got the commercial, which is amazing, but—"

Serena raised both palms. "Hold up. Are you about to give me the you-have-to-be-realistic-almost-no-one-becomes-a-star speech?"

Erik felt sheepish, but he wasn't going to drop it. "Yeah, because I've seen people get broken by—"

She did the traffic cop thing with her hands again. "I'm twenty-nine years old. You're giving me the speech I give my students." She put down her hands and leaned closer to him. "Let me tell you something. I don't expect to become a star. Would I love it? Yes! But my dream, what I came out here for, is to become a working actor. Commercials, small parts, that's fine with me. That's wonderful." She straightened back up. "Save your advice, and I promise not to give you any tips on how to solve the Storybook Court robberies, okay?"

"Okay."

They stared at each other. "Are we good? I still appreciate you inviting me over and cooking me dinner. I didn't mean to be quite so . . . combative."

"You're good. We're good. It's all good," Erik said. "But we need a new topic of conversation."

Serena brushed her golden-red hair away from her face. "I'll take childhood anecdotes for one hundred, Alex."

"You like *Jeopardy!*?" The tension that had started building up in his muscles faded.

"I love *Jeopardy!*"

"Are you any good?" Erik rubbed his thumb over his chin, feeling the stubble coming in.

"Is that some kind of challenge?" She narrowed her brown eyes at him.

"Alexa, we want to play *Jeopardy!*," Erik said in response.

And they did, all the way through the cooking of and eating of the omelets. "I can be a little competitive," Serena admitted as they wrapped up a game.

Erik laughed. "I hadn't noticed." He stretched his arms over his head. "That was a lot more fun than having Kait fire questions at me. We've been studying together for the detective's exam."

"Detective Ross. I like the sound of that. How's the studying going?"

"After more than five years in uniform, a lot of it is already ingrained. I'm not really worried about passing. Kait shouldn't be, either, but she believes in preparing as much as possible, so she started a study group."

"And you go, because you're a good friend." When he didn't

answer, she said, "It's okay. You can say it. Yes, I'm a good friend."

"Yes, I'm a good friend," Erik repeated obediently.

"And I am jonesing for chocolate. Let's break out the tarts." She stood up and got them off the counter. "Plates?" He told her where to find them, glad that she was making herself at home, when they'd known each other such a short time.

It felt longer somehow, though. There was an easiness between them that usually took time to build up. He never quite shook the feeling that he had to impress Tulip, not even when they were living together. Even at the time, he knew that was nuts. He knew she loved him. But he was always aware of if she was happy with him or not, and when she wasn't, he always felt stressed out until he found a way to fix it.

"This is so nice," Serena said, as she dug into her tart. "No waiter you know is wishing you'd just free up your table already."

Erik agreed. He thought he'd be happy sitting there with Serena for hours and hours. Except that he'd also like to get her into his bedroom. That kiss. It had gone from zero to sixty in nothing flat. He couldn't help wondering what it would be like to do more than kiss.

That little argument had shown him that Serena wasn't like Tulip. She didn't have stars in her eyes. She knew what she was up against, and her goals were a lot more reasonable. This could . . . this maybe could be the start of something.

Was it crazy that she was thinking maybe this could be the start of something? After Erik had bolted away from her twice, talking about plans to see other women? But he'd explained that. It was old girlfriend garbage spewing up. And he'd owned it. Eventually.

He was great the other night at dinner. Yes, he'd lectured her about not letting Hollywood crush her soul. Which was patronizing. Yet, also a little sweet. And today? So much fun so far.

Erik pulled up in front of the third yard sale on their list. "Remember, stay focused. We are looking for weird. We are also looking for plates with cool patterns I can use to do a mosaic tile restoration on that birdbath we found at the last place."

"Got it." Serena climbed out of the car and headed for a box that she could see held dishware. She crouched down beside it, but before she could pull out the top plate, a woman swooped down and slapped the box, like she was in a game of tag.

"I'm taking this."

"You didn't even look inside," Serena protested.

"It's not a rule that you have to look inside." She managed to lift the box and staggered off with it. Was it horrible to wish that she dropped it and something inside broke? Not everything, just something.

"Hey, is this weird?" Erik asked. He squatted next to her and showed her a puke-green mug lined with teeth. A pair of fuchsia tonsils stuck up from the bottom.

"There's a fine line between weird and disgusting. And that went far, far over the line. The line cannot even be seen." Serena patted him on the arm. "Don't worry. You're still learning." He stood, then reached out his hand to help her up. She took it, and didn't want to let go once she was on her feet, but she did. She needed to move slow. That kiss had shown her Erik could make her take leave of her senses.

"I should go help that woman load the box into her car," Erik said. "I saw her snake it out from under you. Not nice, maybe. But definitely within the rules of garage-sale etiquette. Don't worry. You're still learning." He gave her arm a pat, then jogged toward the woman.

He was just way too nice. The thought made her smile. She started to look for more dishes. Then she saw something that made her gasp. She rushed over to the card table, snatched up the blue plastic flower, and fisted her hand around it. No one was getting this from her!

"What'd ya find?" Erik asked, wrapping his arm around her shoulders, and she shivered—in a good way. The little touches they'd been exchanging were escalating. But not too fast.

"It's a Polly Pocket compact." Serena whispered, just in case there was another Polly fan in the vicinity who might not follow garage-sale etiquette. She opened it to show him the little green house inside. Polly was still in there!

"It doesn't look weird," Erik commented, arm still around her.

"It's not weird." Serena gave him her best I-am-offended-beyond-words look. "This is a treasure. I wanted it more than anything the birthday I turned seven. I got it, but then I lost the Polly, and it's just not the same without the Polly."

"This is what happens if you don't stay focused. You end up with more stuff than you can possibly cram into your house. Or even your house and garage."

"But this is special. It—" Serena's cell vibrated. "I just need to check my phone," she told Erik. "My parents call on Sundays a lot." But when she looked at the screen, she saw that it was Micah. Her stomach did a flip. Her agent calling on the weekend.

"Hi, Micah. How's it going?"

"It's going great for you. I got you an audition."

"For what?" She didn't want to jump to conclusions. The odds were so against her getting to read for Norberto Foster.

"Untitled werecat."

Serena squealed. She couldn't help herself. She gave a little bounce, and Erik's arm slipped off her. "I'll text you the deets," Micah told her. "If I don't get back to brunch in two seconds, bad things are going to happen to me." He hung up.

Serena spun to face Erik. "I just got an audition for the new

Norberto Foster movie. Norberto Foster! My favorite director. This day just went from great to fantastically wonderful!"

"Wow." He gave her a short hug. "Great news."

"Not great. Fantastically wonderful," Serena corrected. "Do you mind if we go? I don't think I can do the focus thing any more right now."

CHAPTER 11

"I don't know how this is happening. Boom—agent. Boom—commercial. Boom—audition for my absolute dream project. My head is spinning. Do I have a fever? Am I hallucinating?" Serena adjusted the string of jingle bells she'd just placed around the neck of a plastic deer. "I must be hallucinating. Because there's no way I'm really helping you decorate for Christmas on a Monday morning in September."

"Christmas is much too wonderful to be contained by one day, or even one month," Ruby answered. "And I have way too much stuff. I could never get it all up if I started in December, or even November."

Serena put a sprig of mistletoe behind the reindeer's ear, then gave it a pat on the head, satisfied. "Now what?"

"Elves in the tree. But I have to get the ladder for that. Let's take a cookie break." Ruby started for the house, and Serena followed her.

"Doesn't it seem incredible that I've had all those booms?" she asked when she was seated at Ruby's kitchen table, a

chocolate-peppermint cookie in one hand, a cup of hot chocolate in the other, even though it had to be in the eighties.

"Definitely incredible. But you've been putting in your
time," Ruby answered. "A lot of people out here watch your
vlog. I mentioned you to one of the actors in that movie I'm
working on, and she knew exactly who you were. She says you
give the best advice about finding ways to express characters
through action."

"The vlog *did* get me my agent, in a roundabout way." Serena took a bite of her cookie. "Is there pudding in this? I believe I detect pudding."

"You believe correctly," Ruby answered.

"I also had a, not a boom, but maybe a boomlet. Maybe even
that makes it sound too big. Maybe—"

"Stop," Ruby ordered. "I will determine the level of boom-
ness for myself. Go on."

"I went over to Erik's for dinner. Then on the weekend, we
went to some yard sales. And it was fun. I haven't had so much
fun with a guy in forever."

"Was that the only kind of fun. Or are you saying you slept
with him?"

"No. No, no, no," Serena answered. "I haven't forgotten how
he went hot, hot, hot, then cold, cold, cold on me. Although I
did get a little explanation from him. He told me that he went out
with the last lighthouse girl." She pointed at Ruby. "Something
you did not bother to mention."

"Sometimes it's better to let things unfold on their own."
Ruby smiled, and added, "Or with a little help from Mac."

"One of the kittens did more than Mac to get me and Erik
together. We teamed up to help it get down from a tree. Or to
be more accurate, to watch it come down from a tree by itself."
Serena took another bite of cookie, partly because she was
stalling, and partly because, good cookie. "Is it okay if I obnox-

iously treat you like the best friend in a rom-com, by which I mean treat you like you have no life beyond helping me with my romantic life?"

Ruby laughed. "Since you asked so nicely . . ."

"Next time, you get to be the star and I'll be the sidekick," Serena promised. She put her elbows on the table and leaned toward Ruby. "Tell me everything you know about this Tulip person Erik was so in love with."

"They met before she'd even been out here a whole month. She pulled the wrong orange out of a stack at the farmers' market and they all fell on the ground. Erik went to the rescue. He's that kind of guy. They ended up going out to lunch, and it was on." Ruby considered for a moment. "You know how in some relationships, it seems like one person loves more?" Serena nodded. "It felt like Erik was that person. I'm not saying Tulip didn't love him. I know she did. We were friends, and we talked, like friends do." She waved her hands between her and Serena.

"Maybe it's that Tulip was so driven," Ruby continued. "Her goal was a position in a major orchestra, and she worked her heart out to get there. The award gave her time and the resources to travel for auditions and freelance gigs, and she went after everything. It didn't come together for her in the year."

"A year isn't long."

"Not long at all. The competition is fierce. I almost think it was worse for her because right near the end she got so close, and with the LA Philharmonic. Musicians came from all over the world to audition for an open flute slot. About fifty applicants were invited to apply, and the process went on for two weeks. She put everything into it. I remember sitting with her the last day. She was barely holding it together. The stress was almost overpowering. It all came down to five minutes of playing, and she thought she played better than she ever had."

"Then she didn't get it," Serena said softly, sympathy for Tulip flooding her.

"Then she didn't get it. And it devastated her. Instead of thinking, 'I got so close. This proves I can do it,' she decided that was it. She'd had her chance, and that was it."

"But I've heard getting into an orchestra is as hard as getting a slot in the NBA. Not getting one open position . . ." Serena let her words trail off. Ruby knew all this.

"I tried to talk to her. I know Erik did everything he could think of to convince her to keep trying." Ruby gave a helpless shrug. "She moved back home. I hoped she'd gather herself together. Use the experience she'd gotten during her year to get back out there. As far as I know, she didn't. Or at least hasn't. I tried to keep in touch, but—" She shrugged again.

"Sounds like the breakup didn't really have much to do with Erik." Serena realized she was still holding her cookie and set it on her plate.

"I think that made it almost more painful for him. She wanted the orchestra more than anything; he wanted her more than anything." Ruby took a sip of her hot chocolate. "I'm glad that he seems ready to move on."

"That's not a new thing." Serena felt a twinge of hurt, even though she and Erik weren't actually even going out. "I have the feeling he's with some woman or other constantly."

"Which is not at all the same thing." Ruby stood up. "Breaktime's over. Let's go get that ladder. We have elves waiting on us."

Serena quickly drained her cup. After hearing more about Erik and Tulip, she felt extra sure that taking things slow with him was the right call.

Would Serena like Lucifers?

And again, Erik was thinking of her. It had only been two days since he'd seen her, and he'd thought of her about every five minutes. "How many five minutes are there in two days?" he asked Kait, who was doing her mushroom transfer from pizza to salad.

"Five seventy-six," she answered. "It's pretty basic math. Why do you need to know?"

"I don't." He definitely wasn't going to tell her he was obsessing about Serena. Kait would gloat, and she was obnoxious when she gloated. Besides, he wanted to keep whatever was going on between him and Serena *between* him and Serena, at least for now. He'd had so many conversations with Kait and Jandro about Tulip. Talking to them about Serena somehow felt like bad luck.

Erik's radio crackled to life. "6FB83. Code 2. 459 at 189 Glass Slipper Street. PR Helen and Nessie Kocoras." His eyes met Kait's. She gave a sigh-snort combo, and answered dispatch, then they each grabbed a pizza slice and headed for the door.

A few minutes later, they were walking up to the house Helen and Nessie now shared. Back when Erik was with Tulip, they were in the middle of a long feud and had separate places, although both were in the Court.

Marie opened the door before Kait and Erik could knock. Probably she'd have food waiting, which would fill in for the rest of their lunch.

"Sad Bunnies has been stolen!" Helen was tall enough that she could speak to them over Marie's head.

Kait gave an exasperated huff. "Sad bunnies?"

"A porcelain figurine of two bunnies." Marie moved back to let them inside. "We already looked it up. We found one for sale for eight thousand and forty dollars."

"Was anything else taken?" Erik asked. He thought he already knew the answer.

"Nothing. Our great-aunt gave us—" Helen began.

"—her whole bunny collection. Two hundred and four of

them," Nessie continued. "We counted when we noticed Sad Bunnies was gone. There are two hundred and three now."

"And when did you notice the figurine was missing?" He couldn't bring himself to say Sad Bunnies. He wasn't sure he'd be able to keep a straight face. The phrase was sounding more ridiculous every time he heard it.

"What about non-bunny items?" Kait replied. "Jewelry? Electronics?"

"Just Sad Bunnies," Helen and Nessie said together. "We do that sometimes. Talk together. We're twins," they added, in perfect synchronization.

"Do you have any kind of security system?" Erik asked. He thought he already knew the answer.

"No," Marie answered for them. "I know you think we all need them, but we look out for each other."

Didn't stop you or the others from getting robbed, Erik thought. But he wasn't going to get into that with Marie. At least not right now. Maybe not ever. He might not come out alive.

"Do you have any idea when the robbery might have taken place?"

"We know we saw Sad Bunnies—" Helen said.

"—the day we went to the coffee shop," Nessa finished for her.

"That was last Tuesday," Helen added. "We were talking to Daniel about them."

A tingle went through Erik, what Kait would call his Spidey sense. He couldn't stop himself from interrupting. "Daniel? Daniel Quevas?"

"He works there, serving up overpriced coffee," Marie told him, disapproval all over her face. "But that new Coffee Emporium is about to put his place out of business. Even though it sells even more overpriced coffee."

"Is, uh, Sad Bunny insured?" Erik asked. He took the time

to make sure that he and Kait got all the info they'd need to pass on to the detectives in charge of the case. They were decent, and overworked, guys who had no problem letting uniforms do not only witness interviews, but follow up. In some ways, it was like Erik and Kait were detectives already, without the exam.

As soon as they'd finished and were back outside, he said. "Let's get over to the coffee place where Daniel works." Kait said the same thing at almost exactly the same time. Sometimes they were a little like twins. All those hours on the job had gotten them thinking in sync.

"If Daniel's our perp, that means he stole from his mother," Kait commented, as they walked across the Court toward Gower Street. Most studies acknowledge there are minefields to be navigated when an adult child is living at home, but Daniel and his mother seemed to have a healthy relationship, although we only had a short time to see them together."

"Yeah, but Serena mentioned that Daniel had gotten her a huge bouquet of flowers. Pretty extravagant for a struggling actor working at a struggling coffee joint," Erik answered. "Where'd the money come from?"

"There was definite friction between Daniel and his brother, and a lot of it was about financial success." Kait took in a long breath, thinking. "Maybe Daniel felt like he needed to even things out. He knew his mother didn't like the necklace that was stolen. He also knew it was insured."

"He could have thought no harm, no foul," Erik said. "He could even have twisted it around in his head so it felt like he was doing his mother a favor."

Kait slowed down. It only took Erik a moment to figure out why. Charlie was circling around the courtyard fountain, coming their way. She checked her watch. "This falls in the timespan where he should be coming home from work. No violation."

"You're not still thinking he could be behind the robberies?"

She shook her head. "My intuition is still prodding me, though. There's something I'm not seeing." She went silent as Charlie got closer. He gave them a nod and didn't slow down.

"No comic book references today?" Kait asked, and he stopped. "Nothing to show that things aren't always what they seem. That good can look bad, and bad can somehow be good?"

"Remember that time Spider-Man ate Mary Jane and Aunt May?" Charlie asked. Usually when he brought up superhero stuff with Kait, it was with a mix of teasing and challenging. This time his tone was flat, eyes dull.

"Earth-2149. But he was a zombie," Kait said. "Are you trying to suggest you were a zombie when you were dealing drugs and so it wasn't really you?"

"He was a zombie, but he knew what he was doing. Then he ate everything in the galaxy." Charlie started walking again.

"But, wait, forty years later, he turned it around, remember?" Kait called after him.

He answered without looking back. "For a while. But he ended up getting that universe's Spider-Man destroyed, and that MJ and Aunt May destroyed."

"But then—" Kait didn't finish. She stared after him. "He's not listening." Finally, she turned to Erik. "Now I really feel like I'm missing something about that guy, but it's extremely doubtful what I'm missing has anything to do with our case. Let's go see what we can get off Daniel."

A few minutes later, they walked into Yo, Joe! "Kait! Erik! Welcome!" Daniel called from behind the counter. "I'd offer you each a free coffee for really going all in on being Storybook Court's cops. But the owner would disapprove. See, Mrs. Trask, I know the rules."

A woman with a turquoise streak in her hair looked up from

a table halfway across the big room. "Usually, Daniel would be right. But we appreciate the extra protection. If it doesn't break any rules, the coffee is on me."

"Are you serious?" Daniel asked.

" 'Say what you mean and mean what you say,' " she told him.

"General George S. Patton," Kait said, identifying the quote, and the two women smiled at each other.

"We'll buy our own, but thanks," Erik said. A couple he recognized from The Gardens, the man in a sweatsuit bright enough to make your eyes water, the woman in a tasteful beige pantsuit, were the only customers. Marie had been right about business being bad.

"We've been meaning to come in. We're trying to go to every local business on our beat," Kait told him. "And Nessie and Helen were just telling us they'd been by."

"Because Marie refused to loan Helen sugar," Daniel answered. "She's always telling Helen she's getting too fat. Not always, tactful, our Marie. But gotta love her." He got their coffee orders and started making the drinks.

He looked and sounded very relaxed. He was an actor, but acting natural in front of two cops if you'd committed a series of robberies on their watch—that was different than giving a great performance in a movie.

"Do you remember the sisters talking about a figurine. Two porcelain rabbits?" Kait asked. Erik bet she couldn't force the words "Sad Bunnies" out of her mouth.

"Yeah. They were talking to me and Serena about it," Daniel answered.

"Serena?" Erik asked.

"She's one of the few regulars we have left. I'm hoping we'll get some back, once they've tried all forty-three lattes at the new place." He lowered his voice, and shot a glance at the owner. "If we can last that long."

"We just finished a call over at their place. The figurine was stolen. Sometime between when they were over here for coffee last week and today," Kait told him.

"Seriously?" Daniel exclaimed. "That day they were here they were saying they wished someone would steal Tragic Bunnies. I think that's what they called it. Weeping Bunnies? Something like that."

Kait gave a sharp intake of breath. "And they actually said they wished it was stolen?"

"Yeah. It's worth something like eight thou. I told them they should sell it, but it was a present from an aunt and they didn't feel right about it, even though it sounded like they'd still have a whole bunny trail full of bunnies from her left," Daniel answered. "And considering the age of the sisters, I wonder if the aunt would even know if they sold it, unless she's looking down from heaven."

"Was anyone else around, anyone other than you and Serena, who could have heard them say how much it was worth?" Erik took a swig of his coffee.

"Possibly Mrs. Trask, but she was probably too caught up in her paperwork to pay attention."

Mrs. Trask definitely needed money. Erik glanced over at her. She was chewing the end of a purple pen as she stared at a messy stack of papers. It didn't seem as if she was following their conversation.

"My brother was around for a little while that day." Daniel thought for a moment. "He was here while Nessie and Helen were getting coffee, but I'm not sure if they were still talking about the figurine."

There was no point in asking Daniel about his whereabouts during the time of the crime. He lived in the Court, and Sad Bunnies could have been stolen basically any time during the last week.

They'd keep an eye on him. Maybe Erik would stop by Serena's, see if she remembered seeing anyone else around when the sisters were talking about having a figurine worth eight thousand dollars at their place.

Yes. He should stop by. He was a thorough cop, and it was necessary to talk to Serena. For solving the case.

"Mac. Come here, Mac-Mac. Come on home, my kitty, kitty, kitty."

Mac's left ear flicked. Jamie had been calling and calling, and the sound was grating on his nerves. David had been calling earlier. He'd even opened the door to the shed, but Mac had made sure he wasn't seen.

"Mac-y. Kitty, kitty." To distract himself from Jamie's voice, he turned his attention to the kittens. He gave Bittles a few licks on the top of the head, chased Zoomies around until the kitten's little legs demanded a rest, did a little sparring with Sassy, and caught a bug for Lox. Then he gave all his kittens a meow of good-bye and wriggled through the tunnel and out into the cool night air.

It was time to check in on the humans he was considering for the kittens, but he could smell Jamie's scent trail on the air. There was still something in it that didn't smell like her. It had been part of her odor for months, but that wasn't long enough to make it completely familiar. There was a tang of anxiousness in her smell tonight, sadness too, and Mac thought it had to do with him. She started to call again.

"Mac! MacGyver! Come on home, kitty, kitty, kitty. I have sardinesies."

He turned toward home. It's like a leash was tugging him there. He hated leashes. And he hated cages. He ignored his person's—No, she wasn't his person anymore. He ignored Jamie's calls.

CHAPTER 12

Serena walked into the reception room, expecting to find a bunch of women around her age, maybe even all blondes or redheads with a similar type and build. Nope. There was a mix of races, sizes, and shapes. Interesting. Clearly, Norberto Foster didn't have a specific look he wanted for the part of Remy the werecat.

After she signed in, she took a seat as far away from the door leading to the audition room as she could find. It had been a while, well, years, since she'd been auditioning regularly, but she still remembered the feeling of being able to hear, or partially hear, other actors doing the scene she'd soon be doing. It was way too easy to start comparing herself to them, wondering if she'd made the right choices, and generally making herself crazier and more insecure by the second.

For the same reason she tried to tune out the women who were running lines while they waited. She resisted the impulse to run lines herself. She'd found that also got her into a downward spiral of doubt and second-guessing. She'd prepared as much as she could. She had decided the way she wanted to take the character. Now wasn't the time to abandon everything and try to come up with something new.

"That's not my style. That's not *my* style. That's not my *style. That's* not my style," the woman next to her murmured. Her face was all angles, and she had a lean, athletic build that she'd emphasized with an asymmetrical blazer that left most of one shoulder bare, an obi belt that emphasized her waist, and skinny jeans.

Serena had gone a different way. She'd chosen a sheer, feminine dress with a flowered pattern worn over a black full slip. She'd thought the way it was part sexy and part demure played into the way her character was part human and part cat. The skirt was flowy, the bodice tight. Parts of the dress were sheer, parts had two layers. It was sleeveless, and fell to mid-thigh, but had a prim Peter Pan collar.

But maybe she should have gone sleeker. Cats were sleek. And maybe she should have gone more all-out sexy. *Don't do this*, Serena told herself. *You tried on a million different outfits. You chose this one for a reason. Trust yourself.*

Out of the corner of her eye, she saw the woman press the pad of her thumb into the spot right above her nose. "Headache?" Serena asked.

"Does the sudden refusal of words to sound like words come from a headache? Because if so, yes, I have a headache."

"I can offer acetaminophen or ibuprofen," Serena told her. "And when I'm having that word thing, if I stop saying the words for a while, it goes away."

"I know there is a difference between those two," the woman answered. "But I don't know what it is. I'll take whatever's handy. And I can't prep if I don't say the words." She raised one hand to her dark chignon, then brought it down before she could muss her perfect hair. Her sleek hair. Serena had left her own hair in tousled, been-at-the-beach waves. Maybe she should have—*Stop. Trust yourself.*

Serena handed her a painkiller. "I'm sure you've prepped already."

The woman dry-swallowed the pill, seeming to have forgotten she held an almost-full water bottle in her hand. "Thanks. I'm Emily."

"Serena."

"I have prepped. And prepped, and prepped," Emily confessed. "But I always feel like if I don't run the lines right up to the second I go in, I'll forget them."

"It actually makes me feel more and more panicked if I do that," Serena told her.

"Oh, it does that to me, too!"

Serena laughed. "I feel like a little nerves give me some good energy, but panic just makes me panic. Go back to your lines if it helps."

"I keep sticking on that 'That is not my style' line. Nothing feels right. I don't know what to do with it."

Serena could see the tension in Emily's face. "The best advice I can give, is don't try to lock it in. Stay present and go with your impulse in the moment. Once you're in there, trust that all your prep is with you and then let it go. Just be in it." She smiled. "Easy to say, I know."

Emily smiled back. "You shouldn't be helping me, you know. We're going after the same part."

Serena shrugged. "But a cast is like a puzzle. All the pieces have to fit together. It's not about who's the best. It's more about who's the best for the particular puzzle. We don't know what that is. *They* don't even know what that is yet. At some point, they'll start thinking of the movie as a whole, and it'll come down to who fits." She shook her head. "Sorry. I fell into teacher mode. I've been teaching acting for the past few years, and I guess I haven't given up lecturing."

"Don't apologize. It's good advice. I—"

The door at the other end of the room open, and Emily went

silent. A man with a shaved head and a lopsided smile stepped out. "Serena Perry, you're up."

Serena stood. "That's me."

"Good luck," Emily told her.

"You too." Serena walked in to the room, and did what she always told her students to do. She was friendly, but professional. She didn't try to start a conversation. When the casting director asked if she had any questions, she didn't feel like maybe she should ask something to show how deeply she'd thought about the scene. She knew it was basically another way of asking to get started.

"No, thanks." She took her place in front of the casting director and a man and woman who hadn't been introduced. The audition was being filmed. As she took her place on the X taped on the floor, she made sure to choose a couple sightlines around the camera.

Then she tried to follow her own advice. She'd done the prep, now it was time to let it go and trust her gut. It didn't take her long to realize the man reading with her was an actor, not an assistant with limited acting ability. He was sitting near one of the sightlines she'd picked, so she was able to look at him, throwing as much energy as she could at him, and feeling it come back.

At one point, the small part of her brain that wasn't working her character, noted that he'd just given a different line than what had been in the script, a line that shook things up a little. Interesting. She shot back the answer that felt like Remy, ditching her own line, and went right on, working her way back to where she needed to be for the scene.

When she finished, she waited a beat, then tuned to the casting director and said "thank you." She added a thanks and a smile to the actor who fed her lines, then walked out, feeling a little shift inside as she let go of Remy. At least for now.

Emily raised her eyebrows as Serena walked back into the

lobby, and she gave a little shrug. She had no idea what the casting director thought or what any of the people who saw the audition tape would think. What she did know, was that she'd given it all she could.

Erik caught sight of Serena walking down the street, her short, flowered dress swishing above her knees as she moved, her pale red hair falling around her shoulders. Pieces of that dress were intriguingly sheer, and in the late afternoon sun, he got a glimpse of shapely thigh. He knew how it would feel, supple, warm, smooth. He imagined his hand slipping under that dress. . . .

A hard kick to the shin jerked him out of his PG-13 fantasy before it could go R. He jerked his gaze away from the window and returned his focus to the group gathered in the Quevases' large dining room. They'd agreed to host a meeting of robbery victims, and everyone had shown up—Al and Marie, Lynne and her husband, Nessie and Helen. Marcus had come by as soon as he got off work. It was the first time Erik and Kait had met him. He was attentive, but let the others do the talking, occasionally getting up to refill a glass. It was sort of hard to get a read on him because he was keeping to the fringes of the conversation, but Erik's first impression was that he was a decent guy, close to his family.

"Let me recap," Kait said. "And if I'm getting anything wrong, please jump in." She looked around the table, then began. "None of the three houses that were robbed have a security system. It is possible that a door was unlocked at the time of the robbery at all the houses, and it's almost certain at least one window was unlocked at each place." Erik was impressed that she was able to get those facts out without giving at least one sigh or huff of exasperation.

"I know we were careless," Lynne said, twisting her napkin into a knot.

"They're not blaming anyone, Mom," Marcus told her. "They're just laying out the similarities."

Kait nodded. "Exactly. Only one item was taken during each robbery, and each item was both valuable and insured. At all three homes there were other valuable items that would usually hold appeal for a thief, whether jewelry, electronics—"

"My mother's wedding silver," Marie interrupted. Al gave what Erik thought was a grunt of agreement. "What I want to know is if you searched Jamie and David's place the way I told you to. We all know that cat is a thief."

"The house was thoroughly searched," Erik answered. He didn't bother to say that it wasn't him and Kait who had done the searching. He was sure Jamie and David had looked everywhere.

"Let's go on," Kait said. "I just want to make sure I have this all straight. None of you remember seeing anyone in the neighborhood who didn't look familiar."

"That Lucifers has a new delivery boy," Marie told her. "I forgot to tell you about him last time. The girl who moved in next door orders pizza at least twice a week, even though I send Al over with leftovers at least that often." She gave a cluck of disapproval.

"Did you see whether he left right away or spent extra time in the Court?" Erik asked.

"Right in and right out," Marie answered. "And he had the sign on top of his car. He got a parking space on the street where I could see it once."

"Is there anyone else that seemed possibly out of place?" Kait got shakes of the head or "no"s from everyone. She looked over at Erik. There was something else they needed to talk about with the group, something that wasn't quite so straightforward as the whats and whens.

"Helen, Nessie, you two were talking about the figurine that ended up being stolen while you were at Yo, Joes!" Erik smiled at the sisters. "From what Daniel told us, you two said you wished someone would steal it, the way Marie's ring and Lynne's necklace had been taken."

Nessie's eyes widened in shock. So did Helen's. "We didn't," Nessie said. She put one hand on Helen's arm. "Did we?"

"I—Hmmm." Helen looked up at the ceiling as if the answer were written there.

"If you didn't say it, it's still true," Marie volunteered. "They keep a little lace hanky draped over it because they can't stand to look at it." Al gave a grunt that Erik interpreted as can you believe that.

"Just because the bunnies are so sad," Nessie explained. "But that doesn't mean . . . They were a present from our favorite aunt."

"You didn't make a joke about wishing the figurine would be stolen?" Erik knew Kait had chosen the word "joke" to make the question as non-accusatory as possible.

"We may have," Helen admitted. "But we wouldn't have wanted—"

"—someone to break into the house." Nessie shivered. "Never."

"Since we're talking similarities, it is accurate to say no one was especially . . . fond of the items that were taken?" Kait asked. No one answered. Erik noted that the sisters' cheeks had gone an identical deep red, while Lynne untwisted her napkin and began twisting it again.

Marie jerked her chin up. "Al gave me my ring after Little Al was born."

That didn't exactly answer the question. Erik was trying to decide how much he wanted to push when Lynne jumped in. "But you told me that you wished it would be stolen the way my necklace was." She looked at Marcus. "Remember, I told you and Daniel about that, how Marie sounded a little jealous about my necklace being taken."

Daniel heard that. Daniel who had the money to buy Serena a huge bouquet of flowers even though he had a job that couldn't pay much. Daniel who had also heard the sisters talk about how they wished Sad Bunnies would be stolen. Daniel who knew his mother hated the mushroom necklace.

"Is that right, Marie?" Kait asked.

Instead of answering Kait, Marie turned to Al. "That ring is uglier than death warmed over, left in the fridge, then warmed over again. We both know it."

"Seemed happy to get it," Al commented.

"I was happy we had a son, and that you gave me a present. And I was happy someone took it. Anyone would have been. But I told these two to get it back anyway." Marie gestured toward him and Kait. "Besides, wishing for something doesn't make it happen."

"When you had the conversation about the . . . appearance of the ring with Lynne, was anyone else present?" Kait asked. Lynne and Marie both shook their heads.

"We talked about it more than once. But just between ourselves," Marie added. "Because we'd both gotten jewelry from our husband's family that we never wanted to wear."

"That necklace was worth thirty thousand dollars," Lynne's husband, Carson, protested.

"That doesn't make it pretty," Marie shot back. Al backed her up with one of his grunts.

Erik and Kait exchanged a let's-wrap-it-up look. They had everything they needed. At least from the people in the room. Erik wanted another chance to talk to Daniel. "Is there anything anyone wants to add?" No one said anything. It seemed that everyone else was ready to wrap it up, too.

"Thanks for meeting up with us tonight. You have our cards if you think of something else you'd like to tell us." Kait stood. "Coffee shop?" she murmured as they started for the door.

"Yep." They didn't bother to get the car, just walked the few blocks to Yo, Joe!

"I give you permission to look now," Kait said when they went inside. She angled her chin toward the table where Serena sat with Daniel. There was only one other customer in the place. Clearly, Daniel didn't think he needed to stand behind the counter.

"Okay if we join you?" Erik called. The smile that spread across Serena's face when she saw him made his night.

"Come on down," Daniel answered, doing a game-show-announcer voice. Erik was struck again by how comfortable he seemed in the presence of two cops. And he knew they were in the middle of investigating the Storybook Court robberies. Erik was used to people coming off as nervous when they weren't guilty of anything, sweating and stammering. It came with being a cop. He wished it didn't.

But someone guilty who didn't give off any sign of nerves? That didn't happen. Maybe a sociopath could pull it off, but in Erik's experience there were always signs, maybe subtle, but there. Daniel wasn't giving him any kind of guilty vibe.

"I like this dress," Erik said to Serena as he took the seat next to her.

"Thanks. I got it special for my audition."

"Serena was just telling me how it went," Daniel told them.

Erik knew the audition was that day, and he knew how excited she was about it, what a huge deal it was to her. He should have called her, texted, something. If he was going to get closer to her, and he wanted to get closer, he couldn't just ignore something that was the most important thing in her life. "How did it go?"

"Hard to tell. That casting director didn't give me even the basic 'nice job' after I finished, but that doesn't mean anything," Serena answered. "I was happy with what I did. Now it's just wait and see."

The chain of demitasse spoons hanging from the door jangled. Erik looked over and saw Marcus walking in. He hesitated briefly, then headed over to them.

"Marcus! Twice in one week," Daniel said in greeting, then frowned. "Are you okay?"

"Yeah. Why? Just because I showed up where you work two times?"

"Well, it's not exactly routine. But you just looked a little, stressed, maybe." Daniel leaned back and grabbed a chair from the table behind them. He hauled it over so Marcus could sit.

Marcus ran one hand through his hair, the same shade of brown as Daniel's. There was a strong family resemblance between the brothers. "Client who keeps changing her mind, that's all," he explained.

"Marcus is a big shot creative director at Ballista," Daniel explained to the rest of the group. Erik thought he sounded proud of his little brother, but that first day he and Kait met Daniel, it had been clear he had some resentment toward Marcus.

"I just read an article about affective conditioning. There was a study that said even when people knew a particular pen was inferior, they would tend to buy it based on ads that paired it with other things people like," Kait said. "The part I thought was especially interesting was that even when people had plenty of time after viewing the ad to think about the factual information regarding the quality of the pen, they still bought it."

"Put a puppy next to what you want to sell, and step back," Marcus answered. "You make people feel good, and that good feeling extends to the product." He tilted his head from side to side, like he was trying to get rid of tension in his neck, then looked over at Daniel. "I wanted to let you know how it went at the meeting about the robberies, but it looks like you're already getting the report."

"We were actually talking about Serena's big audition," Daniel said. "This girl's been in town for about a minute and already got an agent, shot a commercial, and just today auditioned for a part in the new Norberto Foster movie."

"Impressive. All that in about half a minute." Marcus looked at Daniel. "What's your problem, bro?" Erik thought Marcus had been going for a jokey tone. Didn't make it.

Serena leaned toward Marcus. "Daniel just got cast in a new play. It's a great part. Really meaty. I think it's going to get him a lot of notice."

"But from what he's told me, it's a toss-up whether that play or this job will make him more money," Marcus answered.

"Money! Money, money, money." Daniel slapped his hands on the table. "Why does it always come down to money with you?"

"Because money is necessary," Marcus said. "For food. And for rent—at least for someone who doesn't live with their parents."

"You must be pretty good at managing your money. I don't think most baristas would be able to give Serena the kind of bouquet you did. She said it was huge."

"And beautiful. And thoughtful." Serena shot Erik an annoyed look. He didn't want to get on her bad side, but he needed to know what Daniel would say about spending that kind of cash.

"I have a friend who's a caterer, okay? Once in a while, I fill in as a server. I asked him if I could take one of the centerpieces home, and I gave it to Serena. I also cut coupons, darn my socks, and water down my orange juice." Daniel stood up. "I need a refill. Anyone want anything? My treat. I think I can afford almost everything on the menu. With my employee discount anyway." He didn't give them much time to answer before he strode off.

When he returned with a fresh coffee, Erik decided he had to push Daniel a little more. He was the best suspect they had. "I'm curious, Daniel. Is there ever a time where you'd decide to call it and move on?"

"Call it?" Daniel repeated.

"Just decide that making it as a professional actor isn't in the cards. Not that I'm saying that's the case," Erik added quickly, catching Serena stiffening. "But is there a point where you'd consider getting a job that's more of a career than working here?"

"Look. This place is in trouble. I know that," Daniel answered. "I probably will have to find something else at some point. But it's going to have to be a job with flexibility, like this one. Working here, I can take off for auditions whenever I need to. I can switch my hours around. Like for the play. There will be a few months where we'll be rehearsing during the day, then it will switch to performances at night, and that's not a problem."

"Flexibility is great. I understand that. But what about things like health insurance, like a 401K?" Marcus shoved his hand through his hair again. "How can you not even think about things like that?"

"I have a rich brother. He'll take care of me if I end up in the hospital," Daniel shot back.

"Don't count on it." Marcus let out a sigh so long it was probably making Kait envious. "I didn't mean that. I worry about you, that's all."

"You came over here to tell me about what happened at Mom and Dad's. Is there any progress on the robberies?" Daniel was clearly trying to stop any further conversation about real jobs with benefits.

"Tonight was about finding similarities," Kait answered. "It was helpful to get all the victims in the same place. We'll keep everybody updated on our progress as we're able."

"No one could remember seeing anyone unfamiliar around the Court, except for a new pizza delivery guy, but Marie seemed to have kept a tight watch over him. Have you noticed anyone, Daniel?"

"If I had, don't you think I'd have said something?" Daniel didn't bother to hide his frustration with the question.

Erik realized he'd just given Daniel an opening. Daniel could have made up a story about seeing someone hanging around Storybook Court. He could have given all kinds of details to try to throw suspicion off himself. But he hadn't. Erik's gut was telling him Daniel wasn't their guy. But who was?

Mac heard Diogee barking. Did he know Mac was outside the house? Possibly. But he had seen the bonehead bark at his own shadow.

He didn't have any reason to be there. He'd just caught the smells of his pack—his old pack—and found himself following the scent trails.

He trotted away. He didn't have any reason to be there, and he had somewhere else to be.

CHAPTER 13

"Do you think we should take him home or to the kittens?" Serena asked, cuddling Mac in her arms as she and Erik walked to Storybook Court.

"I'm not sure it matters. He seems to find a way to go wherever it pleases him," he answered.

Mac began to purr, and Serena laughed. "I couldn't believe it when he came strolling up to our table. How'd he even get in the coffee shop? The door was shut. I need to watch him more carefully. He could help me with my werecatting."

"Did I mention that I like this dress?" Erik lightly ran his hand over the part of her back where the dress was sheer, without the lining of the black slip. Damn it. It felt good. But she was mad at him. Didn't he realize that?

"You do realize that I'm mad at you, don't you?" Serena asked.

"What? Why?" He sounded completely surprised. Weren't cops supposed to be good at reading people. "Wait. Because I asked Daniel if he'd ever considering getting a different kind of job?"

"Very good. Got it in one," Serena shot back. "Actually, two. Since you had to stop and think about it." Mac stopped purring. He brushed his head against her arm. He obviously agreed with her!

"Don't you think his brother had a point?"

"What I think it that it's not any of his business. And it definitely isn't any of yours. You barely know Daniel," Serena said. They crossed the street and walked into the courtyard. Mac began to squirm. "He's going to get away from me!" She tightened her arms around him, but he was too squirmy. He broke free and loped off as soon as he jumped down.

"I wonder where he's off to now?" Erik said.

"Did you think I wasn't going to notice that you changed the subject?" Serena asked. "I was asking why you thought it was okay to question the way Daniel is living his life."

"I had reasons. You could consider not assuming that I'm an asshole."

"How is it assuming when I was sitting right there watching you?"

They turned onto Serena's street. "We've both said what we have to say on this, right?" Erik asked. "Can we drop it now?" He sounded a little annoyed. What did *he* have to be annoyed about?

"How's this for a new topic. You know I had the audition today. You know it was a huge deal to me. But you didn't ask me anything about it." She hadn't planned to bring that up, but, to be honest she was as pissed off about that as she was about the way he treated Daniel.

Erik's jaw tightened. "Yeah, I did. I asked you how it went almost as soon as I sat down at the table."

"Okay, I'll give you that. I'll give you that you asked the most basic, perfunctory questions." They'd reached the lighthouse. Serena stopped. If he thought he was going to follow her into the house, he was crazy.

"Clearly, nothing I say or do right now is going to make you happy. It would be better if we talked another time." His tone was stiff and formal.

Serena gave her hand a dismissive flip as she started up the crushed-seashell walkway. "I'll call you," she said over her shoulder.

As if she'd call him. He could call her—and apologize.

Mac watched his kittens with the num-nums, turkey and ham tonight. His friends Zachary and Addison had left packages of the meat out on the counter. Mac knew that they weren't meant for him. But the two of them had started fighting, then slobbering. They had left the food unguarded. What happened next was their fault, not Mac's.

Lox backed away from the other kits, dragging a slice of turkey bigger than she was. Mac waited to see what the others would do. Bittles gave a pathetic little mew. He'd been right about to take a bite of that turkey. Sassy and Zoomies didn't even look up. They'd nabbed their share and were busy eating.

Time for Mac to do some teaching. Kittens, they needed so much attention. He gave a growl of warning, then launched himself at Lox. He—gently—knocked the kitten over, and took back the turkey. He held the meat in his jaws. Would Lox come for it? Would Bittles? Mac was trying to show the littlest kitten the correct response if someone took her food.

Lox gave a growl. Mac could tell the kitten was trying to sound like him, but the sound was more like a buzzing bumblebee. Then Lox came at him. Mac allowed himself to be knocked off balance, then allowed Lox to run off with a piece, but just a piece, of the turkey.

Bittles watched as Mac took a bite. It wasn't sardinesies, but it was very nice. His kittens would go out into the world expecting to be served the best. As they should. If their humans didn't understand that, well, Mac was sure his kittens would be able to train their people.

Mac took another bite of turkey. He pretended not to notice as Bittles, little tummy brushing against the ground, began to creep toward him. Bittles was stalking! When he snatched away the turkey, Mac purred with pride.

Next lesson, cleanliness. As soon as the kittens were all finished with their food, Mac would demonstrate the correct way for them to wash themselves. He wouldn't always be around to do it for them. Sassy had already begun giving herself a thorough tongue bath after meals. Zoomies usually zoomed off without even licking the bits of food off his mouth. Lox and Bittles were progressing, although they seemed to believe licking a paw and running it over one ear meant bath done. He'd keep showing them the correct ways to be a cat until he was sure they were ready to go out into the world.

The shed door opened. Mac watched in approval as several of the kittens went to greet Serena. Humans needed a little appreciation to be happy. But a cat shouldn't make a habit of it. Humans had to understand that it was up to the cat when the human would be given attention.

Serena sat down on the floor. She looked at Mac as if she was ready for a lesson, too. This human might be a bit brighter than most. At least she realized she needed to be taught. Mac began his grooming lesson, and Serena followed along as best she could with her human paws. Maybe with his help, she would realize there was never a need to pour water over yourself or dunk yourself in the stuff.

After bath time, it was play time, where Mac had to continue teaching the kittens not to bite or scratch too hard. It was necessary for them to understand this. Their humans only had patchy spots of fur for protection.

Finally, even Zoomies collapsed onto the floor, unable to

play even a moment longer. He was always the last to fall asleep and the first to wake up. Mac needed to work with him on the need for frequent naps.

Now that his kittens were settled, Mac had to fix whatever had Serena smelling angry. Sigh. His work was never done. Even though she was smarter than most, she didn't seem to realize that she usually smelled happier when she was with Erik. He'd have to remind her. He sauntered over to the shed door and looked at it. No need for the tunnel tonight. Serena had been taught that when he stared at the door, she was expected to open it.

He took in a quick breath, found Erik's scent trail, and began to follow it. He moved slowly. Humans' eyes were never that useful, but in the dark, people behaved as if they didn't have eyes at all. But Mac could see well enough for both of them.

Erik strode down Glass Slipper Street. He needed to move, so he might as well patrol. Maybe he'd actually see something that would help figure out who was behind the robberies. It had to be someone nearby, maybe someone living in the Court. The items stolen had matched what the victims wanted stolen too perfectly for a stranger to be the thief. The person had to be familiar, even trusted.

A new thought struck him. Did the thief know what the victims wanted stolen, because the victims were in on it? The necklace, the ring, and Sad Bunnies were all insured. It wasn't just that the women had been relieved of things they disliked. They also got a nice chunk of cash.

He couldn't imagine Marie being part of an insurance fraud scheme. He didn't know the other three well, but it didn't feel likely. Still, he had to consider every possibility. He'd talk it over with Kait.

Erik had already walked every street of the Court, but he

still wasn't ready to go home and work on one of his DIY projects. He'd let that argument with Serena rile him up. They hadn't known each other that long, but after that dinner, and hanging out at the yard sales, and a bunch of texts and a few phone calls, he thought she would have cut him a break. It's not like he'd said Daniel clearly didn't have the chops to make it as an actor. He didn't even think that. But after years struggling, didn't you at least have to consider hanging it up?

He slowed down, pushing all the thoughts of Serena away. He thought he'd seen movement in the shadows alongside Ruby's house. He kept walking. If there was someone hiding back there, he didn't want to tip them off.

Swish! Plop! Something small fell out of one of the trees. The branches were still swaying. Somebody'd brushed against them. Someone *was* back there. Erik sprinted toward the tree. He saw a figure backing up fast. Not fast enough. He tackled her to the ground. Her. The body beneath his was definitely feminine.

"What are you doing?"

The voice sent a hot jolt through him. Serena. "No, what the hell are *you* doing?"

"I was practicing my cat moves." She squirmed, trying to sit up.

"Your what?" His brain was having trouble keeping up. His body was demanding all his attention, pummeled by the feel of her, the smell of her. He braced himself on his arms, not letting her up, but not exactly holding her down.

"For the werecat part." She planted her hands on his chest and gave him a push. Before he could move back, her arms went around his neck. He realized she was breathing hard. He thought he was the only one. His breaths were coming fast and ragged, and it had nothing to do with that sprint.

Then his mouth was on hers. Had she moved first, or had he? Didn't matter. All that mattered was the slick warmth of her as his tongue explored. Her hands slid down his back. He wanted to use his hands. He had to touch her.

Erik lowered himself until his body was flush against hers, not breaking the kiss. He managed to get his hands under her back, then rolled her on top of him. He wrapped both hands around her waist, then immediately ran one up her back. He wanted all of her.

But there were outside. In the neighborhood that he was responsible for.

Reluctantly, Erik broke the kiss. He briefly pressed his lips against her neck, then said, "We should—"

Serena didn't wait for him to finish. She scrambled to her feet, looking a little dazed. He felt more than a little dazed himself. "Wow," she murmured.

"Yeah," he agreed.

She tried to tame her hair with her fingers. He wished she wouldn't. That tousled mass of golden red was amazing. He took her hand, and they walked in silence back to the lighthouse. They paused at the front door. Serena looked down at herself in the porch light. "I'm filthy."

He laughed. She looked like she was trying to frown, but the corners of her lips kept quirking up. "You know what I mean. Dirt. From the ground. On my dress." She let go of his hand and started trying to brush it off.

Erik caught her hand. "Let me." First, he straightened her collar, letting his fingers drift across her throat, then he moved lower, running his palms over the sheer section of the dress that stopped just above her breasts.

His eyes locked on hers, he moved his hands lower again, briefly sliding over her breasts. He could feel the silky black slip through the sheer fabric of the dress. It called to him. He slid one hand under her short skirt, but over the slip, allowing himself to savor the feel of the slick softness, warm from her skin.

Erik wanted her skin, but he forced himself to take it slow. Serena swayed toward him. He moved his hands to her waist, steadying her, then returned one hand to her slip. "What's under this layer?" he asked, allowing his fingers to toy with the hem.

"Um." She licked her lips. "Uh. I'm trying to think. I can't think."

He kissed her cheek, her neck again. "I could help you remember."

He slid his hand under the slip, caressing her thigh, then moving up, up, up. "It's not much." He curled his fingers over the waistband of her panties.

"Good night." Serena stumbled away from him, and stood there, resting her back against the front door, as if she didn't trust herself to stay upright.

"Good night?" Erik repeated. What was happening?

She gave a firm nod. "Good night."

"Did I go too fast?" He thought she'd been right there with him.

"No!" she exclaimed. "Well, yes. But not just you. I was here, too." She straightened up, and smoothed the hem of her dress. "We've had kind of a strange start. With that first kiss, and then you taking off."

"I tried to explain about that," Erik protested.

"You did. And I understood," she reassured him. "But I'm not feeling completely ready to . . . go inside with you."

He gave a reluctant smile. "I don't think there's much else we could do outside, at least not without getting arrested. Although I could probably get us off with a warning."

"So, I'll call you?" The words sounded a lot different than when she'd flung them at him after their fight. That fight seemed like it had happened years ago.

"Or I'll call you." Erik stepped forward and gave her a quick kiss on the lips, not allowing his hands to touch her. "Sleep well."

He knew he wouldn't.

CHAPTER 14

"I've already discovered that Marcus has several of the qualities on my list," Kait told Erik. They sat down in their usual booth at the Gower Gulch Denny's. As he'd predicted, he didn't get a lot of sleep the night before. Too many mental movies of Serena. But he felt great, like he'd gotten a solid ten.

"How'd you manage that in one short ride home?" he asked. Marcus had volunteered to drive Kait to her place while Erik and Serena escorted Mac home.

"We decided to stop for a drink at Public," Kait explained. She said it like she went there every weekend, and as far as he knew, she'd never been. Neither had Erik. He knew enough to know it was ritzy, and ritzy wasn't his style. "I already knew Marcus has a good job. We talked about a campaign he worked on, and I could tell he enjoys his work."

"That's Number Three, part A and B on the list, right?"

Kait narrowed her eyes at him, probably trying to decide if he was teasing her. "That's right. I'm also giving him credit for being close to his family, even though he and Daniel weren't exactly getting along last night."

"Yeah, I'd give him that, too. Marcus was getting on Daniel's case, but I think it's mostly because he wants Daniel to be secure. And when we had that meeting, he was there for his parents." He was glad Kait had gone out with someone she might actually want to go out with a second time.

Susan, one of the waitresses they'd gotten to know since they'd been working the beat, came over. "The usual?" Susan flipped their coffee cups over and filled them.

"Yes, please," Kait said, and Erik nodded. "Did your son's team get everything done for this weekend?" Susan's son was on an Odyssey of the Mind team, and Susan had been worrying about the team's time management skills. She claimed they'd spent two months trying to decide on a team name.

"Of course not. The competition is"—she counted on her fingers—"almost two whole days away. They have lots of time, according to Jake."

"If they don't get it together, they'll still have learned something about working as a group," Erik told her.

Susan rolled her eyes. "He'll find a way to make it my fault. He's hit an age where everything is my fault. Or his dad's. Or his sister's." With that, she left to put in their order. Erik clicked coffee cups with Kait. "We're doing it. We're becoming part of the neighborhood."

"I hope they decide to expand the program," she answered. "It's good for the citizens and good for us. I read a study that said cops who do the kind of community-oriented policing we're doing have measurably less stress."

Erik grinned. "How does Marcus feel about psychological studies?"

"We didn't discuss it per se, but psychology is key to his kind of work, the same as it is to ours," Kait answered.

"Okay, here's the big question. Where does he stand on the Maguire, Holland, Garfield issue? And is he pro or con Glover?" Erik took a swallow of his coffee. Interest in Spider-Man wasn't on Kait's perfect-man list, but Erik thought it should be. Charlie Imura would get a top score. But even perfect scores in all other categories wouldn't be able to wipe out the fact that he was a convicted felon.

"Every conversation I have doesn't involve Spider-Man." Kait's voice was crisp.

"True." He knew he was annoying her, but he still said, "I know having fun together isn't on your list, but did you have fun?"

Kait dodged the question. "He meets the requirement for being attractive, too."

"Fun?" Erik prodded. He wasn't willing to let it go. Kait might not think fun was important, but he knew it was. He should look up some studies, so he could make her understand that.

"We decided to move to the Spare Room. It has games like Dominos and Monopoly and chess, and two retro bowling alleys. They made me think of you. They had wood floors, tongue, and groove."

"Nice." Erik didn't let himself get sucked into a carpentry conversation. "Sounds like a spot for fun."

"I think it would have been." A small furrow appeared between Kait's brows. "We walked in, and a couple guys waved to Marcus from across the room. He waved back, then he said the room was too crowded, and he'd rather go."

Yowch.

"It's a small space. However, we could have found a spot," Kait continued. "But according to environmental scientists, feeling crowded isn't directly related to how many people are occupying a space. For example, a room might feel more crowded if it was filled with strangers than it would have filled with the same number of friends."

Erik suspected crowding wasn't the issue. Maybe Marcus didn't appreciate Kait's quirkiness and didn't feel like introducing her to his buddies. His loss.

"He asked if I would like to go to the Hollywood Bowl with him next weekend. The LA Phil's doing John Williams music with movie clips," Kait added.

Erik hadn't been expecting that. Maybe Marcus really just hadn't felt like dealing with a crowd. He'd come up with something for them to do that Kait would really like, something fun. Maybe something could get going between them.

He wondered if Serena would want to go to the Bowl. He'd ask her when he called. He'd been wanting to call her since the door closed behind her when she went inside the night before. Maybe it was a little too soon, but he wasn't playing any games. He wanted her to know exactly how much he wanted to see her. Maybe he'd call after breakfast.

"You're smiling," Kait observed.

Erik felt his smile go full-on grin. "Yes, I am."

Mac pawed open the screen door and headed to the living room. He leapt to the back of the couch and sat there, staring down at the human called Charlie. He did not smell happy. Mac wondered if Zoomies would make him laugh. Watching him had made Serena laugh. Why not Charlie?

Or maybe Bittles would be a good match. Bittles loved to snuggle, and Charlie looked like he could use some kitten cuddles. Mac reminded himself that he had to put the kittens' needs first. Of course, they would end up helping their humans, they were cats, but the important thing was that the humans gave the kittens good homes.

Charlie had shared chicken with Mac the other day. That showed the attitude Mac was looking for. Mac stretched out on his stomach, so he could look right down at Charlie's face. He was napping. Mac approved. Napping was a basic necessity, and a nap with a human could be pleasant, especially when there were no good spots of sunshine available.

There was only so much intel Mac could gather while Charlie

was asleep. He reached down and gave Charlie a soft tap on the nose with one paw. When Charlie didn't respond, Mac gave him another tap. Then a tap-meow combo. That got Charlie's eyes opening. He looked up at Mac for a long moment, then smiled. "Chewie, my friend. You're back." He sounded glad to see Mac. As he should be.

Mac jumped down onto Charlie's stomach, and Charlie began scratching him behind the ears. Correct behavior.

"On the couch again?" a woman blah-blahed as she came into the room. "You're going to become permanently attached if you aren't careful. You'll have to carry it around like a turtle shell."

"I go to work, and it's not like I can go anywhere else." Charlie kept scratching Mac. "Besides, can't you see I have company?"

"What a beauty. I've heard people say he's a thief, but I don't believe it. He's much too sweet. Just look at the two of you."

Mac could feel the woman's appreciation as she studied him, and he began to purr in response. Recognizing that a cat should be appreciated was important. It was also a sign of intelligence. Between the two of them, this man and this woman might be able to make a good home for a kitten.

"You could have gotten yourself up to offer your friend some refreshments." The woman walked out of the room. When she returned, she had a bowl of fresh water and a small piece of salmon. Mac jumped down to the floor to accept her offering. Oh, yes. One of his kits could be happy here. He just had to decide which one.

The woman grabbed Charlie's feet and shoved them onto the floor, then sat in the empty space she'd created. "I've given you all the moping time you're going to get. What's going on?"

"Nothing." The bad smell got stronger. Mac wanted to figure out what was wrong with him and fix it, so one of the kittens wouldn't have to.

"Charlie."

"Nothing new, is what I meant. House arrest. Convicted felon. Social outcast. Do I need more?"

"That was all true last week, and last month. But something's changed. I repeat, what's going on?"

"Okay, okay, no more interrogation!" Charlie's blah-blah was so loud that Mac stopped his post-snack grooming with his paw halfway up to his ear. "I'm pretty sure Shelby is ghosting me. Or at least doing a semi-ghost. She texts me once for every fifteen times I text her."

"Ah. Do you think it could be because you have more, let's call it free time?" The woman's voice was soothing, and Mac returned to his tongue bath. He didn't need to step in right now.

"Remember when she would come over after work almost every night?"

"She knew you needed her. But visiting that often would be tough for anyone. I'm sure she has errands, grocery shopping—"

"Why are you defending her? You never liked her." Charlie's blah-blahs were getting loud again. Mac jumped up onto his lap, and the human immediately began stroking him.

"Charlie, I hardly know her. I met her once before the trial. And on her visits here, well, I know it wasn't the best time for her. For either of you."

"But you don't like her."

"I didn't warm up to her as fast as I do to some other people."

Charlie gave a laugh that sounded almost like a dog bark. "Which in Aunt Grace speak means you hated her."

"She's just not the kind of woman I expected you to be with, I suppose."

"Well, no worries. Once she actually dumps me, I'm sure all kinds of quality women will come running. They all love a bad boy. I just need to buy me a leather jacket. Is that still the correct attire for a bad boy? I need to google it."

"No matter what you wear, no one who gets to know you is

going to think you're bad. I'm afraid you'll have to find some other way to attract women."

Mac yawned. Kitten duty hadn't been allowing him to get his usual sixteen hours. And with Charlie petting him ... He yawned again, then closed his eyes. He felt welcomed. He was definitely going to allow one of his kittens to live here.

And he was going to figure out a way to help Charlie. As soon as he woke up from his nap.

"The Snow White Café? Seems appropriate, since my life is feeling like a fairy tale right now." Serena looked at the unassuming little tavern, its name written in white on a plain brown awning.

"It's one of my favorite local places," Erik answered. Then he frowned.

"What?" Serena asked.

"I probably should have picked a better place to celebrate you getting a second audition. Someplace more special."

"A second audition with pretty much no notice. Like I told you, I got the call this morning, and had to be there at eleven," Serena told him. "I don't need fancy. I just need to wind down."

She almost added that anyplace where she could hang out with him was perfect, but didn't want to go all gushy. Last night had been knee-bucklingly hot, but Serena had pulled back for a reason. She hadn't forgotten how Erik had run hot and cold in the past. He'd explained—but that didn't necessarily mean he wouldn't do it again. She needed more time.

"Are you're sure? We're close to the Roosevelt Hotel. They have a—"

"I've seen it on Kimmel. You know that Hostel La Vista segment?"

"Where the kids staying in youth hostels compete, and the winner gets to stay in the Roosevelt for the rest of their trip."

"Right. The Roosevelt looks amazing," Serena said. "But not for tonight. I want cozy, not ritzy."

"You got cozy." Erik opened the door for her. Serena stepped inside, immediately liking the vibe. Everyone there looked relaxed and happy.

"Those murals all around? They were done by some of the artists who worked on the movie," Erik told her, leading the way to an empty table. "There are rumors that Disney wants to close this place, because it doesn't exactly match their image. It's not perfect. There's some wear and tear on most of the chairs, if you haven't noticed."

"I hope that doesn't happen. It would be destroying a piece of history," Serena answered.

Erik picked up the salt shaker and turned it over in his hands, then he said, "How did the audition go?"

Serena got the feeling that he'd had to gear himself up a little to ask. But he had asked. That's what mattered. He was trying to get past the garbage leftover from his relationship with Tulip. Otherwise he wouldn't be sitting there with her.

"It was crazy. I got the call, and they wanted me there two hours later. I had to do a cold reading of a scene. Well, not completely cold, Emily, an actor I met last time I auditioned, and I got a chance to run lines a few times."

"Is that usual? Helping the competition?" Erik asked. "Tu—" He stopped abruptly.

"It's okay with me if you mention Tulip." Serena touched his arm lightly.

He nodded. "Mostly I don't talk about her. Well, not anymore. There was a stretch after we broke up when she was almost all I talked about. I'm lucky I have any friends left."

"Been there," Serena admitted. She didn't mind him talking about Tulip, but she didn't want to get into a big conversation about exes. Not tonight at least. Tonight was too close to yesterday night when Erik had set her on fire. They'd set each other on fire.

"And on the competition thing—depends on the people. Emily and I had gotten friendly. And running lines would help us both."

The waiter came over to get their drinks order. He clapped Erik on the shoulder. "Good to see you. Usual?"

"You ever tried Point the Way IPA?" Erik asked Serena.

"Nope. But if it's your usual, I'm in," she answered.

"Two," he told the waiter. "That's one thing I like about this place," Erik said as the waiter walked away. "I only come in maybe once a month for a burger, and they remember my usual."

"It's like that in Atlanta, too. A big city, but with places that make it feel small." Part of her was engaged in the chitchat, but only part. The rest of her was registering everything about Erik, the little flecks of deep green in his hazel eyes; the muscles in his forearms; the tiny chip in one of his front teeth; the smell of him, like soap and sawdust and skin.

"I've never been there. Actually, I haven't been too much of anywhere," Erik said. "Most vacations, I end up having things I want to do around the house. And my niece usually cons me into a trip to Disneyland. It doesn't take much. I just get season passes every year." He shook his head. "Boring, huh?"

"Vacations should be about enjoying yourself. Once when I had some time off, I went to triple features every day, sat in the sun on my porch, went out to dinner with my friends. Not exactly *Travel* magazine stuff. But it was great."

"Disney and DIY was pretty great, too."

"I think I know what this guy wants," the waiter said when he returned with big glasses of beer. "What about you?" he asked Serena.

"I need a little more time," she answered. But actually, she didn't. "It's been a long day. I think I want to have our beer, then go home," she told Erik after the waiter had walked away.

"Oh, okay. Yeah, I'm sure you must be tired."

He didn't get it. Well, she hadn't exactly made it clear. "I didn't mean by myself. I want you to come home with me. To my bed," she added to make it as clear as possible.

"I could do that." When he smiled at her, she could feel it down to her toes. She took a big gulp of beer. He drained half his glass without pausing for breath. They both laughed. "You ready?" he asked.

She'd thought she needed more time, but somehow just sitting with him for a few minutes had made her doubts fade away. Maybe because he'd been willing to talk about the audition. Maybe because all her instincts were telling her he was a good guy.

Breathe it in, she told herself, then said, "I am so ready."

CHAPTER 15

"I thought maybe we'd get complaints on the amount of Christmas lights on Ruby's place, especially since it's not even the end of September," Kait commented as they started doing a neighborhood walkthrough.

"Ruby's lights are a Storybook Court tradition. So is the truly amazing Christmas party she throws for everybody who lives here. Even I had fun, and you know I'm not a big party guy." He couldn't help smiling at the tree where he'd tackled Serena the other night.

"Cute elves," Kait commented.

Elves? He looked again. Yeah, there were elves on the tree. And now that he thought about it, he remembered one falling on the ground the other night, alerting him that someone was back there. He was sure he and Serena would have gotten over their quarrel pretty quickly no matter what. They were both pretty reasonable. But the make-out session over there had made them both forget all about it.

"There was a study in the *Journal of Environmental Psychology* that made a connection between people who put up

Christmas decorations early, and people who have had disappointing holidays in the past."

"Now that's a cheery thought. Thanks, Kait. Just a tip. When you're invited to this year's Christmas party, which you will be, don't use that as a conversation starter," Erik teased.

"I don't see it as a bad thing," Kait protested. "It's optimistic actually. The person in question is taking charge. They are doing whatever they can to make the upcoming holiday better."

Maybe that's what her list was about. Taking charge, trying to make her life better. Maybe she was doing everything she could so that she didn't end up the way her parents had, staying in a miserable marriage for too many years before a long, ugly divorce. Erik could talk to Kait about almost anything, but he couldn't bring up this theory, even though he thought the list of hers might be keeping her from giving someone great a chance.

"In my family, my parents used to put up the tree after my brother and sisters were in bed. When we got up in the morning, it was in the living room, all decorated. It was like magic," Erik told her. "By your theory, does that make my parents pessimistic?"

"It's not my theory. And I think it makes your parents wonderful," Kait answered.

"It was pretty cool. Later, when we got older, we'd all decorate the tree together. I always thought I'd do that with my kids."

"Your kids!" Kait pointed at him. "See, you want them."

"I never said I didn't."

She snorted. "Well, it's not like it's going to happen the way you go through women."

"I've actually gone out with Serena"—he did an elaborate finger count—"three times. Four if you count the night we hung out in her backyard waiting for the kitten to come down from the tree." Five if you counted almost having sex behind Ruby's tree, he silently added.

Kait gave an approving nod. "Four times. Nice. My real objection to your interest in her was my fear that you'd treat her like your usual women, and dispose of her after a few dates. I don't think you've gone out with the same woman four times in a row since—"

"Since Tulip," he finished for her. "Maybe it's a good thing Serena's a Lighthouse Award winner. It's forced me to deal with all that crap head-on. We've even talked about it some. She's actually really different from Tulip. She has a realistic take on what might or might not happen for her out here."

"It probably wasn't a good idea to form a whole hypothesis based on one woman's behavior. It's not like you'd gone out with enough performers to have a decent random sampling. Oh, and Marcus texted me last night."

Erik laughed. "Were you hoping to slip that by me?"

"No. I wanted to tell you. I just didn't want to jinx it."

"Jinx it?" he repeated. "What have you done with my partner, the least superstitious person on the planet?"

She made a growling sound. "I can't believe I said it! It's a self-protective mechanism to avoid disappointment. But it's a kind of self-protection that leads to negative outlook, an assumption that something bad always follows something good."

"Maybe you should ease up on the psychological journals a little. Up the comic books. Sometimes thinking too much can mess you up." He smiled at her. "Not that I have even one study to back that up."

"The texts showed me Marcus has another quality from my list." Kait paused to pick up a gum wrapper that had been left on the sidewalk. Probably the person who'd dropped it didn't realize it had happened. The people who lived in the Court had a lot of civic pride. "He's a good listener. Not that he was listening exactly. But we texted back and forth about his job and my job, and he asked really good follow-up questions. I could tell he was really interested."

"That's great." He hoped at some point, maybe after the Hollywood Bowl, he'd hear about some actual fun Marcus and Kait had together, but it was good to hear Marcus was paying attention to Kait.

"Nobody panic. Convicted felon coming up behind you. I'm on my approved walk from bus stop to home." Erik slowed until Charlie caught up to them. Kait probably wished Erik would have picked up the pace, but being on the beat meant being around for everyone who lived there, including, maybe even especially, for people who'd already had some problems with the law.

"How's it going?" Erik asked. He couldn't think of a better question.

"Have you been checking in with your parole officer?" Kait asked. That was definitely a worse question. It was as if Kait wouldn't forgive him for somehow making her think he was a cool comics-loving guy before she found out about his drug dealing.

"Yep, happy to do it, too. Ms. Ayala is a woman I can trust," Charlie answered. "Hey, it's Chewie." He stopped and knelt down, making a clicking sound with his tongue. A moment later, Mac trotted over and rubbed his cheek against Charlie's shin.

Kait looked down at Mac. "That indicates affection. It's called bunting."

"I knew you were an expert in human behavior," Erik commented. "You're studying animals now, too?"

"You can learn a lot about people from animals." She raised her gaze from Mac and studied Charlie, a small frown on her face.

Mac moved over to Erik, and rubbed his head against Erik's leg. Erik crouched down and scratched him under the chin. "Did you call him Chewie?"

"He looks like—"

"Captain Marvel's cat," Kait finished for him. "Although in the movie—"

"He was called Goose," Charlie filled in. "I assume it was a shout out to *Top Gun*, and it's a cool cat name. But there was no reason to change Chewie. Let's face it, there's not a better side-kick name." Erik noticed his voice lost its edge now that he was talking about Mac and superheroes.

"I—" Kait gave a little gasp as Mac wound around her ankles, and her body stiffened.

"Mac likes you, too, Kait," Erik said. He looked over at Charlie. "That's his name. Mac. Mac for MacGyver." He watched as Kait reached down and gave Mac an extremely gentle pat on the head. She may have done some reading on animals, but she hadn't had a lot of real-life experience with them. He thought he remembered her saying her mom was allergic.

They started down the sidewalk again, Mac trotting along with them. "I'm waiting for you two to start up one of your conversations about comics that I will only be able to follow in the most limited way," Erik said.

"I've been trying to decide which superhero has the most dysfunctional relationship." Erik thought Charlie's expression had gone way too serious for a topic that comic geeks should love.

"Harley Quinn and the Joker," Kait replied.

"Obviously top of the list," Charlie agreed. "But what about the number two slot? Pretty much every couple is screwed up in some way."

"That's ridiculous. Lois and Superman. Enough said."

"Right. Superman let Aquaman sic an octopus on Lois to teach her a lesson. He decided to be the prosecutor when Lois was accused of murder," Charlie countered. "The prosecutor. That time that all Superman would have to do to save Lois was let the Joker die—He sat on his hands. He basically had to choose between Lois and the Joker, and he chose the Joker."

"That wasn't the choice. He was choosing between right and wrong," Kait countered. "I'll concede that their relationship isn't one hundred percent perfect, but that doesn't make it screwed up. Superman is a superhero, and it's clear he admires Lois. And Lois loves all of him, not just Superman, Superman *and* Clark. And they aren't the only solid couple. There's Hulking and Wiccan, Bigby Wolf and Snow White, Reed and Sue, Alicia and—"

"I give!" Charlie exclaimed. "There are some good couples out there. But there are a lot more that are completely messed up." Erik had the feeling he wasn't talking about comics anymore, or at least not just comics.

"Agreed," Kait answered.

They continued down the street to Charlie's place. "Here I am. With several minutes to spare." Charlie opened the gate and stepped inside. Mac followed him. "I guess Chewie-Mac is going to keep me company for a while." He gave them a wave and started for the house.

Kait waited until Charlie was out of earshot, then said, "I still don't know what it is, but there's something off about that guy."

"It'll come to you. Don't try to focus on it. Let it come up. That's what usually works for you."

She answered with a huff of annoyance as they started walking again. "Let's focus on our real problem. Who is behind the robberies? Every time the radio comes on, I think it's going to be another one."

"Daniel still seems like a good bet. But we have no evidence that points to him. We have pretty much no evidence at all." He felt like they were making good progress building relationships on the beat, but if they didn't solve the robbery case, how could anyone have confidence in them?

"Erik!"

Serena's voice pulled him away from his thoughts. He turned and saw her running down the street toward him. She didn't slow as she reached him, just hurled herself into his arms. He had to take a step back to keep them both from hitting the ground. "Hi to you, too," he said, and she laughed. He loved that laugh of hers, the way it seemed to start deep inside her and kind of exploded out.

"Guess what?" She didn't wait for him to respond. "I got another call back for the werecat part. It's a big one. I'm reading with Jackson Evans. He's already locked in. It's what they call a chemistry read. It's pretty much to see if we can sizzle together." She still had her arms around him, and she brought her lips close to his ear. "The way I sizzle with you."

She released him and took a step back. "Hi, Kait." She pushed her wavy red-gold hair away from her face. "Sorry. I got a little—You know what? Not sorry! I'm so excited about this audition!" She backed up a few more steps. "You two are working. I'll see you when you're off."

With that, she was heading back down the street, doing that thing where she was almost skipping.

It was an adorable sight, but Erik felt a heaviness fill his body. A sense of . . . of foreboding filled him.

"You look like you're almost about to puke," Kait told him.

"I'm fine." Erik strode away, forcing Kait to trot to catch up with him.

"She's not Tulip," Kait said.

But Erik had almost been able to feel the hope pulsing out of Serena. She wanted this part with everything in her. If she didn't get it—He refused to let himself think like that. "She's not Tulip," he agreed.

"I can't believe I have the star of a Norberto Foster movie as my acting coach. I also can't believe you've never had one of these." Daniel handed Serena a horchata latte. "It's like drinking a buttery cinnamon cookie."

Serena took a sip and smiled. "Bliss in liquid form. How's the play going?"

"More drama behind the scenes than in the play," Daniel answered. "The director quit yesterday."

"What's going to happen? Will the producers bring in someone else?"

"This is the second time he's quit." Daniel came around the counter and they took their usual seats on the sofa. "Someone, someone not me, fortunately, will have to call and apologize for I don't even really know what, then tell him he's a genius, and we won't be able to go on without him. Then a day later, he'll come back."

"I worked with someone like that once. An actor, not a director. The only good thing is that her crazy behavior created a bond between the rest of the cast and crew. I'm still friends with a bunch of them. It's like we went through a war together," Serena told him. "Wait. I shouldn't have said that. No one was dying or killing. It's like we went through a really unpleasant work experience together."

"That's happening to us, too." Daniel put his feet up on a hassock. "I'll be glad when the show is up. Although he might be the type that comes to every performance and then rants at everyone for an hour before we're allowed to leave."

"I had one of those once, too." Serena took another sip of her drink, and gave an *mmmm* of approval.

"Have you ever thought of directing a play?" Daniel asked. "I bet you'd be good at it."

"The closest I've gotten is directing students' scenes, which I love," Serena answered.

"Speaking of which . . ." Daniel pulled a few folded pages out of his pocket. "A new scene just got added."

Serena held out her hand, and Daniel handed the pages over.

She quickly read them. "Ah, the dreaded convulsive laughing. That one's hard for most of us. Can you think of a time you laughed so hard you had trouble stopping?"

Daniel rubbed his forehead with his fingers, like he was fighting a headache. "Honestly, I haven't been laughing that much lately. My family has really been upping the pressure for me to, uh, how do they phrase it—accept that some dreams just don't happen. Maybe it's because my thirty-fifth birthday was a few months ago. Marcus is barely thirty, and he—"

Serena held up one hand. "Stop. Not helping with the laughing. Anyway, I can think of a time that you were laughing really hard not that long ago. It was the day we met when we were talking about what to wear on an audition."

"Oh, yeah." He smiled. "How forgetting to wear deodorant can lose you the part."

"Too bad we didn't record that. Sometimes it helps just to remember exactly what your natural laugh sounds like." Serena thought for a moment. "Have you ever tried laughing yoga?"

"I thought as a native Angeleno that I'd heard of every possible type of yoga. But no," Daniel said.

"Basically, it's based on laugher being a physical process. It doesn't have to come from how you're feeling. In fact, the emotional feeling of happiness can come from the physical process of laughing."

"Uh. Hmmm. Yeah, I don't get it," Daniel told her.

"Even with my super-clear explanation?" Serena shook her head. "I did a session once. All we did was walk around the room, look each other in the eye, and say, 'ha, ha, ha.' Pretty soon everyone was laughing for real. I was going through kind of a hard time. It was right before I decided to try teaching. Anyway, I wasn't in the mood to laugh, but a friend brought me, and after maybe a minute of fake laughing, I was laughing for real. And it felt so good."

"I won't have a minute when I'm on stage, though."

"The idea is that you can train your body to laugh whenever you want it to. The same way you can train it to, I don't know, do a sit-up," Serena explained. "We should try it. All we do is look at each other and say 'ha, ha, ha.' "

Daniel obediently looked Serena in the eye and began saying the "ha"s in a flat, emotionless tone. Serena joined in. And almost immediately they were both laughing. When the laughter started to fade, they reverted to the forced "ha"s, and pretty soon they were for-real laughing again.

It took them both a moment to realize Mrs. Trask was standing in front of them. "Daniel, I'm sorry to interrupt, but I'm going to have to cut your hours," she said in a rush, eyes on the ground.

"It's—" Daniel let out one more laugh. "It's okay. I understand. It's not as if I haven't noticed business is way down." So far down they were the only three in the place right then, or Serena wouldn't have suggested practicing the laughing yoga.

"If I can—No. As soon as I can, I'll get you back to full time. For now, I'll take over some of your shifts. As the General said, 'Do everything you ask of those you command.' " Serena noticed the turquoise streak in Mrs. Trask's hair was starting to fade, and she looked tired, her eyes puffy. *Poor woman. I've been in here so many times, and I never really paid attention to her,* Serena thought, with a pang of guilt.

"I need to go over some orders. Stay for your shift tonight, and before you leave, we'll figure out a schedule for the next week or so."

As Mrs. Trask rushed off, Serena heard her murmur, " 'There are three ways that men get what they want; by planning, by working, and by praying.' "

Daniel forced a smile. "Ha. Ha. Ha."

The kittens were sprawled in a heap, sound asleep. Zoomies had led the group in a race around the shed, scrambling over or around or under any obstacles. Then they'd all nap-plopped at once, although Zoomies's paws were twitching a little, as if he was still zooming in his dreams.

Mac gave a slow blink as he looked at them, even though none was awake to see the I-love-you signal. He was going to miss the kittens when they were in homes of their own, even though he was only choosing homes that were close enough for him to visit. But it's not as if he could bring them all to his house. With his toys. And his treats. And his food. And his people.

It *would* be fun to see Diogee deal with the pack, though. Mac could picture Zoomies running down Diogee's back, Lox biting Diogee's tail, Sassy giving him a paw whap on the nose, and Bittles . . . Bittles would probably be snuggled up between Diogee's paws, not even minding that he was getting drooled on.

For a moment, he'd forgotten that he didn't have that home anymore. If he saw Diogee again, it would only be at a distance. When the kittens were in homes of their own, he'd be alone. No pack. But cats weren't like dogs and humans, they didn't need packs. Mac knew how to get food. He knew where to find warm places to sleep. He didn't need anyone to take care of him.

Mac allowed himself one more moment of watching the kittens sleep, then he headed outside. He was still figuring out which kitten belonged where. There was a place he wanted to take another look at.

As he trotted there, he passed the spot where he'd found the kittens. A faint whiff of their scent remained. Another, much stronger, odor captured Mac's attention. He knew it came from Daniel, and that Daniel was extremely upset. He followed the human's scent trail. It led to a closed door. Mac opened it with a solid head-butt. Some sparklies made a jingle-jangle as he walked in. They looked like they would be fun to play with, but Mac didn't have time for fun.

He spotted Daniel lying on the sofa in the big room. He was

only halfway to the human, when he heard the jingle-jangle again. He looked over his shoulder and gave an impatient hiss. Sassy had followed him!

Mac wasn't going to take the time to deal with the naughty kitten, not until he checked on Daniel. Sassy would be fine. There was nothing around that could hurt her. He started toward the human again, but before Mac reached Daniel, there was another jingle-jangle. The other kittens better not have followed him. It was enough trouble just keeping an eye on Sassy while he did what he needed to do.

It wasn't kittens coming through the door. It was two human women. "Isn't she the most adorable thing you've ever seen?" one of them loudly blah-blahed.

Daniel leapt up from the sofa. "Welcome. What can I do for you ladies tonight?"

"We actually just came in to visit the kitten," one female blah-blahed. She knelt down and wiggled her fingers at Sassy. Sassy gave a tiny growl and pounced. "Oooh! Those baby teeth are sharp. But she's so cute I can't be mad."

"Since we're here, I'll take an iced vanilla chai latte," the other woman blah-blahed. Then she crouched down and invited Sassy to bite her, too. Humans. How was it beyond their understanding that wiggling things needed to be pounced on?

The two women and Daniel continued to blah-blah. When they finally left, Daniel sat down on the floor next to Sassy. He didn't stick his fingers out. He, at least, seemed capable of learning by observation. Mac strolled over.

"I know this little one can't be yours, Mac. I'm sure Jamie made sure that was impossible a long time ago. But she sure looks like you," Daniel blah-blahed. "You two really aren't supposed to be here. But since you are, how about a little treat while I figure out what to do with you?"

Mac gave a yes-please meow. "Treat" was one of the blah-blahs he knew. He could probably learn more if he wanted to, but he knew all the important ones—"tuna," "Mousie," "sardine," "din-din," "dinner," "breakfast," "snack," "lox," "turkey." Without really trying, he picked up some other blah-blah's, like what people called each other, "bad kitty," and "no."

"I have a sandwich in the back. I can pull some chicken off that. I'm pretty sure I've heard that milk isn't really good for you guys, or I would hook you up." Daniel walked away, and Mac turned his attention to Sassy. She was washing her face with her paw, as if she hadn't just done a bad kitty.

Sassy was the smartest kitten. Maybe she'd already figured out being a bad kitty was fun. He wished she hadn't made that discovery until she was in her own home and wasn't his problem anymore.

Daniel came back. He gave Mac a bite of chicken, then fed one to Sassy. He clearly understood that it wasn't proper for a kitten to eat before Mac. He would make a good human for one of the babies, but Mac needed to get him smelling better first.

"If it wasn't against the law, I'd put you right in front of the window. That would get some people in here," Daniel blah-blahed.

Mac meowed, and Daniel gave him another piece of chicken. Sassy meowed, and Daniel gave her a second piece. That Sassy was a quick learner. So was Daniel.

CHAPTER 16

"What crime doesn't the Hierarchy Rule apply to?" Jandro asked. "This would be a multiple-choice question on the test, but if you really know it, you won't need the choices."

"I'm entering a carb coma," Angie complained. "Whose idea was it to get the Sicilian crust?"

"It was yours," Erik reminded her. "And it was good." He took a surreptitious glance at his phone. They'd probably be out of here by ten, so in about an hour and forty-one minutes, he should be able to get Serena naked and into bed.

Angie yawned. "Seriously. My brain just switched into low gear. I'm all about digestion right now."

"You don't have to worry about the test this year anyway," Jandro told Angie. "Now, Hierarchy Rule doesn't apply to—"

"Arson, motor vehicle theft, and justifiable homicide," Erik answered. If he answered enough questions quickly enough, maybe he could cut a few minutes off the time until naked Serena.

"Got all three," Jandro said. "Nice. That's the end of my questions. Who's next?"

Erik suddenly felt like a sixth grader who'd forgotten all about the homework assignment. "Uh. Sorry, everyone. I forgot we were supposed to bring questions. I'll bring double next time."

"There is no next time," Jandro reminded him. "We take the test in two days, and Angie and I are on tomorrow night."

"I'm sure Kait came up with extra." Erik looked over at her. She was staring down at her tablet, pizza mostly uneaten. "Kait!"

Her head jerked up. "Huh?"

"It's your turn for questions." Erik didn't mention that he hadn't brought any.

"What are you doing over there, anyway?" Angie asked. "You didn't even try to answer the last question. Usually, you don't give any of us a chance."

"Have any of you heard of brie and Molly parties?" Kait asked.

"Something bored soccer moms are doing, right?" Jandro answered.

"Yeah, I heard about this woman who thought her book group wasn't close enough. She decided a little MDMA would get them all bonding. And everyone loves brie," Angie added.

"I'm the only one who didn't know this was a thing?" Erik looked around the table. "Are you all messing with me?"

"You're lagging, *buey*," Jandro told him.

"Right now, we need questions." Erik didn't want to get sidetracked. He could feel minutes being added until Serena-naked time. "Kait, ask us some."

Kait ignored him. "I'm looking at Shelby Wilcox's Instagram."

"Who?" Jandro asked.

"Charlie Imura's girlfriend. Ex now, from what I'm seeing," Kait answered.

"Who?" Jandro asked.

They were never getting out of there. "Charlie Imura's a guy who lives in the Court. He's on house arrest for drug dealing," Erik answered.

"And on his ex-girlfriend's Instagram, some of her friends are asking when they're going to have another brie night. With Molly." She snorted. "They keep going on and on about how Molly's the guest of honor, and how she's always the life of the party. Very subtle."

That got Erik's attention. "You think that's why Charlie had such a large quantity of MDMA on him? You think he was buying it for some girls' night?"

"He bought it, he bought it. Wouldn't matter to a judge why," Jandro said.

Kait frowned down at the tablet, scrolling drown. "I think we've lost her for the night," Erik told Jandro and Angie. "You know how she is when she gets fixated on something. She's been telling me she thinks there's something off about Charlie, and now she's digging."

"Let's call it then." Jandro grabbed his backpack and shoved his notes in. "It would be nice to actually get home while my wife is still awake."

Erik was already on his feet. "Not gonna argue with you."

Serena wanted to take the lighthouse's circular staircase two steps at a time, but she was afraid she'd drop the breakfast tray. "Wake up. I've got brain food!" she called as she stepped into the bedroom.

Erik rolled over onto his side and gave her a lazy smile that made her want to throw the tray on the floor and pounce on him. She restrained herself. "I've got eggs, a little fruit, one whole-grain pancake with walnuts, and a multivitamin. I want you fully alert for your exam." She set the food on the bedside table, and he pulled her down on the bed.

"Only one pancake? I'm a growing boy," Erik protested,

wrapping both arms around her, and burying his face into her hair.

"I can feel that," Serena joked, nudging him with her elbow. "But you don't want to eat a really big meal when you have serious thinking to do." She reached over to the plate and tore off a big piece of pancake. "I can have however many I want. All I have to do today is pretend to be wildly attracted to Jackson Evans. Easy-peasy."

Erik grabbed her piece of pancake and popped it into his own mouth. "Oh, that was so wrong. After I cooked?" She didn't mention the pancakes were extrafancy frozen ones she'd found at Whole Foods. "I'm going to find a way to make you pay." She raised her eyebrows. "I just realized I don't know if you're ticklish."

"Nope. I'm a cop, remember?"

"That makes no sense. And you look like a ticklish kind of person to me." Serena went for his ribs, fingers flying up and down. In two seconds, he was laughing, and in two more seconds, he was begging her to stop.

"Say you were bad. Say you were rude and bad."

"I was rude and bad." It took Erik a few tries to get the words out, since Serena hadn't let up on the tickle attack.

He was breathless now. "Won't . . . give . . . you . . . present if . . . you don't . . . stop."

Serena instantly stopped tickling, but held her fingers poised above his naked chest. "You got me a present?"

He pulled in a deep breath. "A good-luck present. For your easy-peasy audition."

Wow, him getting her a present was a better present than anything he could have bought. She knew it was hard for him to be completely supportive of her acting, even though she'd done a lot to convince him she wasn't going to be devastated if she couldn't make it work out here.

She flexed her fingers, trying to look menacing. "Well, let's see it."

He leaned halfway out of bed and pulled something out of the pocket of the jacket he'd left lying on the floor the night before. It's like he'd been trying to break the world record for how fast two people could get naked. Not that she was complaining.

"I didn't wrap it." He thrust something into her hands. As soon as she realized what it was, she gave a cry of delight. "You got me Polly!" She gave him a smacking kiss on the cheek. "This is the best present ever! Ev-er!"

"It's the right one? There were a couple different compacts on eBay," Erik told her.

"The exact right one. Thank you. It was such a sweet thing to do." Serena gave him another kiss, this one on the lips. The pancakes were cold before either of them was willing to move apart long enough to take another bite.

The reception area was empty of actors when Serena checked in that afternoon. Her stomach gave a little flip-flop, part nerves, part excitement. She was getting close. She didn't know how many women had been called in to do the chemistry read, but it was definitely a lot less than there had been the last time. She gave her purse a squeeze, feeling the Polly Pocket compact inside, and smiled.

She was early, so she decided to hit the ladies' room, do one last check of her hair and makeup, Wonder Woman for a few, maybe pop a mint. Bad breath was a chemistry killer.

"You!" Emily exclaimed as soon as Serena stepped inside.

"You!" Serena said back, then gave Emily a hug.

"My agent told me it's down to two for the werecat. I was hoping the other one was you," Emily told her. "Even though I shouldn't have been. I should have been hoping it was the least talented person in town. Are you nervous about reading with

Jackson Evans? Because I am incredibly nervous. I had a poster of him from that CW show on my bedroom wall. I feel like I might squee when I see him. Not really. But on the inside. In case you couldn't tell, I'm freaking out."

"First, breathe," Serena instructed. Emily obediently sucked in a gulp of air. "I think it's great that you had a crush on him. Obviously, you think he's attractive."

"Well, yeah." Emily gave her a doesn't-everybody look. He wasn't quite Serena's type, but she had to agree he was objectively extraordinarily handsome.

"That's part of chemistry. Being attracted to the other person. And you have it without even trying."

"When I was in junior high, I almost puked on the boy I liked," Emily confessed. "There was no drinking or anything involved, just nerves. If I puke on Jackson Evans, that's it. I'm out." She pressed her hands over her stomach. "I feel like I'm going to puke right now."

"You're not going to puke, not now, not in there." Serena actually had no way of knowing that, but she knew for sure that being anxious was only going to make Emily feel more like she was going to heave. "Let me state the obvious. You're testing with Jackson because they're really interested in you for the part. You've done everything right. For all anyone knows, you could be the next Emma Stone. Walk in there like you already are."

Emily shook her head. "It's so unfair that men don't have to go through this."

"Men have to have chemistry tests with actors who are bigger stars," Serena said. For a second, Serena flashed on Erik asking her if helping the competition was a good idea. All she knew was that it felt right to her. Like she'd told Emily the first day they met, it was going to come down to how well each of them fit into the puzzle that was the movie as a whole.

"But it's not the same. It can't be. That's not the way the world is. It's women who are constantly objectified. It's—"

This was not helping. "I'd love to discuss sexual politics with you, but not now. Do you feel completely comfortable with the scene itself?"

Emily nodded. "I've done the work."

"Then you've done everything you can do. Just walk in there and show it to them."

"You mean show them my boobs or—" Emily began in a breathy Marilyn-Monroe-esque voice. Serena laughed, and after Emily gave an exaggerated pout, she joined in.

"I've got to get in there." Serena took a look in the mirror. She had on the same dress she'd worn for the first audition, the one that was sheer in a few places. It made her feel like Remy the werecat, and it was better not to change up your look for callbacks. Maybe there was something about her in the dress that they responded to. Her lips started to curve into a smile. Erik had certainly responded.

"See you on the other side, Serena."

"We're having coffee—make that hard liquor—when this is all over," Serena promised. As she walked back to the reception area, she let her gait loosen a bit. She wanted a little slinky feline in her walk.

The woman behind the desk smiled and waved her inside. This time there were about ten people in the room, more than double the number of the other two auditions. She gave a friendly hello, channeling the same energy she did for her classes. She was a professional, but she was also there to play, to discover what Jackson would bring out in the character of Remy.

She got smiles and nods from a few people, but Jackson, Norberto Foster, and another man didn't acknowledge her greeting. They continued their conversation. She felt way more disappointed in Norberto than she should have. Just because she loved his movies, that didn't mean he was a nice guy.

It took Serena a few seconds to realize they were talking

about swimming pools. One of them was planning on remodeling his. She didn't have any thoughts on pavers versus stone decking, so she took an empty seat and waited for them to finish, letting her fingers rest on her purse, so she could feel her lucky charm. She wasn't superstitious, but she loved that Erik had given it to her.

Minutes passed, and annoyance began to build up inside her. Just because she was a nobody didn't mean they should be rude. It definitely made it an option, though. She curled her toes, then let them relax to release some tension. She wasn't going to let them see any sign that she was bothered by their behavior.

In fact, she could use it. In the scene, Jackson's character seriously underestimated hers. He thought Remy was a nobody. She knew he was an easy mark. Talk as long as you want, Serena thought. The longer they ignored her, the more revved up she'd be when she finally got started.

She tuned back into their conversation. Now they were talking about fire pots versus fire pits. Jackson turned to grab a water bottle from an empty seat and his gaze flicked across her face, then down to her body. When he looked back up at her face again, she raised one eyebrow. "Want me to get up and turn around?" she asked.

He might not realize it, but she was starting the audition. She figured Jackson might like a challenge. Women had to be falling all over him wherever they went. Well, she wasn't going to be so easy.

He surprised her by laughing. "Yeah, would you?" he asked, but his tone was playful and teasing. Didn't mean he wasn't a butthead, though. Serena stood and did a quick twirl. "Let's get going," Jackson told Norberto.

Serena took her spot, and looked Jackson over, sizing him up and not bothering to hide it. She told herself he was just like Erik. Seeing her in this dress was making him crazy. He wanted her, and she, unlike with Erik, had all the power, because she didn't really care if she had him or not. It might be amusing, but she could happily go home alone.

She let a beat go by, making him wait, then gave her first line. And near the end of the scene, when he put his hands on her, she imagined they were Erik's hands, and she gave an involuntary shiver. Jackson thought his touch had done that, and he pulled her tighter against him. Serena let her lips almost brush his lips as she gave her last line, then she jerked away and laughed.

"Nice," Norberto told her. "Very nice. Let me see it again. Jackson put up a little more resistance. You want her, but you want her to beg. And, Serena, I liked where you were going, but push it further. There's no way you're begging. You can feel your power over him."

She nodded. She was going to nail this.

"I really do think I nailed it," Erik blah-blahed. Mac followed him and the human, Kait, as they strolled past the fountain. He caught a whiff of dog on one of the palm trees, and paused to give it a good scratching. This was his place, and it was not going to smell like dog pee. When he caught back up to the people, they were still blah-blahing. Not surprising. They seemed to think it deserved as much time as napping.

"We covered pretty much everything in the study sessions. No surprises." Kait flipped a few of her braids over her shoulder. The motion made Mac want to pounce, but he stayed on the ground. He had things to do. No playtime for him, not until he had everyone, kitten and human, sorted out.

He was almost positive he wanted Charlie and the other human in his house to have Bittles. They would both give the littlest kitten the attention he deserved. But Charlie had been smelling unhappy for days. Since he'd moved to Mac's neighborhood, he'd always had a whiff of sadness, but now it was so strong it made Mac's whiskers twitch.

Mac had noticed that his smell changed when he was near Kait. And Kait's smell changed when she was near him. Kait lost some of the lonely smell that reminded him of Jamie's scent before he had found her a packmate, and Charlie lost some of the sad smell.

Of course, the humans only had meat lumps for noses. Humans couldn't smell each other, so how could they be expected to know what the people around them were feeling? If they could, they'd be much happier.

"Would you just go visit Serena?" Kait blah-blahed. "I'll make the rounds by myself for a while."

"If you're sure." Erik rushed off toward the kittens. But Mac knew it wasn't the kittens he wanted to see. It was Serena. He was starting to think a little like a cat. He knew where he was happiest, and he went there.

Kait was still behaving like a human. She clearly didn't even realize what made her smell better. Could humans smell themselves? Their noses had to function at least that well, didn't they?

Maybe not. Kait kept walking away from where Charlie was. Mac turned around, tail up, and took a few steps toward Charlie's. He gave the meow Jamie would know meant "come here." Kait didn't even turn around.

Mac escalated from the meow to the howl, and that got her attention. He howled again and started to run. He heard her start after him. Good humansie. Mac streaked over to Charlie's house, climbed over the fence, then kept running.

But Kait stopped. He knew she understood how to open the gate. Why wasn't she coming? He took a breath and gave his highest, loudest yowl, the one that made David blah-blah "you'll wake the dead."

Kait still didn't come into the yard, but Charlie came out of the house. "Did he hurt himself?" he blah-blahed.

"I don't know." Kait rested one hand on the gate. "He came over here on the run. He wasn't limping or anything. Maybe he got stung by a bee? I didn't see anything to make him act so crazy."

Charlie rushed over to Mac and began gently running his hands over Mac's body. "Nothing seems tender."

"Well, he's not crying anymore . . ."

"I'm going to get him some water. You want to come in?"

Mac began to purr when Kait opened the gate and stepped into the yard. "Actually, there's something I want to talk to you about."

"If you're going to try to convince me the droid parents was one of the five worst Spidey storylines, I'll listen, but I have to tell you it's not gonna happen."

"It's nothing to do with comics."

"Is it about my parole officer? Because I make every appointment." Charlie picked up Mac, and stroked his head. Mac purred more loudly. This was the human for Bittles. Bittles loved to cuddle with his brothers and sister.

"It's about your girlfriend," Kait blah-blahed.

Charlie's grip on Mac tightened. Mac didn't try to squirm away. Charlie's scent smelled of fear. He needed Mac. "I don't have a girlfriend."

"Your ex. Shelby Wilcox. Her Instagram allows anyone to view it. It looks like she's getting ready for another party with her good friend Molly. And some brie." Mac could feel Charlie's heartbeat speed up. "What I wanted to know, is how she's going to get the Molly with you on house arrest?"

"I don't know what you're talking about."

"I'm talking about how you were arrested for having a large amount of MDMA on you. Enough for a party, the kind your girlfriend likes to throw."

"Shelby was shocked when she found out I was dealing. We broke up. She couldn't handle it," Charlie blah-blahed.

"If you're going to lie to me, there's no point in me staying." Kait walked away.

Mac stared after her. Sweet Sardinesies! Exactly what was he supposed to do to make her behave? Put her on a leash and give the other end to Charlie?

CHAPTER 17

"I'm going to waste away to nothing," Erik said, once he was capable of speech. "It's been three days since I've eaten lunch."

"We can eat lunch on your lunch hour, if that's what you want to do," Serena answered. She still straddled him, and the midday sunlight streaming through the windows high in the lighthouse turned her skin golden and her hair to pale flames. To get all poetic about it. He couldn't help it. The sight of her made him feel poetic.

"No, I couldn't do that. I'll keep making the sacrifice. You might need more material to draw on next time you have to make yourself feel attracted to a big movie star." It still gave him a kick that she'd thought about him when Jackson Evans had touched her. Jackson friggin' Evans.

"I'll stash some crackers under my pillow," Serena promised. "You need to keep your strength up."

Erik laughed. "You're saying you won't kick me out of bed for—"

He was interrupted by Serena's cell hollering "show me the

money!" "My agent," she explained. "I should get it." She slid off him, and grabbed the phone off the bedside table. "Hi, Micah."

Erik's gut tightened as he watched her smile fade, then her lips tighten, tighten because she was trying to stop them from trembling. She nodded, nodded again, then seemed to realize she hadn't said anything. "I understand. It's the who-fits-best-in-the-overall-movie thing." She used one hand to wipe away the tears that had started dripping from her eyes.

His stomach felt like a rock now. She didn't get the part. She'd been so sure she nailed the audition, and she didn't get the part. He picked up his own cell and checked the time. He needed to get moving. The beat patrol team was having a progress meeting.

"I owe you a carton of Big Hunks for getting me in there," Serena said. Her face had crumpled, but her voice was calm. No, more than calm. Cheery. "An audition with Norberto Foster and Jackson Evans? That alone makes me feel like I'm big timing it." She listened, fisting the comforter in both hands.

Erik stretched out one foot and managed to hook his boxer briefs. He was pulling them on when Serena said, "Talk to you soon." A moment after the words were out, she was sobbing, face in her hands, shoulders shaking.

Get over there, Erik ordered himself. *Comfort her*. He stood and zipped and buttoned his pants, then forced himself to sit back down on the bed and wrap his arms around her. She pressed her face into his shoulder, smearing warm tears against his skin. "I wanted it so bad."

"I know you did." He managed to get a glimpse of the time on her phone. He really had to get going. "I know you did," he repeated.

"I was great at that audition, too." She pulled back and looked up at him. "Norberto had me and Evans go through one scene six or seven times, trying it different ways. Even though they were both jerks when I went in, they got really into it. And I was right there with them. I got to show them how I improvise, how I take direction. I swear I was on fire." .

"I know." His brain was refusing to come up with more words. "I know." Of course, he knew. She'd told him every detail when they'd met up the night after her audition and his test. She'd told him every detail a couple more times since then. She'd been so excited and hyped up.

And that's when you crashed hard. She'd told him she knew the odds. She'd told him just being in the commercial was a success. She'd told him that luck was as much a part of getting cast as talent, because it was about what they were looking for as much as how talented someone was.

Erik gave her a hug and kissed the top of her head. "I have to go. I'm sorry. I have that meeting." He pulled away and got out of bed. "It's not acceptable for me to be late, forget about skipping it," he added as he continued dressing.

Serena wrapped the comforter around her naked body. "Yeah, of course. Go."

"I'll call you." Erik walked down the first flight of steps, but when he hit the second flight, he began taking them two at a time. He had to get some air. It didn't feel like there was any air in the lighthouse.

He kept the windows rolled down on his way to the station, and he took a parking spot at the far end of the lot, so he'd be able to walk a little. It didn't help. It didn't feel like there was enough air anywhere.

He did another time check, and decided to hit the men's room. He didn't want to get to the meeting early. Kait would take a look at him and know something was wrong, and he didn't feel like talking about it. Not to her, not to anyone.

When it was one minute before the meeting was supposed to start, Erik left the bathroom and walked down the hall to the makeshift squad room. He timed it perfectly. Corporal Hernandez, their field officer, was just heading in. Erik followed him, and took his usual seat next to Kait. His phone vibrated. He checked the text.

Serena
When do you think you can come back over?

Seriously? He hadn't even been gone an hour, and she knew he was at a meeting. Hernandez pulled a chair to the front of the cramped room. "Before we get started, I have an announcement. All three members of our team who took the detective exam passed."

"*Menos mal!*" Jandro pretended to wipe sweat from his brow. "Every day I came up with another question I thought I screwed up."

Kait elbowed Erik. "I told you you'd pass."

That rock in his stomach felt like it had become a boulder. See? This thing with Serena was already changing everything. He couldn't even feel happy about something great, because he knew how miserable she was. "I had no doubt you'd pass," he answered, managing to smile at Kait.

"Next year, when I take the test, I'll be beating all y'all's scores," Sean announced.

"You do know there won't be questions on if lamb shawarma or corned beef and cabbage makes your farts smell worse," Tom said, and everyone, even Hernandez laughed.

"Remember passing the exam isn't an automatic promotion to detective. You'll all have interviews," Hernandez said. "Let's move on. I've been reading your reports, and it sounds like you've all made progress becoming a presence on your beats. I want to hear more than what you've submitted. How's it going out there?"

Erik didn't feel like talking. He'd let Kait handle it. It wouldn't be a problem for her. She was good at giving organized, detailed answers. And, yeah, she was already talking, the first one to speak up. He only half listened. He knew everything she was going to say anyway.

A few minutes later, his cell vibrated again. He hoped it wasn't Serena again. He took a fast look.

Kait
What's going on with you?

Erik
Nothing.

Kait
Donkey dust. What?

Erik
Serena didn't get the part.

Maybe that would shut Kait up. She knocked her foot against his, a way of saying "that sucks" in Kait. Good. He couldn't deal with more questions right now.

He had about an hour and a half of peace, mostly meeting, with some congrats about the exam at the end. But the second they were back outside, Kait was on him. "How's Serena taking it?" she asked as they started for the parking lot.

"Hard." He hoped she wouldn't want details.

"You said she thought that last audition went really well."

"Yeah. So now she's crushed." Saying just that much felt like it broke something in Erik, and suddenly he couldn't stop talking. "Which I knew would happen. I knew she was setting herself up. It's a—" He censored himself for Kait's sake. "It's a freakin' Norberto Foster movie. It could have made her a star. But she didn't get it. And when I left, she was sobbing her guts out. It's just like with Tulip. It's exactly like it. Why did I let myself get involved with—" He paused again, got control of himself. "Involved with another friggin' wannabe?"

"Serena and Tulip aren't really anything alike," Kait said as they reached the patrol car.

"Maybe not in some ways, but they're both performers, and they both came out here dreaming of fame and fortune, like every other person who lands in LA. Serena had me convinced she was more practical, more grounded. But what I saw when she got the call? She's not going to be okay, Kait. And I'm not going through that again. It's not like I have a long-term thing with Serena. I shouldn't have to try to pick up the pieces. It won't work anyway."

"Serena's not one of your three-dates-and-you're-out girls. You can't treat her like she is." Kait fingered her key fob, but didn't unlock the door.

"I haven't gone out with her that many more times."

Kait just looked at him in response. She knew that he knew what he'd said was bullcrap. Or bull feathers or whatever she'd call it. He and Serena might not have gone on many dates, but they'd spent almost every free moment together since she invited him home to her bed. It hadn't been many days, but he couldn't pretend, even to himself, that it was a casual fling kind of thing. That didn't mean he had to go through the wringer with her. He had to think about himself.

"Do you want to go over there now? I can do a walk around while you talk to her."

They'd been to Storybook Court that morning, and had planned to go to the assisted living community that afternoon. "We're doing The Gardens. I don't want to see her, Kait." He hoped he'd manage to avoid her every time they patrolled the Court. He was sure she wouldn't be around that much longer. Probably just long enough to pack up and book a flight.

Kait gave an impatient huff. "You're going to have to see her at least one more time to break up with her."

Break up with her? They were beyond casual fling, but were they in something that required a breakup?

"You have to talk to her, Erik," Kait told him, when he didn't respond.

"I'll text her."

Kait waited until he met her gaze, then said, "That's not good enough."

It would have to be. He couldn't deal with talking to her face-to-face. She wouldn't have recovered yet. She'd probably still be crying. He pulled out his cell.

"Erik, no," Kait protested.

"Best I can do. Do you still want to drive?"

Kait unlocked the car and got in without a word. Erik took the passenger seat. As Kait started the car, he pulled up Serena's name. He wanted to get this over with. But all he could do was stare at the row of texts they'd exchanged recently. Fun, playful, sexy. He had no idea what to write. The words didn't matter, he decided. There was no good way to say it anyway.

Erik
I can't come back over. This isn't going to work for me. Good luck with everything.

Mac was trying to show the kittens how fun a cardboard box could be. He'd emptied one of the ones in the shed, and tipped it over. Sassy had gone right in, but the other babies weren't interested. Lox was looking for crumbs in the food bowl, Zoomies was zooming, and Bittles was sitting close to Max.

He caught a whiff of unhappiness from Serena. He'd been smelling it for hours. Mac gave a huff of frustration. How was he supposed to focus on kitten training while he was constantly smelling that?

He couldn't. But he knew what to do. He just had to make a

visit to one of the possible kitten homes first. They were growing so fast. It was time to get them settled.

Mac gave Bittles a lick on the head, then took the tunnel to the backyard. He quickly traveled the two blocks to the building where the human called Marcus lived. He slipped inside when another human carrying a bag of food—tacos, Mac thought—opened the door.

He enjoyed tacos, and was confident he could convince the human to share, but there wasn't time. He had too many responsibilities. He trotted up the stairs to the door that led to Marcus's place. He could smell that Marcus was inside, so he gave a loud meow.

Marcus didn't open the door. Mac meowed a few more times. Marcus didn't come. That wasn't good. A human should always respond to the first meow. But Marcus could be trained if he turned out to be acceptable in other ways. He had shared his peanut butter with Mac the last time.

Mac reared up on his back legs and wrapped his paws around the door knob. It turned a little, before his paws slipped off. It took two more tries, but then he was in. He still approved of the amount of open space. Zoomies would love it here with so much room to zoom.

Now he needed to observe Marcus. Maybe he'd even do a little meow training with him so Zoomies wouldn't have to—if Mac ended up choosing this as Zoomies's home. He found Marcus lying on a mattress on the floor. He had the blinds shut, even though everyone should know an afternoon nap was better in a spot of sunshine. A plate of crackers and peanut butter sat nearby. Mac ignored it. He curled up close to Marcus's side. It needed to be determined if he was a good napping companion. Jamie was perfect to nap with, but David moved around too much. He'd almost rolled over Mac once!

Why was he thinking of Jamie and David? It didn't matter how they were to nap with, not anymore.

Mac took a brief nap with Marcus and found it enjoyable. He decided not to wake the human. He'd gathered the information he needed. Marcus smelled anxious. He clearly needed a kitten. He had a lot of room for a kitten to play, he was willing to share, and he didn't interrupt the nap of a cat sharing his bed. Not only did he need a kitten, he deserved a kitten.

On his way out, Mac spotted something sparkly. Just what he needed. Serena clearly needed a sparkly, at least until Erik came back. Erik would make her feel better than the sparkly, but the sparkly would help.

He loped back home and went straight to Serena's door. He put down the sparkly so he could meow to be let in. Maybe he shouldn't have taken that nap. Serena smelled even worse than before. But he'd needed to evaluate Marcus. He was only one cat. He could only do three or four things at a time.

Serena opened the door. Good human. He stretched out one paw and gently pushed the sparkly toward her. She gasped. She liked it! He knew she would.

Now he had to return to his kitten training. His work was never done.

Serena called the police. She had no choice, even though she knew what was going to happen. They'd send Erik and Kait over. She was going to have to see Erik when she was still reeling from that text. That text! She'd thought as soon as he got off work, he'd come back and cheer her up, maybe take her out to dinner or something. Instead—that text!

She knew he'd been hurt by Tulip. She got that. But what the hell? Serena and Erik hadn't known each other long, but come on. He knew her well enough to know that she wasn't like Tulip. She wished she'd never met him. She wished he'd never made her dinner, or bought her that Polly Pocket, or made her laugh. She wished she'd never brought him to her bed. Because now—It hurt so much. Damn him!

He'd be there soon. She wasn't going to answer the door looking like a wreck. She ran upstairs and pulled on her green floaty dress, then hurried into the bathroom. She groaned when she saw her puffy face and red eyes. She did what she could—a couple splashes of water, some Visine, a little concealer, powder.

The doorbell rang. She took a moment to add some tinted lip balm, then returned downstairs. She was an actress. She could handle this. She wasn't going to scream, she wasn't going to cry. She was going to make it look like he hadn't just stomped on her heart. She didn't want him to think he had the capacity to hurt her. Not in the slightest.

"Thanks for getting here so quickly," she said when she opened the door, making sure to look at both Erik and Kait. "I couldn't believe it when Mac showed up with Sad Bunnies. What I'm sure has to be Sad Bunnies."

"Can we see it?" Kait asked.

Serena realized she was blocking the door. "Of course." She stepped back so they could come inside. When Erik passed her, she caught his scent. He still smelled like, like *them*. From his lunch break. It was faint, but Serena felt like she'd been slapped.

"I put it in the kitchen. I tried to only touch the edges. I didn't want to leave it on the doorstep." She managed to keep her tone matter-of-fact as she led them over to the kitchen table.

"Where is Mac now?" Erik asked as Kait put the figurine in an evidence bag.

"I don't know. He meowed at the door. I answered it. Sad Bunnies was on the welcome mat." She made herself look at him as she talked. His hazel eyes felt like they were burning her skin as he looked back. "I called the police right away."

"So, you didn't actually see the cat carrying the figurine?" Erik asked.

"No. But it was still a little damp. I assume from being in his mouth," she answered. "That's really all I know." She wanted him out of her house.

"We'll be in touch if we have any other questions," Kait said. "I was sorry to hear that you didn't get that part you were auditioning for."

"Thanks," Serena answered. "I admit I had a sob-fest when I heard. But rejection is part of being an actor." She was impressed with herself. She'd given the answer in a casual, friendly way. Even though she was talking about the reason Erik broke up with her. What? She wasn't allowed to be sad for two seconds? She was still upset. She'd really wanted that part. Was she not supposed to be human? Was she not supposed to have emotions?

"Do you two want something to drink?" *Bonus points to me for that*, Serena thought.

"We need to file a report on this," Kait told her. She started for the door. Erik and Serena followed. Serena hung back a little, not wanting to get hit with his scent again. When she shut the door behind them, she sunk down on the floor and wrapped her arms around her knees. She needed a moment to recover.

Breathe it in, she told herself. *You can use this.* But she didn't want to save this emotion for some future part. She wanted to forget she'd ever felt this way. She wanted to forget what had happened to make her feel this way.

She wanted to forget Erik.

CHAPTER 18

"She didn't seem devastated to me," Kait commented as she and Erik walked away from the lighthouse.

"You didn't see her. She was crying like she'd lost everything, not a part, everything," Erik answered.

"You're really never going to see her again?"

"Not if I can help it," Erik answered. "Can we not talk about—"

"It's the cat! Mac! He has something in his mouth!" Kait exclaimed. She raced after him, and Erik followed. He didn't go far, just across the street to Charlie's. When he reached the gate, he set something down and started to meow.

"I'm coming!" Charlie called from his usual spot in the yard.

Erik crouched down so he could see what Mac had been carrying. It was one of the kittens. It started to come toward Erik, but Mac caught it gently be the scruff of the neck. When Charlie opened the gate, Mac deposited the kitten at his feet. He rubbed his cheek against the kit, almost knocking it over, then turned and ran off.

244 / Melinda Metz

"Zoinks!" Charlie crouched down, too, and tickled the kitten under the chin. It was the tiniest one in the litter, Erik realized. "What just happened?"

"I think you just adopted a kitten," Kait answered. She knelt down and stroked the kitten's head, her fingers brushing against Charlie's.

"Mac's been taking care of a litter of kittens. It did look like he decided you should have that one. But I don't think cats can think that way, can they?" Erik asked.

"Whether they can or can't, this little guy needs a home." Kait met Charlie's eyes. "Are you going to keep him?"

"Do you think I should?"

" 'With great power—' "

" 'There must also come—great responsibility.' "

Kait smiled. "You got the quote right. I should have known you would."

Erik stood, letting Charlie and Kait continue their conversation. He didn't feel like talking to anybody. He couldn't wait until he could get home, maybe do some work on the patina he wanted on the light fixture. He wanted his old life back.

"I wouldn't say I have great power." Charlie tapped his ankle bracelet.

"To a cat, I think you do. If you can provide food, that's great power," Kait answered.

"I can't even go to the grocery store. But my aunt can, and I bet she'd love this one." He stood, cuddling the kitten against his chest. "She had a cat years ago, but could never bear to get another one after it died. I don't think she'll be able to resist the story of how this one turned up."

Kait rose to her feet. "You only have three more months of house arrest."

Charlie looked at Erik. "Does she always do this? It's like she's memorized my file."

"She's always thorough," Erik answered. "But I think she's gone a little above and beyond where you're concerned."

Kait's earlobes went red. That didn't only happen when she was pissed. It happened when she was embarrassed, too, not that Kait embarrassed easily. She probably wished he'd kept his mouth shut, but Erik didn't care. She was interested in him, whether she'd admit it or not, and why shouldn't he know.

Erik took a quick glance at Serena's. He had an itchy feeling, like she was watching him out one of the windows, but he didn't see her. *You're kidding yourself,* he thought. *She probably never wants to see you again.* Which is what he wanted. His stomach churned. He'd handled the breakup badly. Kait was probably right about texting. But he and Serena had only known each other a few weeks.

He tuned back in to Charlie and Kait's conversation. He needed distraction.

"Did you find out anything interesting?" Charlie asked.

"Not about you, exactly. But I did find out your girl-friend—"

"Ex-girlfriend," he corrected.

Kait gave a slow nod. "Ex-girlfriend. I found out she has a sealed juvenile record. Did you know that if someone with a juvenile record is found guilty of a crime later in life, the record can be unsealed and can be considered when the person is sentenced?"

He didn't answer. He lowered his head, directing all his attention at the kitten.

Interesting. Kait had been telling Erik there was something off about Charlie. It looked like she'd figured out what.

"I'm almost positive your then-girlfriend knew that. And I'm almost positive before you plead guilty, you knew that, too," Kait continued.

Charlie finally looked up. "What's the point of speculating? The case is closed."

"I found it interesting," Kait told him.

"It's kind of romantic, taking the fall for someone else. Not that anyone is saying that happened," Erik added quickly when Charlie gave him a sharp look. "Romantic is one of the items on your list of perfect-man qualities, isn't it, Kait?" It was almost impossible to tell, but Erik thought her ears got a little redder. She was probably both pissed and embarrassed.

"You have a list of perfect-man qualities?" Charlie asked Kait.

"Romantic is near the bottom. It's not that important," she muttered. Then she turned to Erik. "We should get the evidence we collected back to the station."

"See you later," Erik told Charlie. "Kait and I will be around a lot."

"Patrolling," Kait said.

"That's what I meant. You'll be around a lot, patrolling." Erik noticed that Charlie was giving Kait a considering look.

"You know I'm going to go out with Marcus again," Kait hissed when they reached the sidewalk. "I've been talking to him most nights. He's really interested in me. And has the majority of qualities from the list."

"But can he talk comics with you? Do you ever laugh when you're doing all this talking?"

Kait didn't answer, but Erik thought he'd given her something to think about. He took another glance at the lighthouse as they walked by. *You're much better off without her*, he reminded himself.

"He broke up with you by text?" Ruby frowned. "By text?"

"By text," Serena confirmed. She felt her eyes sting, and blinked rapidly to keep tears from forming.

"Sweetie, why didn't you call me yesterday? You shouldn't have been all by yourself," Ruby told her.

"If I'd tried to talk about it yesterday, I'd have seriously ugly cried, with snot." Serena took a gingerbread man off the plate in the middle of the table and bit its head off in one bite.

"Satisfying, isn't it? Bite the head off another one," Ruby urged. "I'll eat the bodies."

Serena laughed, then sniffled. "Don't be too nice to me or I'll cry right now."

"Won't be the first time someone cried at this table," Ruby reassured her. "Actually, I think Briony did. I told you about her, right? Jamie's cousin who is now married to the guy Mac found for her. They run The Gardens retirement community together. But for a while, things were pretty messed up between them."

"Please don't tell me that Erik and I are going to get back to-gether because Mac has super-special matchmaking abilities." Serena bit the head off another gingerbread man. "In his text, all he said was that it wasn't going to work for him. Oh, and he wished me good luck." She tore the arm off the gingerbread man. It felt good, but not as good as decapitation.

Ruby took the arm from her and ate it. "This is another rea-son the Christmas season must start in September. Christmas cookies. And, so you know, I changed the subject because I can't think of anything to say to make you feel better."

"That's because there isn't anything," Serena answered. "I'm going to feel bad for I don't know how long. It seems like it should be short, because Erik and I haven't known each other very long, but . . ." She gave a helpless shrug.

"It's no excuse, but Tulip really broke his heart," Ruby said. "I got the impression from something Tulip said once that he'd never had a serious relationship before her."

"You're right. It is no excuse." Serena tore a leg off the ginger-bread man and handed it to Ruby. "It's childish for him to as-sume all performers are the same. I'm not like her. I was upset that I lost the part. That's totally normal. But look at me." She flung out her arms. "I'm sitting here, mangling gingerbread men, and talking to you. I'm not lying in a heap on the floor because I didn't—" She paused, then exclaimed, "Emily!"

"Emily your friend from the auditions?" Ruby asked.

Serena felt a grin spread across her face. "It was down to the two of us. If I didn't get it, that means Emily did! I didn't think of that until now." She pulled her cell out of her purse. "I've got to text her and tell her we have to go out and celebrate."

"Not only are you not in a heap on the floor, you want to celebrate with the woman who beat you out for the part," Ruby said as Serena typed the text.

"Emily's great. I'll have to introduce you sometime. You'd really like her."

Ruby smiled at her when she closed her phone. "You're kind of amazing, you know that?"

"Because I'm not mad at Emily? That would be crazy. Maybe she had more sizzle with Jackson Evans than I did. Or they liked how the two of them looked as a couple more. Or she's just a better actress. I guess it's *possible.*"

"I hate to kick you out—" Ruby began.

"—but you have to get to work," Serena finished for her. "Thanks for letting me vent. I swear I'm going to stop treating you like you're my rom-com best friend."

"The best friend has a lot less angst," Ruby reminded her.

"Okay, but at least tell me a couple things about what kind of guy you like, so I won't feel so guilty."

Ruby laughed. "It's not like I have a list." She considered the question. "I like an accent, which is silly because all kinds of men have accents. It doesn't signify anything. I also appreciate creativity. Are you happy?"

"For now," Serena answered. She and Ruby walked out together. Serena didn't feel like going home, so she decided to go to Yo, Joe! She needed more venting and Daniel would listen.

Mrs. Trask was washing the front windows when Serena arrived at the coffee shop. " 'Success is how high you bounce when you hit bottom,' " she heard the woman mutter as she rubbed away with a crumpled sheet of newspaper.

"I can't decide if today's General Patton quote is inspirational or not," she said to Daniel once she was inside.

"The one about bouncing when you hit bottom?" he asked, and she nodded. "I'm not sure, either. I didn't think we were about to hit bottom. Getting close maybe. I feel worse for her than I do for myself. There are always places that need talented baristas. Speaking of which—what can I make you?"

Serena leaned on the counter. "Got anything that will make me feel better for losing the werecat part?"

"If I do, I haven't found it. I'm sorry, Serena."

"It happens. We both know it happens," she answered.

"Yeah, and we both know when it happens it sucks. I'm making you something with a lot of whipped cream. Whipped cream is in itself cheerful." Daniel got to work.

"Maybe you should just fill the cup with it, because that's not all that happened yesterday." Before Serena could tell him about Erik's text breakup, Marcus came in.

Daniel glanced at the clock. "Kind of early for lunch break."

"I'm not a nine-to-fiver. I can go when I want," Marcus answered. "Look, I told Mom and Dad I'd come over—"

"Don't say it," Daniel interrupted. "Or at least let me say it for you. 'Daniel, you have to get realistic. You're not making it as an actor, and you're getting too old to be working serving coffee.' Have I got that right?"

"Yep. I told them I'd tell you. I also told them telling you wouldn't make any difference," Marcus answered. "Money is important, Daniel. You don't have any real expenses living with Mom and Dad, but they aren't always going to be around. You—"

"We had this conversation, less than a week ago," Daniel told him. "Let's not today."

"Okay," Marcus answered. "Okay."

"You want coffee?" Daniel asked.

"Sure. Why not. I'm here. I've got nothing better to do."

The door chime tinkled. "The cat is back," Mrs. Trask announced. "And it brought a friend."

Mac trotted in and went straight to Daniel. He put down one of the kittens—the one with the roly-poly tummy—at Daniel's feet. Then he returned to the door and meowed. Mrs. Trask opened it for him, and he left.

Daniel scooped up the kitten and it began to purr. "Once when I was prepping to play a vet, I did some reading on cats. They don't only purr when they're happy. It can also be something they do to comfort themselves when they're upset or in pain."

"Maybe I should take up purring." Serena leaned across the counter. "Is she okay?"

Daniel lifted her up and studied her. "I don't think she's hurt, but I'd be a little scared if I was her." He brought the kitten close to his chest. "They're supposed to like your heartbeat. It reminds them of their mom."

"That little kitten didn't have a mom for long. I found her and her littermates in my shed. Mac seemed to have adopted them. He brought them food and everything. I started supplementing when I realized they were there, but he's spent a ton of time with them," Serena explained. "I can't believe he carried one over here. I know it's not far, but . . . ."

"We've now exhausted most of my cat knowledge," Daniel admitted. "I wish she could be the Yo, Joe! cat. Some women who were here the other night would be regulars if she was."

"Huh. Interesting," Marcus said.

"His brain is trying to find a way to use that information in his next ad campaign," Daniel explained.

"Why don't I set up a little bed for her in the supply closet, since she can't stay out here," Mrs. Trask suggested. "General Patton had a cat named Willie. Maybe you should call her that, Daniel."

"Does that mean I'm keeping her?"

"Can you afford another mouth to feed?" Marcus asked, then added a muttered apology.

"I have a big bag of kitten chow you're welcome to dip into," Serena volunteered.

"I hear meowing, but she's not meowing," Mrs. Trask said. "I think it's from outside." She hurried over and opened the door. Mac sauntered in, another kitten in his mouth. This time he went directly to Marcus and set the kitten down. He immediately raced away, zigging and zagging.

"Look at it go!" Marcus exclaimed, bursting into laughter. Serena wasn't sure she'd heard Marcus laugh before.

"Yours is crazier than mine." Daniel stroked the kitten he held.

"Mine?" Marcus repeated.

"Well, we know *you* can afford another mouth to feed," Daniel said.

"It might be nice to have some company." Marcus laughed again as "his" kitten zoomed around the sofa and under a chair.

Serena felt her phone vibrate. She was almost afraid to look at the text. What if it was from Erik? If he was going to try to justify what he'd done, she didn't want to hear it. She took a cautious peek at the screen. The text was from Emily.

Emily
Yes, I want to go out and celebrate! Soon! Tomorrow night!

Serena
Congratulations again. I'm so happy for you.

Emily
I couldn't have done it without you. Seriously. You saw me in the bathroom before the last audition. If you hadn't come in, I'd still be there.

Serena
Not true.

Emily
So true. I'd be using a roll of toilet paper as a pillow. Thank you for being my coach. So tomorrow?

Serena
Definitely.

Serena closed her phone. "That was Emily. I told you about her."

"Right. Your competition for the werecat," Daniel answered. He shook his head at Marcus, who had moved closer to the kitten. It was now trying to climb up his pant leg. She could tell the suit was expensive, and the kitten had to be snagging it, but he was still laughing.

"You know the weird thing?" Serena continued. "I feel the way I always do when one of my students gets a part, just happy and proud. Even though I simultaneously feel disappointed that I didn't get it myself."

"Did you help her with the part?" Daniel handed over a drink with a fluffy cloud of whipped cream on top.

"I gave her a little audition advice is all. It was no big, but she was so grateful." Serena licked up a little of the whipped cream. The kitten Daniel held mewed.

"I think I need to find this girl something to eat," he said. "I'm not surprised Emily was grateful. You're a kick-ass acting coach."

She smiled. "You're right. I am."

Mac heard Jamie calling him again when he was returning to the shed. He wished she would stop. When he heard her, something inside pulled at him, trying to pull him to his person. But she wasn't his person anymore. How could she be?

"Mac, come on, Mac-y, come home. Come home, sweet boy. My little Mac-Mac."

He took a step toward her voice. He didn't mean to, but he did.

She smelled different, but she sounded the same. The way she sounded when she blah-blahed his name. She loved him. Even though she put him in a cage, she loved him.

He reminded himself that she was a human. Humansies didn't always understand things, even though they thought they did. Maybe Jamie didn't understand how he'd feel if she put him in a cage. Maybe she thought he'd *like* it.

She put a leash on him once. And she'd acted like he should be happy about it. He'd had to show her she was wrong. He had to teach her.

"Mac, I need you to come home, baby. Come on, kitty, kitty, kitty."

Jamie wouldn't still be calling him if she didn't love him. He should have realized right away that her human brain had made a mistake. She was still his Jamie. He had to always remember that as much as he loved her, she just wasn't as smart as he was. Neither was David.

He would go home. They needed him to help them understand what they should do. Diogee needed him, too. He was much stupider than the humans, and that meant he was incapable of handling himself.

As soon as he could, he'd answer Jamie's call. But first he had to find a home for one last kitten—Sassy. And he couldn't go back to his own home until he'd done that.

CHAPTER 19

Mac looked over his shoulder to make sure Sassy was behind him. She was. She knew the straight up tail meant "follow me." He'd taught her well. But as smart as she was, he wasn't going to let her cross the street on her own. When they got to the corner, he picked her up by the scruff of the neck and carried her across, ignoring her little growls and her squirming.

By the time they reached the place where Erik and Kait were, Sassy was hissing mad. Mac didn't care. This was the place she belonged. He'd had a hard time making the decision, until he realized Sassy was so sassy she needed both Erik and Kait to keep her in line. And when she grew up a little, she'd be able to take care of any problems the two of them got into.

Mac followed a person through the door, and Sassy followed him, even though she didn't look happy about it. He picked up Erik's and Kait's scent trails, but he would have remembered which way to go without them. Had Sassy learned to follow scent trails yet? Maybe he hadn't taught the kittens everything they needed to know before he let them go. Well, even though they were babies, they were still cats. They'd figure it out. But he'd check on them just to make sure.

The door Mac needed was ajar. He gave it a head-butt and sauntered inside, then checked for Sassy. Still with him.

"I thought you were paws-itive the cat didn't do it." One of the humans slapped the table where he sat and laughed. A few of the other humans laughed, too, but not as loudly. Had the man seen him? Where they laughing at The Cat? He'd just blah-blahed "cat," then most of the people laughed.

Kait and Erik didn't laugh. Mac noticed that Kait wasn't smelling as lonely as she had been when she'd chased him over to Charlie's last night. Thanks very much to him. But Erik still smelled horrible. He might have to give Sassy an assist with him if Erik didn't manage to figure out what made him happy.

"I know why the cat stole all that stuff. He wanted to trade it for a fur-rari," a woman blah-blahed. And this time everybody laughed, even Kait and Erik.

Mac was not amused. There was nothing funny about him or any other cat. And that was the other reason he'd brought Sassy to this place. A few days with her, and these humans would never laugh at a cat again.

He gave Sassy a few licks, and a good rub with his cheek. Anyone who smelled her would know she was under his protection. Then he left, turning to push the door shut behind him. He didn't want Sassy to follow this time.

It was time for Mac to go home.

He broke into a lope as soon as he was back outside. He wanted his person. This was the longest he'd been apart from her. Maybe she'd be so happy to see him she'd break out the sardines!

He went straight to the front door and meowed. A few moments later, the bonehead began to barkbarkbark, but no one told him to be quiet. Mac could tell Diogee was the only one inside.

Mac turned and trotted to the tree that grew outside the bathroom window. What had happened here? More changes. Wood, and screen, and the thing that made the bang. He did *not* approve, but he would ignore all of the new things for now. He wanted in.

He climbed up the familiar branches and pushed his way inside. The window was always open a crack. He heard Diogee galumping up the stairs. His ropey tail started wagging as soon as Mac walked into the bedroom. Usually Mac wouldn't be able to resist pouncing on it. It was like the biggest, best piece of yarn ever. But today he wasn't in the mood. All he wanted was Jamie.

He leapt onto the bed and curled up on her pillow. It had the new Jamie smell, the smell that wasn't quite right. It was better than nothing. Mac closed his eyes. When he woke up Jamie would probably be home.

"Are you sure?" Ruby asked. "This is so sudden. You only found out you didn't get the part two days ago." She and Serena were up on the widow's walk, their favorite place for morning coffee.

"I know it's hard to believe, but this really doesn't have that much to do with losing the part," Serena answered. "I'm always telling my students to listen to their gut instincts, and that's what I'm doing. I like acting, although that commercial reminded me how tedious it can be, but I love teaching. Rehearsing scenes with Daniel and giving Emily tips, I loved that. There was a girl at my agent's who I taught the Wonder Woman pose. I could tell it helped her, and that made me feel so good."

Ruby nodded slowly. "I'm just concerned you haven't given the acting enough of a chance. You barely got here."

"I know. But it's not like I started acting when I arrived. I've been acting since I was in college, even before that if you count my elementary school debut as a wolf," Serena explained. "When I first started teaching, it was a stopgap, but then I started really enjoying it. I started doing my podcasts, and that was a kick. It got so when I would read audition notices, I'd think about which of my students would be right, instead of if I wanted to audition myself."

Ruby took a swallow of coffee. "Okay, last thing. I'm a believer in the gut, but something made you apply for the award. Wasn't that your gut, too?"

"I thought it was. But I think maybe it was my ego. That's located somewhere near the gut, right?" She could tell Ruby still needed more. "I heard two of my students talking about how maybe they should be studying with someone who had made it. They saw me as someone who was teaching because I'd failed at acting. Suddenly, I panicked. I was like, 'I'm twenty-nine. It's almost too late. If I'm going to do this, I have to do it now!' I read about the Lighthouse Award two days before it closed. It seemed like fate that I found the information just in time to FedEx out my application."

"I know I said one last thing, but I guess I have one more last thing. The award is an amazing opportunity. There are very few like it. Why not give yourself the year to see what happens? You've made a phenomenal start, getting the agent and that commercial."

Serena scrubbed her face with her hands. "I know. I was up all night poking and prodding at myself, trying to make sure I wasn't just afraid to keep trying. And I'm not. And since I know that, why spend a year going for something I don't really want to get? Especially since there are so many women that would get so much out of this year. I hope the Mulcahys will go back to the applications and make another choice."

"I'll have to talk to them. This has never come up before," Ruby admitted.

"Please let them know how incredibly grateful I am. They're doing a wonderful thing." Serena felt a pang of guilt. She hadn't even thought about how the Mulcahys would feel until now. But she knew giving up the award was the right thing to do. She'd start packing up her stuff so she'd be able to get out of the lighthouse quickly.

She hoped someone else would be moving in soon. Maybe she should leave a note with a warning about Erik for whoever did.

Erik offered the kitten a tiny bite of pepperoni off the study group's pizza. She sniffed it suspiciously, then ate it, and gave a loud meow. Erik quickly gave her another piece.

"She has you trained already," Kait told him. "And she hasn't even been the station kitty for one whole day."

"Did you see how Sean and Tom were arguing over whose lap she got to sit on?" Angie asked. "I've never heard the two of them agree on anything, but they were both smitten with the kitten."

Erik looked down at the cat. He was almost positive she was the one who had gotten stuck in the tree. All the kittens had tan and white stripes, but he knew for sure the littlest one hadn't been up the tree. The one who was always running around like crazy wouldn't have been able to stay still all those hours, and the one who was a chow hound, or whatever you should call a cat that loved food more than anything, wouldn't have been able to stay up that long without a snack.

This kitten wasn't the speed demon. If she'd been the one who loved food, she would have gobbled up the pepperoni without sniffing it first. Yeah, this one had to be the one he and Serena had sat in the dark watching.

He needed to apologize to Serena. He didn't want to try to get back together, even if she would take him. But she didn't deserve to be treated like crap, and that's what he'd done.

"Erik!"

He automatically started to pass Jandro another piece of pizza, then realized his friend still held one. He set it back down. "I guess I stopped paying attention for a minute."

Kait snorted, but didn't comment. "I was asking what you said at the last interview when they asked what your biggest weakness was," Jandro told him. "I heard they ask a lot of the same questions as in the interview we had before we joined the force."

Erik tried to remember. Right now, all he could think of was that he was a chickenshit who broke up with a woman by text so he didn't have to see her cry. "Uh . . . sorry, I guess I'm kind of tired tonight. It's not coming back to me."

"What they want is for you to tell them how you're working to improve whatever the weakness is," Kait said. "That's the important part."

"The ones I hated were the ones about what you'd do if you found out a family member committed a crime." Angie took a swig of Diet Coke. "I don't even like to think about having to bring in someone in my family."

Jandro stood up. "I just realized that if the questions are pretty much the ones we answered to get on the force, and we all got on the force, we don't really need to study for the interview. It was the exam part I was worried about anyway. I'm going home to my wife." He put his half-eaten slice of pizza between his teeth, and picked up a new one. "For the road," he mumbled.

Angie tossed her soda can in the trash. "I'm heading out, too. I have two years to prep. But thanks for letting me sit in." She gave them a wave as she followed Jandro out the door.

"Do you want me to ask you some questions that might come up?" Kait asked.

The thought made Erik feel exhausted. "Not tonight, okay? Maybe when we're patrolling tomorrow."

"You'll feel better if you apologize to Serena," Kait told him. "In person."

"I know." It was going to be hard looking Serena in the face. She had to hate him. And he didn't blame her.

CHAPTER 20

Erik stared at the lighthouse. He'd been staring at it for a solid minute. He was having trouble getting himself to actually walk up the path of broken seashells. This was ridiculous. He was a cop. He'd been in all kinds of confrontations. Yeah, Serena had to be furious with him, but he didn't have to worry whether or not she was carrying a concealed weapon.

He didn't move. This was different than any of the work situations. He didn't have to admit to any of them that he'd been a huge jerk. It shouldn't be that hard to admit it to Serena. It was completely true. He felt horrible about it. Apologizing should come easy.

It wasn't that he couldn't admit he was wrong. He just didn't want to look her in the face and see how her feelings for him had changed. He loved the way she'd smile when she saw him, used to smile. So open, showing him how happy she was. Not going to happen today.

Before Erik had managed to take a step, the door swung open. "What are you doing here?" Serena demanded. "If you're looking for your toothbrush, I threw it away. You didn't leave anything else here."

Seeing her jerked him out of his paralysis. He hurried toward her. "Can I talk to you, just for a minute?"

"Why don't you send me a text?" she shot back.

"That's fair. That's completely fair," Erik answered as he reached her.

"I don't need you to tell me what's fair."

Erik held up both hands. "You're right. Not that you need me to tell you you're right," he quickly added.

She stood blocking the open doorway, clearly not planning to ask him inside. She didn't look like a woman who was devastated either by losing a big part or by getting kind of dumped via text. She looked beautiful, her brown eyes clear, her hair pulled into a curly ponytail. She had on that pair of jeans he loved and a well-worn "Actor's Express" T-shirt. He could hear Nicki Minaj blasting from somewhere upstairs. He realized they'd never gotten around to talking music. Because they really hadn't known each other that long.

"I'm waiting for you to say something," Serena told him, and he realized he'd just been standing there looking at her, which was progress from standing looking at the lighthouse, but not much.

"I'm sorry about the text. That was an asshole move."

"Yeah. It was."

Serena wasn't going to make it easy for him. But why should she? "I don't have any good explanation," Erik continued. "There can't be one. I treated you like we barely knew each other."

"Like you were cancelling a drinks date with one of your swipe-right women."

Erik nodded. "You deserved better. You—" Over her shoulder, he caught sight of two cardboard boxes. He took a closer look. Packing boxes. There was a stack of folded clothes next to one.

He backed up a step. "You let me stand here apologizing to you, when you're doing exactly what I knew you would?"

"And what's that?" Serena snapped.

"Running away. You gave me a big speech about how you were a pro and you had realistic expectations, but then you lose a part and—*bam!* You're out of here." Erik's heart was slamming against his ribs, fury burning through him. "When exactly did you decide? I bet you had a flight booked less than an hour after your agent gave you the news. Were you even going to tell me? Where was *my* text?"

"There's no point in talking to you about this," Serena told him. "You've got it all figured out." She shut the door in his face.

He was right. He'd been right all along. He never should have gotten involved with her. At least he didn't get in too deep, and now it was over.

Mac snuggled closer to the warm, furry body. What? Wait. He opened his eyes. He was sleeping on Diogee's cushion, next to Diogee! It came back to him slowly. He'd woken up on Jamie's pillow. She hadn't come home. Neither had David. Mac had felt so alone that he'd crept up next to the bonehead, and fallen back asleep.

He jumped up. Diogee kept snoring. At least the dog would never know what Mac had been reduced to. He needed a bath. Now. He began licking one of his front paws. He'd just moved on to his other paw when he heard the click that meant the front door was opening.

Jamie was back! He leapt to his feet. So did Diogee. The meatbrain let out a long string of barks and galloped down the stairs, Mac right behind him.

"Mac! You're back!" David blah-blahed. He knelt down and stroked Mac's head with one hand while he petted Diogee with the other. Diogee was slobbering all over him, and even managed to lick Mac once. Disgusting.

Mac took a deep breath. Was Jamie outside? Would she be coming in next? He didn't smell her. Where was she?

"Jam is going to be so happy to see you. She was so worried about you. Didn't you hear her calling you?" David blah-blahed. "I was calling you, too. I kept looking for you." He scooped Mac up in his arms and stood. Diogee kept jumping up, like he wanted David to carry him, too. Didn't he know he was gigantic?

David opened the door to the prison. Mac didn't struggle as David set him inside and closed the door. He could find a way out later, but right now, he didn't even want to. All he wanted was to wait right there until Jamie came home. He sat on the bed. A nap would feel good, but Mac didn't even want to blink until he saw her.

Even when David put water and a plate of sardines into the prison, Mac didn't move. He would eat and drink when his person came back.

The doorbell rang. Serena's heart lurched. It better not be Erik again. She put down the packing tape she'd been using to seal up one of the boxes, and strode to the door. She jerked it open—and saw Ruby standing there.

"I was afraid you were Erik," she admitted. "He was here a little bit ago."

"To apologize, I hope," Ruby said as she came inside.

"He started to, but then he got a look at that—" Serena gestured to the boxes. "And he went off. He assumed I was running home because I couldn't handle losing the part. I told him I wasn't like Tulip, but he obviously didn't believe me."

Ruby looked at the boxes for a moment. "Not to be a disloyal, non-rom-com best friend, but I get why he thought that. He had no reason to think you'd decided you would rather teach than act."

Serena felt some of her anger fade, and it left her feeling chilled, like her fury had actually been generating heat. "He should have asked. Even if he thought he knew what was happening, he should have given me the benefit of the doubt and talked to me. I wasn't being all that friendly, though."

"After that text, he's lucky you didn't give him the gingerbread treatment and literally bite his head off." Ruby smiled. "See, I'm still on your side."

"Thanks for coming to check on me," Serena said. "You're a great friend."

"Actually, I wasn't coming to check on you, although I'm sure I would have if I didn't have another reason to come over." Her dark eyes sparkled.

"Another reason?"

"Let's sit down. This is official business with official business paperwork." Ruby held up a folder, then sat down at the kitchen table. Serena loved that pale green table. And her blue fridge. And the patchwork quilt on her bed. She loved the whole place. She was going to miss it.

"You want tea or anything?" Serena asked.

"Maybe after. But I can't wait to tell you what I'm going to tell you," Ruby answered. "Sit, sit." Serena sat. "In this folder, I have a new contract between you and the Lighthouse Foundation."

Serena figured there would be something to sign to prove she was giving up the award, but she didn't get why Ruby was so excited about it. "How soon do they want me out? I started packing. I could leave in a day, or maybe two. I want them to be able to get someone else in here as soon as possible."

"Sorry. That's not going to happen. Because you're staying!" Serena opened her mouth, but wasn't able to get words out. "The award is to give a woman an opportunity to pursue a career in the arts," Ruby explained. "It turns out that Mr. and Mrs. Mulcahy consider teaching acting part of the arts. As do I. You get to keep the award as long as you show that you're trying to get work or have work as an acting teacher."

"This is—Wow. My head is—" Serena waved her hands in circles.

"Isn't it wonderful?"

"It's absolutely wonderful." Serena still felt chilled, though. She was just having trouble taking it all in. That was it.

"You know what, I never asked you the question I always ask people when I meet them. If your life were a movie, what would the title be?"

"Profound," Serena teased. Then she thought about it. "I think I have to be untitled for now. I feel like I'm too much of a work-in-progress to know."

Ruby nodded. "Fair enough. I'll ask you again at the end of the year."

Serena wondered if she'd have an answer by then. Even knowing she still had the award, the ground felt a little shaky under her feet.

CHAPTER 21

The kitten—it had been two days since she arrived, but no one could agree on a name for her—crept across the table, belly low to the ground, eyes locked on Kait's water bottle.

"She's about to pounce!" Tom warned.

Too late. The bottle was taken down. Hard. Then the kitten spun around, bit Erik on the finger, and raced off.

"She's so damn cute," Sean said.

"A horndog and a gentleman fall in love with a kitten," Angie muttered, with a smile.

"She's sassy." Jandro smiled at the kitten, too.

"That would be a good name for her," Angie said. "She's one hundred percent sassy."

"Not a hundred percent. She's also bossy, and pesky," Erik said. The kitten jumped down onto Jandro's lap and fell asleep. "And cuddly."

Erik envied the way she could do that, just plop and out. No tossing and turning, like he'd been doing the last bunch of nights.

"I think Sassy's an appropriate name," Kait offered. "We

should vote." For the first time since the kitten-naming process had begun, they got a unanimous "yes."

"I'm going to get her bowls with her name on it," Tom announced.

"Tell me what color. I'm going to get her a scratching post, and I'll get one that matches," his partner volunteered.

"We can go together after shift," Tom answered.

Kait and Erik exchanged a look. Other than the department summer picnic, the two of them didn't spend any time together outside of work.

Erik felt his cell vibrate. He pulled it out of his pocket at the same time Kait took out hers. Jandro was trying to retrieve his without disturbing Sassy.

"Times for our interviews," Kait told everyone.

Erik had to tell them now. It was only going to get harder if he waited. "I decided I want to withdraw. I don't want to go for detective right now." That was one of the things that had been keeping him up. Serena was the other one. He never should have gotten involved with her. He knew what was coming, and he'd walked right into it.

"That's bat-guano crazy!" Kait exclaimed. "You did great on the exam. Are you worried about the interview? I told you I'd ask you some questions to help you prep, even though you don't need it. Like we were all saying the other night, a lot of the questions are going to be ones we've already had to answer, and you had no problem with that."

"It's not the interview." Erik knew they weren't going to get it, but he had to try to explain. "I'm not a desk kind of guy. If I spend more than a couple hours in this room, or one like it, I get itchy. I like the beat. I like getting to know a community, being a part of it, being someone people know they can trust."

"Like those people at Storybook Court trust you? You couldn't even catch a cat," Tom joked. No one laughed.

"Why didn't you talk to me about this?" Kait asked, her voice so low only he could hear it.

"I can't believe you didn't say anything all those nights we were studying together," Jandro said at the same time. "When did you decide?"

"I guess it's been bubbling under the surface. Then I suddenly realized, I didn't have to do it. I didn't have to go for detective just because I've put in five years. And right then I knew I didn't want to."

"You're going to be one of those guys who's in uniform forever? One of the losers?" Angie asked. "Sorry. I didn't mean to say that last part out loud."

"I don't think staying on the beat makes Erik a loser." Kait knocked her foot against his. "If you can, why not do the work you like?"

"Money," Jandro suggested.

Erik expected Kait to have more to say, but when he looked at her, she was focused on her laptop. "H-E-double-toothpicks," she breathed.

"What?" Erik asked, leaning toward her. H-E-double-toothpicks was saved for the big stuff.

"They were able to get fingerprints off Sad Bunnies," she told him. "They belong to Marcus Quevas."

"Marcus?" Erik repeated. "Daniel I would get. He needs money. But Marcus has a great job."

Kait closed the laptop and rested her folded hands on top of it. "This is what I think we should do. Let's tell Mr. and Mrs. Quevas we have an update on the case, and would like to give it to the whole family."

"You want to confront him in front of everybody?" Erik was surprised. Kait wasn't the vindictive type.

She shook her head. "Just so we'll be able to make the arrest and bring him in without a lot of upset. His neighbors at the apartment building won't be looking on."

"Makes sense," Erik said. "Let's set it up."

A few hours later, he and Kait were seated at the Quevases' dining room table. Lynne was nervously twisting the edge of the tablecloth again. "Are you sure you don't want anything to drink?"

Erik was tempted to say yes, just because he knew that's what she wanted. But they needed to get this done. "We recovered the figurine that was stolen from the Kocoras sisters," he began.

"Shouldn't they be here then?" Mr. Quevas asked.

"We'll be filling them in, too," Kait answered. Erik wondered how it felt for her to be sitting at the table with Marcus. It looked like he'd just been phoning and texting her, and asking her out for drinks that time, to keep tabs on the case. At least they hadn't gotten too close. Not the way he and Serena had.

Crap. How many weeks would it take for him to stop thinking about her all the time? It had taken forever with Tulip, but this wasn't the same. He'd cut it off fast.

Erik forced his attention back to the Quevas family, as Kait went on. "We were able to get fingerprints from it." Erik saw Marcus's jaw tighten a fraction. He didn't look like he was about to bolt. Erik didn't expect him to, but it was always a possibility.

Kait looked directly at Marcus. "The prints were yours, Marcus."

"I'm sure that's just because Marcus touched it over at Helen and Nessie's," Lynne said, her voice quivering.

"Marcus is very successful," Carson stated. "There's no reason for him to steal anything."

Kait and Erik had prepared for both these responses. "We spoke to Helen and Nessie, and Marcus has never been in their home," he told the group.

"And we contacted Marcus's job. He hasn't been employed at Ballista for almost a year," Kait added.

"Impossible—" Carson said.

"There must be a mistake," Lynne said at the same moment.

Daniel didn't say anything, just stared at his brother.

"It's true," Marcus admitted. "I could live on savings for a while, but my place is expensive. I sold most of my furniture. I took a lot of my clothes to a consignment place. Then, I just didn't see any options."

"Oh, Marcus. Why didn't you come to us?" his mother asked softly.

"I only took the necklace because I knew you hated it, Mom, and I knew you and Dad would get the insurance. Then Marie mentioned the ring, and I heard the sisters talking about how they wished Sad Bunnies would be stolen. It seemed like a win for everybody."

"The only bad part of the plan is that it's illegal." Erik stood. "Marcus, you'll need to come to the station with us." Kait began giving the Miranda warnings.

"Then Kait began reading Marcus the Miranda rights," Daniel told Serena. "Marcus said he had leads on a couple jobs. He said he would start paying back the money as soon as he could. I guess he sold the stuff through a dealer who didn't ask many questions. He hadn't given the guy the figurine yet."

Serena frowned. "I still don't understand how Mac ended up with it."

"I'm learning that cats are strange and mysterious creatures. Mine likes to walk over my face at two in the morning. It can't be explained." Daniel laughed, then his expression went serious again.

"What's going to happen now? Bail or—?"

"I think he'll get bail. My dad is trying to work it out. My mom went upstairs right after they took Marcus in. She didn't want to talk, so I came over here."

"I'm glad you did. It was nice to be able to make you coffee for a change. I hope you liked the selection of milk and sugar," Serena said.

Daniel took another sip. "Perfect." He set down the cup. "After they left, I started wondering if maybe Marcus could get house arrest, like Charlie, who lives next door to us. He's staying with his aunt, because part of the deal is living with a family member. I know our parents would let Marcus stay with them. Us, I mean."

He sighed. "I really have to find a new job. I'm not giving up acting, but I need to make more. I can deal with living with my parents. But my parents and Marcus? Uh, no. I want him to get the house arrest. I just don't want to be in the room next door."

"I understand. I have a brother." Serena reached out her hands. "Can I hold her for a minute. I miss kitten time."

"Sure." Daniel handed over the roly-poly kitten. "I've decided to call her Macchiato. Her stripes remind me of the caramel drizzle on the whipped cream of a caramel macchiato. It's also in honor of Mac since he's the one who brought little Mac to me."

"I love that." Serena cuddled the sleepy little Mac.

"What kind of person sits around talking about kitten names when his brother is in jail?" Daniel asked suddenly. "It's like I'm a sociopath."

"No, you're not. There's just nothing you can do right now," Serena assured him. "The idea of house arrest is a good one. That's something you can try to make happen. I guess you'd talk to Kait or Erik? I'm not sure of the right channels, but they could tell you who to contact if it's not them."

"Is Erik coming back here after he . . . finishes with Marcus? Maybe I could ask him then," Daniel said.

"To patrol, you mean?" Little Mac began to knead her leg. Serena could feel the tiny claws even through her jeans, but she didn't make her stop. She was just too sweet.

"No. To be with you."

Serena closed her eyes for a long moment. "I didn't get the chance to tell you," she groaned.

"Well you have to tell me now." Daniel reached over and stroked the kitten's head.

"We broke up. Or whatever you call it when you never want to see each other again, but you've only been together a few weeks. I did the unforgivable. I cried in front of him when I didn't get the werecat part." She could hear the bitterness in her voice. She hated that.

"Of course, you did. I would have myself," Daniel told her.

"I also didn't get to tell you that I don't want to keep going after acting jobs."

"That's crazy! Because of losing one part? I lose parts all the time. You already have an agent. People would kill for your agent. You already—"

"Stop!" Serena interrupted. "Please," she added. "Everything you're saying is true. I know that. I know how ridiculously lucky I've been."

"Well, you have a little talent, too."

She laughed. "Thanks. Here's the thing—I realized although I like acting, I like teaching acting so much more. I didn't realize how much. I don't want to give it up."

Daniel raised his eyebrows. "Well, I'm all about people following their dreams. How does that affect all this?" He gestured at the lighthouse's cozy parlor.

"I thought I'd have to leave, but the couple who give the Lighthouse Award decided teaching acting is something they're willing to support. So, I'm here for the year. All I have to do is show I'm looking for work as an acting teacher."

"I have tons of friends who'd want you as an acting coach," Daniel said. "Some of them even have money. Some of them are also extremely attractive. And some of those are even straight. We'll fix your broken heart."

"It's not broken," Serena insisted, although it had definitely taken a hit. "But I'm not ready for any romantic fix ups." She pointed at him. "Promise you won't try."

"Not until you give me the go-ahead," Daniel agreed.

Serena didn't think that was going to happen any time soon. She was going to need a recovery period after Erik. A long one.

Mac smelled her before the door opened. Jamie! She still smelled a little strange, but it was definitely his Jamie. He'd been waiting so long. David had come home a few times to give him and Diogee food, but never Jamie. Now she was back.

David came in first—alone. He rushed up the stairs without saying anything to Mac. "Okay, he's away!" he loudly blah-blahed. Mac heard him coming back down, although it was hard over the wails from Bonebreath.

Finally, Jamie came in to the kitchen, followed by David. Mac couldn't help letting out meow after meow of greeting. He didn't always show how excited he was to see her. It was best to keep humansies on their toes. But today, it was impossible to hide it.

She handed something to David and slowly walked to the door of the prison, one hand pressed against her belly. "I'm still a little ouchy," she blah-blahed as she bent down and freed him. Mac began to wind himself around her ankles, making sure she was marked with his scent.

"I'm so happy you came home. I was so worried about you, you bad kitty," Jamie blah-blahed. As usual, when she blah-blahed "bad kitty" it didn't sound like she thought he was so very bad.

She lowered herself slowly onto the floor, and gave Mac a snuggle. He purred his loudest purr. "Mac, look. Look who's here. It's your little sister."

"Our daughter is not the cat's sister," David blah-blahed. He smelled the happiest he ever had. Even though Jamie didn't smell quite normal, she smelled her happiest, too. "Maybe he could be her uncle. Uncle MacGyver."

"Uncle Mac," Jamie blah-blahed into Mac's ear as David knelt down beside them and showed Mac what he held. Mac had seen one of those before. It was a human kitten.

A human kitten was coming into Mac's house! He squirmed away from Jamie and raced up the stairs. He was out the bathroom window before anyone could catch him.

"Mac!" he heard Jamie blah-blah. She was standing in the doorway as he scrambled down the tree. As soon as his feet touched the ground, he ran. And ran. And ran.

CHAPTER 22

Serena paused as she started to cut across the courtyard. Erik and Kait were standing on the edge of the fountain, presumably doing a safety talk the way they had the first time she'd seen them there. Or maybe giving an update on the robbery, although it had been a week since Marcus was arrested. She wasn't sure. They were facing away from her, and she couldn't hear them distinctly.

She thought about retreating and circling around to the entrance on the other side of the Court. But she held two grocery bags in one hand and three in the other, and they were already biting into her fingers. Besides he was still the beat cop here. She couldn't avoid him forever, although she had managed to avoid him for the last week. She hadn't felt ready even to exchange a few words. She hadn't felt ready even to look at his face.

Just go, she told herself. It's not as if he was going to jump down from the fountain and follow her. Why would he? He was probably hoping to avoid her, too.

She sucked in a deep breath, and began walking.

* * *

"I have an announcement that's both happy and sad," Erik told the group gathered in front of the fountain, a smaller group than had been there the first time he and Kait had done their safety speech. "My partner, Kait, has been promoted to detective. Which means she won't be one of your neighborhood police. But you still have me." He smiled at them. "And I'll have a new partner soon."

He couldn't imagine a better partner than Kait. It was going to be a huge adjustment working with somebody new. But the relief he'd felt after he announced he wasn't going to interview for a detective slot had told him he'd made the right decision, and no matter what, Kait would always be a part of his life.

"What happened? Did you flunk the test?" called a middle-aged guy wearing a Speedo and a towel tossed around his shoulders. It took Erik a moment to recognize him with so few clothes on. Mr. Todd from Red Ridinghood Lane. His question was obnoxious, but obnoxious was his usual sense of humor. Every shift, Erik was getting more familiar with the quirks of the people in his community.

"No, Mr. Todd, I only got two wrong," Erik answered. "But I decided I'd miss you." He threw out his arms to encompass the whole group. "All of you, too much, if I became a detective." That got a lot of laughs, but also a lot of appreciative smiles and some applause.

"I'm going to miss you, too," Kait added. "But know I'll be just as concerned about your safety when I'm a detective as I am now. It's safety Erik and I want to talk to you about. Just because the robberies at Storybook Court have been solved, that does *not* mean that it is safe to leave your doors or windows unlocked."

It had been less than a month since they stood up on the lip of the fountain introducing themselves as the new beat cops. Less than a month, since he first saw Serena. His mind kept bouncing back to her. It hadn't been that long, though. Only a week since he last saw her. The memories would start to fade, especially since she was safely back in Atlanta and he wouldn't be seeing—

His head jerked toward the flash of red-gold he'd caught in his peripheral vision. Serena. It was Serena. What the hell was she still doing there?

"I need a volunteer!" He hadn't been intending to say that. It's like his voice was operated by someone else. Serena froze for a second, then started to walk faster. "You! Serena Perry. You did a great job last time. Let's get you up here again."

Kait was giving him a quizzical look. He didn't blame her. He felt like he was losing his mind. What was he doing? He'd been surprised to see her that was all, he told himself. He didn't want to let her walk off without finding out what she was still doing here.

Serena stepped up on the lip of the fountain without taking Erik's hand. "Just do what you'd do if I showed up at your door," he instructed. Then he pretended to knock.

She mimed opening the door a crack and scowled at him. "Didn't you see my no soliciting sign?"

Good. She was getting into it, and she was giving out solid tips. A no soliciting sign was a great idea.

"I did, but I wanted to tell you about a great opportunity. I was sure you wouldn't want to miss it," he began.

"I'm not buying anything from you. I don't know you." Serena pretended to close the door. Erik did the air knock again, but Serena had already jumped off the edge of the fountain. She was walking away.

"I'm going to help our volunteer carry her groceries home, as a thank-you." Erik looked over at Kait. "Can you take questions?"

"Of course. Who has questions? Or would anyone like to

share a story about someone coming to their door who made them feel uncomfortable?" Kait asked as Erik started after Serena.

"Why are you still here?" he asked Serena when he caught up to her. "Wait. Don't answer. That came out wrong. What I meant was, I'm surprised to see you here."

"I live here," Serena told him, without offering further explanation.

"But you said you were leaving."

"Actually, I didn't. You saw boxes and assumed I was going to weep my way back to Atlanta because I didn't get one part that I auditioned for," she told him, looking straight ahead.

"Oh." He thought about it, trying to remember the details. He'd seen those boxes and—And he'd gone off. Because she'd been doing exactly what he'd been afraid she would from the moment he realized she was an actress. She'd been doing exactly what Tulip had done. "I guess . . . I guess you're right. I assumed."

"It's a good thing you're not going to take a job as a detective," Serena told him. "They're supposed to avoid assumptions, aren't they?"

"I guess I owe you an apology. Make that an apology and a half. I didn't finish the one I started that day." She picked up her speed, still not even glancing at him. "Can we stop for a minute. I really would like to apologize, and I'd like to be looking you in the face when I do it."

Serena jerked to a stop and spun toward him. "Fine. Go."

She was acting like she hadn't done anything. She'd—

She'd cried in front of a guy she trusted when she didn't get something she really wanted. That's all she'd done. She'd been upset, and she'd let him see it.

"I treated you unforgivably. Except I'm hoping maybe you can forgive me somehow. When you got so upset after that call from your agent, it scared me. That's the truth. It seemed like the worst stretch of my life was about to repeat itself, and I couldn't take it."

"That's not what was happening. I was having emotions. That's all. I'm human," Serena told him.

"I get that. Now. When it was happening, all I knew was I couldn't take it. I . . . I thought Tulip and I were in love. I know I was. I was crazy in love with Tulip. I would have done anything for her. She wanted to move away from LA. Fine. I would have gone. But I somehow got turned into something that reminded her of failure, I guess. She never tried to explain why she didn't want me to go with her. She just said no. And then she was gone. So fast."

Serena reached out and lightly ran her hand down his arm. "I'm sorry that happened to you. But you realize that's what you did to me. Not in such a heart-wrenching way. We didn't have the relationship you and Tulip did. We weren't in love. We didn't even really know each other really well. But I was feeling really close to you."

"Me too," Erik admitted.

"And then it was like you turned into another person," Serena told him.

"I know. I'm sorry."

She nodded. "Okay. Okay," she said again. "Let's keep going. These bags are going to amputate my fingers."

He grabbed all of them from her. "Why were there packing boxes at your place that day? If it's okay to ask," he added quickly.

"I decided I didn't want to keep acting. Not because I didn't get the part. I just realized I love teaching. I didn't think I'd be able to stay in the lighthouse, since I'd gotten the award so I could spend a year pursuing an acting career. But the Mulcahys decided teaching was an artistic endeavor, and that I could keep the award while I tried to get work as an acting teacher."

They turned up the walkway to her place. "I'm sure that seems crazy. I know I'd made real progress, and so fast. I know there are actors who would kill for what I've already gotten. The commercial. The agent."

"I get it. People who know I passed the detective exam think I'm nuts to want to stay in uniform. But I know I'd hate spending so much time in an office. And I'm really behind the return-to-beat assignments. Being a presence in a neighborhood, getting people to trust me, to believe I'm someone who wants to help—for me, there's no better job. There's better money, more prestige, but no better job."

They'd reached her door. "I'm not asking you in," she said. "But do you want to go to Snow White's? Have a beer? Talk about our love of jobs that will never bring fame and fortune."

Erik felt a lightness fill his body, as if someone had cut cement blocks off his feet. "Yeah. I'd like that."

"Just let me stick the groceries away," Serena said. "I'll be right back."

"I'll be right here."

Mac was running. Running and running. His legs were burning. It was hard to breathe. He stumbled, but forced himself to go on.

He reached his tree, and climbed straight up, even though he was so tired. He shoved the window open with his head and jumped down to the bathroom floor. He could smell the human kitten. Its scent mixed with Jamie's.

He went to them. It took him two tries to jump onto the bed. When he did, he rested his gift beside the tiny person.

"Mac," Jamie blah-blahed. "Did you bring that for the baby?" She rubbed her fingers along his jaw, and he tilted his chin up so she would keep scratching. She did. He'd trained her well. "David, come see what our cat has done."

David hurried into the room, Diogee right behind him, his ropey tail and his whole back end wagging. "Look what this good, good kitty did. Mac brought this for the baby." Jamie patted the gift Mac had dragged home. He hadn't dropped it once, even though it was almost as big as he was.

"A stuffed elephant?" David picked up the present, and Diogee started to whine for it. It wasn't for him! If he tried to grab it, Mac would have to give him the whap-whap. Maybe he'd keep his claws in—the first time.

"I shouldn't call him good. He's clearly really a bad, bad kitty. He clearly stole it," Jamie blah-blahed. She said "bad kitty" in that "good kitty" way, as usual. Except when he ate the butter. Hadn't she realized how much he liked butter? If she would only put some in his bowl, he wouldn't eat it off the counter. Sigh. She clearly needed more training.

And the new little human. It would need an enormous amount of training. It didn't know anything about cats. Mac wasn't going to get more than two or three naps a day for years! But this new baby was his responsibility, and Mac took his responsibilities seriously. Someone had to.

EPILOGUE

Ten months later

"Come on in!" Daniel called as Erik and Serena walked up the winding path to the Quevases' tree-house-style home.

"We're so excited to see the show!" Serena gave him a hug.

"You've basically seen my part. Since you're the one who helped me refine my hosting style." Daniel looked over at Erik. "She's a truly gifted teacher."

"And now she's a truly gifted teacher with her own space," Erik told him.

"I just signed the lease this afternoon! I'm so excited. I'd do a happy dance, but I don't think there's room right now." She glanced around the living room, spotting Al and Marie, Kait, Helen and Nessie, Marcus, his and Daniel's parents, Charlie and his aunt, Ruby, Riley, and Riley's mom, Mrs. Trask, Jamie and David and the baby, Emily—

"Emily!" Serena called, waving. "I have to go say hi," she told Erik, leaving him with Daniel. They'd discovered a mutual love of yard sales, and now Daniel spent almost as much time with Erik as he did with her.

She'd only taken a few steps, when she almost bumped into Ruby. The place was so crowded.

"Your year is almost over. I'm going to miss you," Ruby said.

"Oh, don't worry. You're not getting rid of me that easily. I'm all ready to be your rom-com best friend," Serena answered.

"I don't have anyone I'm rom-com-ing with," Ruby reminded her.

"Things change. I'm heading over to say hi to Emily. I want you to meet her."

"Later. I want to find the bathroom before the show starts. But I told you I was going to ask you a question near when your time at the lighthouse was almost up." She smiled. "If your life were a movie, what would the title be?"

"Hmmm." Serena tilted her head, thinking. "How about *Storybook Romance*? Since my life did become a rom-com while I was living at Storybook Court, complete with all the crazy ups and downs. And hot sex."

"Love it!" Ruby exclaimed. "Now I have to find that bathroom."

Serena looked for Emily, and saw her weaving her way through the crowd. She gave Serena a hug when they reached each other. "I saw the billboard for *Be-Were* on Sunset. You look gorgeous supersized," Serena told her friend.

"The whole thing feels completely surreal," Emily admitted. "You have to come to the premiere with me. Erik can come, too, but you have to sit next to me. And you have to stay until the end credits."

"Of course. I always do. Is there one of those extra scenes?" Serena asked.

Emily grinned as she shook her head. "My acting coach is listed in the credits."

Serena squealed. She couldn't help herself. She only had two months of her time at the lighthouse left, but even if she left tomorrow it would be fine. This year had transformed her life. She was actually going to have her own acting school, with the whole floor of a building instead of the community college classroom she had back in Atlanta.

"Thanks, Emily. And thanks for what you did to get the café and the show going."

"Hey, I'm a cat person. Literally. I couldn't turn my back on my own kind. Daniel told me that even though Yo, Kitty! has only being going for a week, eight cats have already been adopted."

"And after tonight, I bet there will be a line of people waiting to get in," Serena answered.

"Quiet everyone!" Marcus yelled from a spot next to the bi-screen TV. He was wearing a nice suit, but Serena noticed there were little snags all over both pant legs. She also noticed the slight bulge around one ankle. She knew it was from the ankle bracelet, but didn't think people who didn't know he was under house arrest would be aware of it. "It's about to start. Anyone under fifty, sit on the floor."

Emily and Serena obediently sat, and Erik came over to join them. Daniel navigated the crowd and positioned himself next to his brother.

"We have about two minutes!" Daniel called. "I'm going to practice for the Emmy I'm sure is going to come to me by doing some thank-yous. First of all, I have to thank this guy"—he put his arm around his brother—"for the brilliant idea of turning Yo, Joe! into a cat café."

" 'Accept the challenges so that you may feel the exhilaration of victory!' " Mrs. Trask cried, pumping her fist in the air. All her hair was now turquoise, and it looked awesome.

"You're the one who said if there were kittens there would be dozens of customers," Marcus reminded Daniel.

"Okay, then thanks to the kittens, now teen cats, for the inspiration. And for being regulars on the Yo, Kitty! reality show. That's Little Mac over there, eating someone's canapé."

"No!" Marie cried. "You put that down." Little Mac obeyed, then wandered off, probably to find something else to eat out of Marie's sightline.

"That's my guy, Deoxys, named after the fastest Pokemon, climbing up the curtains," Marcus added.

Marie clapped her hands. "You get down." Deoxys jumped to the floor and chased after Little Mac, trying to grab her tail.

"Where's Chewie Two?" Daniel asked.

"Here he is." Charlie waved from his spot beside Kait. His cat, his truly enormous cat, was draped over his shoulder. "Can you believe he was the runt of the litter?"

"Do you think now that Charlie's finished his sentence that Kait will let him out of the friend zone?" Serena whispered to Erik.

"It's possible. You eventually let me out." Erik squeezed her hand. "And she'll never find anyone else who can hold their own against her in a Spider-Man debate."

"And last but not least, there's Sassy, the official North Hollywood police station cat." Kait tried to scoop her up, but Sassy gave her a paw-tap to stop her. "If Yo, Kitty! does as well as we hope, we're going to have to do a spin-off. Sassy the SWAT cat."

"She's not actually with a SWAT team," Kait protested.

Daniel waved her off with a smile. "Details, details. Don't start to play me off yet, I have a few more thanks. Emily Lee, soon to be a major motion picture star, for convincing her studio that sponsoring the show would be a great way to promote *Be-Were*. And to Erik Ross, our favorite police officer, for offering ideas on renovating the coffee shop to make it cat friendly."

"Daniel, will you shut up. It's going to start in about one minute."

"You shut up, Marcus," Daniel shot back, but he grinned at his brother.

Jamie stood up, her baby girl, Peaches, balanced on her hip. The little girl's name was really Genevieve, which Serena though was a beautiful name. But they always called her Peaches because they said it was David's second favorite jam. As if that made actual sense. "Has anyone seen Mac?" Jamie called. "We brought him with us."

"That means nothing. He could be anywhere," Erik answered. "I'll go take a look around the neighborhood. I know a lot of his spots. I'll call over to The Gardens, too. He has a lot of friends over there. Briony or Nate won't mind checking around." Before Erik could stand, Mac swaggered into the room holding a stuffed monkey at least as long as he was. His whiskers bristled with pride.

"Kait, Erik, you're not on duty, remember?" Jamie called. "That means you don't have to arrest my bad, bad kitty."

"In fact, even when off duty—" Kait began, but stopped when a fifty-something man stepped into the room.

"I'm sorry," he said. "I knocked, but it was too loud for anyone to hear." He had a faint Eastern European accent that Serena couldn't quite place. "The door was open, so I came in."

"What can we do for you?" Daniel asked.

"I thought I saw a tan-and-gold cat run in here. He would have been carrying—"

"A stuffed monkey?" David asked. He plucked it away from Mac, who gave a huff of protest.

"Yes. I make them, and other animals. I have a table at the farmers' market over on Fairfax. That cat has managed to nab one from me every few weeks."

"That's why our daughter's room is full of them. He keeps bringing them home," Jamie told him. She looked at Mac. "Fairfax is way too far from home. Naughty kitty," she scolded. *She could really use some acting coaching*, Serena thought, trying not to giggle.

"We're happy to pay for them," David volunteered. "We didn't know where he was getting them."

"It's really starting now!" Marcus announced.

Erik stood. "I'm a cop. This is my beat. Let's go in the kitchen, and I'll take a statement."

"I'll come too." David and the man followed Erik out of the room.

A chorus of mews started up and on-screen, David opened the door of Yo, Kitty!

"You're happy with this, Sebastian?" Erik asked.

"Happy and in fact somewhat flattered," Sebastian answered. "I think I'm going to make a cat based on Mac."

"I'll buy that one, too," David said. "My wife will love it."

"It will be my gift," Sebastian told him. "Since you're already buying sixteen of my creations."

"Are you finished or am I interrupting," Ruby asked, poking her head into the kitchen.

"I'm sure none of us could find your presence anything but a pleasure," Sebastian told her. He was like a throwback to an earlier era, what Erik's grandmother would call a gentleman.

Ruby seemed to like it. "Thank you. It's actually your creations I wanted to talk to you about. I'm working doing set dressing for a movie. I love all the stuffed animals Mac has been bringing home to my goddaughter. They're so whimsical, but with a little bit of an edge."

Sebastian gave her a little half bow. "I wonder if you might consider making something specifically for the movie. We could have a conversation about the character it would belong to, and maybe you could do some sketches."

"I love movies. It would be an honor," Sebastian answered.

"Let me give you my card." He pulled it out of his vest pocket and stepped toward her. Mac wandered in and circled Ruby and Sebastian, rubbing his cheek against their legs as he went.

Erik and David exchanged a look. They'd both gotten somewhat drunk at Ruby's annual Christmas party, and had a meandering conversation that included ideas on how exactly Mac managed to get so many couples together. Nate had wandered over at some point and joined in. Their favorite theory was that he was Cupid and he'd annoyed one of the other gods so badly that he'd been turned into a cat.

"He's at it again," David said under his breath, and Erik nodded. He excused himself and went back into the living room, but didn't see Serena.

"She went into the yard for a minute to get some air," Emily told him.

Erik found her staring across the street at the lighthouse. The cupola was illuminated, and it gave the impression the tower was watching over the neighborhood. "I'm going to miss that place," Serena said. He wrapped his arms around her, and she leaned back against him.

"I've been wanting to talk to you about that." His gut tightened, but not with anxiety, with anticipation, as he turned her to face him. "What would you think about moving in with me?"

"Hmmm. Would you build me some kind of funky display for my weird things?" she asked.

"As big as you want," he promised.

"Will you make me cook for you?"

He laughed. "As if I can make you do anything. But no. In fact, it will be a condition of your moving in that you never cook anything that can't be microwaved."

She leaned closer until her lips were almost touching his. "Will you love me forever?"

"And then some."

She kissed him. "That was a yes, but I still have one more question."

Erik tightened his arms around her. He couldn't imagine anything she wanted that he wouldn't want to give her.

"Can we adopt a cat?"

"Our home wouldn't be complete without one."

Ruby and the human male smelled good together. They both had smelled content alone, but their good scents got more than twice as strong when they were together. Feeling pleased with himself, Mac returned to the room that was filled with his people and his kittens. They were almost as big as he was now, but they would always be kittens to him.

Mac jumped up on Jamie's lap and snuggled next to Peaches. She patted his head, and he felt something sticky smearing onto his fur. Well, that's what tongues were for, even though humans would never accept that.

For once, no one smelled sad. No one smelled anxious. His kittens were all well taken care of by the humans he'd selected for them. Mac yawned, and closed his eyes. He deserved a nap. It would probably have to be a short one, knowing how bad humans were at taking care of themselves. They weren't that bright.

But they were lovable.

Inspired by the true story of a Portland, Oregon, cat who stole from his neighbors—and stole America's heart. . . .

SHE'S PUTTING HER LOVE LIFE ON PAWS

Jamie Snyder is thirty-four and single but NOT ready to mingle. After suffering through the Year of the Non-Committal Man, the Year of the Self-Absorbed Man, and the Year of the Forgot-to-Mention-I'm-Married Man, Jamie's ready to celebrate the Year of Me—and MacGyver, of course. MacGyver is an adorable tabby with a not-so-adorable habit of sneaking out at night and stealing things from the neighbors. That's right, MacGyver is a cat burglar. He's still the only male Jamie trusts—and the only companion she needs. . . .

BUT HER CAT HAS OTHER IDEAS

MacGyver knows his human is lonely. He can smell it. It's the same smell he's noticed on their neighbor David, a handsome young baker who's tired of his friends trying to fix him up. But now MacGyver's on the case. First, he steals something from David and stashes it at Jamie's. Then, he steals someth¹ from Jamie and leaves it with David. Before long, the tw swapping stolen goods, trading dating horror stories ing not to fall in love. But they're not fooling Mac⸢ humans generate this much heat, *the cat is out r*

Look for *TALK TO THE P*
wherever book┣

Inspired by the true story of a kleptomaniac cat who stole his way into America's heart. . . .

HE'S THE CAT THIEF OF LOVE

MacGyver the tabby is feeling very pleased with himself. His human, Jamie Snyder, has found the perfect packmate—and it's all thanks to Mac. By stealing personal items from the home of Jamie's handsome neighbor David, the matchmaking cat brought these two LA singles together. Now, while the newlyweds are off on their honeymoon, MacGyver is ready for a well-deserved catnap. That is, until he meets his cat sitter, Briony. Like most humans, she's hopeless when it comes to romance. And Mac can't resist a challenge. . . .

SHE'S FOUND THE ESCAPE CLAWS

Briony feels terrible about leaving her fiancé at the altar. When her cousin Jamie offers her the chance to cat sit Mac-Gyver, the runaway bride leaps at the chance to cuddle up with the only male creature she trusts herself around. But MacGyver has other plans. He lures Briony to a friendly neighborhood retirement community—run by a charming young hottie named Nate. Briony and Nate hit it off instantly. But Briony's still not sure she's ready for a relationship. And Nate's got problems of his own—someone is sabotaging his community.

Crazy humans. Why can't they follow their instincts and go after the love they deserve? MacGyver is on the case. And this ne, he's not pussyfooting around. . . .

RAVES FOR *TALK TO THE PAW*

"Filled with romance and adorable kitty antics . . . a light and cozy read!"
—*Modern Cat*

"Surpassingly cute story of a matchmaking cat determined to pair off his human with a neighbor through the power of stinky laundry."
—*Kirkus Reviews*

"Whimsical . . . appealing characters."
—*Publishers Weekly*

Look for THE SECRET LIFE OF MAC *everywhere books are sold.*

Connect with
Us

Visit us online at
KensingtonBooks.com
to read more from your favorite authors, see books
by series, view reading group guides, and more.

Join us on social media

for sneak peeks, chances to win books and prize packs,
and to share your thoughts with other readers.

facebook.com/kensingtonpublishing
twitter.com/kensingtonbooks

Tell us what you think!

To share your thoughts, submit a review,
or sign up for our eNewsletters, please visit:
KensingtonBooks.com/TellUs.